To Michael
For never suggesting that I get
an ordinary job.

# Uphill all the Way

## Sue Moorcroft

LARGE PRINT

Oxford

First published in Great Britain 2005
by
Transita


Published in Large Print 2006 by ISIS Publishing Ltd.,
7 Centremead, Osney Mead, Oxford OX2 0ES
by arrangement with
Transita

**British Library Cataloguing in Publication Data**
Moorcroft, Sue
    Uphill all the way. – Large print ed.
    1. Middle aged women – England –
    Northamptonshire – Fiction
    2. Loss (Psychology) – Fiction
    3. Large type books
    I. Title
    823.9'2 [F]


ISBN 0–7531–7527–4 (hb)
ISBN 0–7531–7528–2 (pb)


Printed and bound in Great Britain by
T. J. International Ltd., Padstow, Cornwall

# Acknowledgements

Thanks to Transita for having the faith and discernment to buy this book when they'd only read half of it and didn't even know how it ended. And to my editor, Marina, for being confident that I would be able to finish it in three months.

Also to my agent, Laura, for making the above deal in the first place, being so pleased on my behalf, and fitting reading the final draft around my holiday.

To Sue Dukes for answering fifty e-mails about sub aqua diving without a single complaint.

To Tony Bosson for his advice on hand injury, and for letting me touch his scar.

Especial gratitude to *all* on the My Global Friends web-site, but especially Tom Restall, Paul Vella, Louis Risso, Peter Birkett, Mark Caruana and Bill Coxhead, for patiently answering my many and varied questions about my beloved Malta, and for making the translations. If any of the words are naughty, it was them, not me!

And to Salvinu Lombardi of Sliema, for very kindly doing much the same.

I would never have got this far, or, indeed, very far at all, without the Romantic Novelists' Association, and in particular the New Writers' Scheme run, at that time, by Margaret James, who always knew just what to say. Thanks also to my great mates at the RNA's Bedford Chapter who supplied encouragement along with the raucous lunches and the champagne, and also to South-East Chapter for their friendship (especially Myra, for reading skills).

And thanks to my kids, Carl and Paul, for turning the guitars down when I asked, and Mum, Trev and Kev for their interest and support.

And to Michael, for being so pleased. And for bankrolling me for the past decade. I love you.

# PART ONE

# Giorgio and the House of Cards

# CHAPTER
## ONE

Tired of listening to a mechanical woman's patient explanation, *The phone you are trying to reach may be switched off. Please leave a message . . .* Judith McAllister tossed down her mobile and prowled out into the heat on the open balcony to stare at the early evening light on Sliema Creek.

The creek, one of those deep fingers of sea that cuts into Malta's coastline, reflected the intense blue of the sky. Red-and-white ferryboats shimmied lazily, returned from their day excursions around the island or to the sister islands of Gozo and Comino, and emptied of early summer tourists. Aluminium tables at the pavement cafés had filled up, perhaps with the same tourists keen to cool off with a Cisk beer beneath yellow or blue umbrellas.

Although the sun was sinking behind the building the heat was still intense. She wasn't as resilient as she used to be. In her twenties and thirties she'd basked at every opportunity, but wisdom came with age and now she was wary of blistered skin or pounding headaches.

The Strand, the teeming road between herself and the boats, was busy with cars, orange buses, and *karrozzini* — the traditional horse-drawn carriages. She glanced down into the street, half expecting to see Giorgio sniffing the sea air as he parked his car, a new MG, bright red.

A glance at her watch.

He was very late.

She'd rushed home from work two hours ago, but found the flat empty and silent. After showering, she'd slipped into a floaty dress she knew to be one of his favourites and dried her hair so that it lay sleek over her shoulders. And still no Giorgio. Maybe he'd stopped off for a drink? One with the boys?

She turned her head and narrowed her eyes to gaze inland up the creek towards the bridge to Manoel Island, the smaller craft bobbing at their buoys and the luxury cruisers, the "gin palaces", in the yacht marina. Giorgio was deliberately late, she presumed, to exhibit his irritation that she had to work this afternoon.

"But it's Saturday, I have the air!" he'd complained, dark eyes unsmiling. "This dive has been arranged for a week!" Now that she'd introduced Giorgio to sub aqua diving, he showed the beginner's impatience to be underwater all the time, go further, deeper, push his boundaries.

She'd stroked his thick, dark hair. "It's a pain. But they're important clients, Giorgio. We've been wooing them for months, I can't let Richard down by missing the meeting. It's not his fault they had to reschedule." She'd invested part of her divorce settlement into Giorgio's business, Sliema Z Bus Tours, but the rest into her Uncle Richard's business, Richard Morgan

4

Estate, so took it seriously. "We can dive on Sunday. The sea will still be there."

His eyes had softened as he'd accepted her apologetic kisses, but he'd refused to be put off. "OK, Charlie Galea will be my diving buddy."

"No, he's not much more experienced than you, Giorgio —"

He kissed her, thoroughly. "Am I or not a diver?"

"But so inexperienced —" Her words had been lost in laughter, every one of her objections smothered with a kiss.

Judith watched the small horses in the shafts of the *karrozzini* whisking their tails at the flies, and sighed. Apart from her instincts rebelling at the thought of novice divers — no matter what their certificates said — diving unaccompanied, her own opportunity to dive this weekend had no doubt disappeared. Giorgio would have let Charlie have her air.

It had been sweltering in Sliema today, inevitably tomorrow would be the same. Fabulous to have escaped it by sinking into her beloved, beautiful, hushed turquoise world of weightlessness, to revel in the water gliding coolly into her wet suit and overexposed skin. To turn to Giorgio to signal *OK*.

It was wonderful now they could dive together. Special.

Even decompression halts had become a pleasure, the cobalt blue panels of her wetsuit entwined with the scarlet of his as they hung together in the water to watch the elongated beams of sunshine filtering down from the surface.

She let her eyes half-close for a moment as she recalled the delicious sensation, the combination of body warmth and water chill. Sub aqua diving helped keep her from feeling middle-aged.

Curling her bare toes away from the hot concrete of the balcony, she wandered back in to the kitchen where the windows stood wide open in a largely futile attempt to release hot air, and switched off the oven with a kept-warm-for-too-long lasagne inside.

Red wine, opened ready, waited on the worktop. She poured another glass, ruby, ruby red, and returned to the sitting room to try Giorgio's mobile again. *The phone you are trying to reach . . .*

A fat lot of use that was.

She sighed, and arranged the layers of her green-shot-with-gold dress, selected to complement her golden-brown eyes and the nutty highlights in her hair. Her favourite colours, like an English late summer harvest.

Slotting a love songs album onto the CD player, she sank into a chair, her bare feet cooling pleasantly on the tiled floor, her head tipping comfortably back. "Giorgio's playing bloody games, Judith," she told herself.

It was to punish her a little and pique her appetite, this withdrawal of his company, to make her especially pleased to see him when he finally sauntered in, eyes alight with challenge and skin tasting of the sea.

He'd press his body to hers. "So, now the work is finished and you have time for Giorgio?" And suddenly being with him would be more important than making complaints about where he'd been until now.

That's how it was. Being with him was always more important than everything else.

They'd met on the promenade that edged Tower Road at Ghar id Dud. She often climbed the hill from The Strand in her lunch hour to walk on the broad paved area high above the rocky foreshore, tall hotels on one hand and the sea on the other. It had been November, then, and the days deliciously warm rather than beating with heat.

She'd paused to watch teenagers jump from the heights of The Chalet, the bones of a concrete pier projecting into Ghar id Dud Bay. Four boys and a girl ran off the top tier, letting out blood-curdling shrieks as they plummeted through the salty air and entered the sea thirty feet below with loud smacks and plumes of spray. Judith winced with the force of every entry, smiling three seconds later as the youngsters resurfaced in circles of foam, screaming with exhilaration.

Part of her longed to share their youth and blithe disregard for danger, to leap into thin air and slap down into the sea with leg-stinging force, wait for gravity to stop bearing her down then kick, kick, ears aching, for the surface.

A voice at her shoulder claimed her attention. "It's a little mad, but not too painful."

She looked around. A man. She returned his smile politely.

He settled his elbows on the rail beside hers. "This I have done." He gestured at the foolhardy teenagers clambering back to the upper level. He spoke good English, but, of course, many Maltese did, making things too easy for English-speaking visitors.

Judith glanced at him again. His skin was golden, his eyes as dark as damsons, his hair well cut and neat. Around his neck glinted a gold crucifix on a thick chain. He smiled.

"Recently?"

A laugh, a soft, husky sound. "When I was much younger, and more stupid. But it is unsafe, The Chalet, is unsafe for many years. You can see there has been a fence to stop people climbing on. It's broken, and the children climb."

The howls of glee began again, and together they watched the spectacle of young bodies springing joyously into nothingness and plunging down into benevolent blue waves.

"The Chalet used to have a dance floor and an open-air café on two levels, for celebrations, for dances. A balustrade ran all the way round, and there was a grand entrance, here." He indicated a spot near to where they stood.

Judith frowned at the skeletal structure, trying to envision such imposing flesh to it. "What happened?"

He shrugged. "A bomb, in the war."

She nodded. The war had been very cruel to Malta. Reminders, such as the ruins of The Opera House in Valletta, dotted the island.

"I think it was fixed, but there was too much damage, and in some *grigal* storms the sea took it away."

"*Grigal?*" She spoke a little Maltese, but this word was unfamiliar to her.

"Storms on the north-easterly wind, they can bring a very big sea. You've seen the breakwater built in the mouth of Grand Harbour? To keep the shipping protected from the *grigal*." He indicated The Chalet. "Now, the government wishes for The Chalet to become something safe and new, but there is nothing decided, I think."

Judith stared at the pier in fascination. At the crumbling remains of balustrades, the immense pillars. Gazed at the rippling turquoise sea, and, even though she'd witnessed violent winter storms herself, had difficulty in imagining it rising and towering in monstrous waves capable of sucking masonry off a big concrete structure.

She often paused to watch the waves roll in around The Chalet Ghar id Dud, and once or twice a week the man materialised beside her. He was Giorgio Zammit, he lived in Sliema and worked as a tour guide, and was younger than her. The days their paths crossed were either his off-duty days or those when he worked afternoons and met the distinctive Z Buses in front of The Chalet at one o'clock, ready for tourists from the nearby hotels, The Preluna, The Park.

One afternoon duty was to escort a trip to Ta' Qali Handicrafts Village in the centre of the island, what remained of the military airport where the famous Gloster Gladiator biplanes, Hope, Faith and Charity, had once flown tirelessly against the might of the Germans. Some enterprising person had begun to use an empty aircraft hangar for glass blowing, and then others moved into the old nissen huts, and eventually new huts, and for years the whole thing had been a thriving tourist attraction.

"Do they still sell the Mdina glass at Ta' Qali? And the filigree jewellery? It must be a year since I last went."

"Come today," he suggested. He let his arm touch hers.

"I haven't booked."

"There is space."

She glanced at her watch. She had no meetings or appointments that day, November and December were the quiet months in the office. Why not? She took out her phone. "I'll pay my fare, of course. You won't get into trouble with your employer, will you?"

"No." He smiled, eyes gleaming. It took her a month to realise that he was one of the owner-operators of Sliema Z Bus Tours, the cream coaches with a rainbow that arced along the side above a big Z.

She rang Richard to say she was taking an afternoon off. Yes, she was fine. No, nothing was the matter. "Have a good time, then," he said. Richard was marvellous, she had such a great relationship with him. Difficult to realise, sometimes, that he was her mother's brother.

10

The modern coach arrived, cream paintwork gleaming, a contrast to the island's bright orange route buses, some of which had been trundling the island's roads for fifty or sixty years. He introduced her to the driver, installed her in a front seat, grabbed a clipboard and swung down to meet his passengers.

"Hallo, madam, I am Giorgio, and I am your tour guide today. Your name, please?" His charm was effortless. It just shone from him, coaxing out smiles and laughs and turning everything into a joke. Still smiling, the guests climbed the steps, giving little puffs of pleasure at the coolness of the interior with the air conditioning and the dark glass windows.

It proved an interesting afternoon. Giorgio spent most of the short journey standing beside the driver, facing the passengers and talking about himself, the bus, the tour company, the areas through which they passed and Malta's history, swaying easily with the bus's motion and making jokes.

At Ta' Qali he took the tourists to a display of filigree jewellery making, then gave them an hour to shop, pointed out their bus number, explained where to get an ice-cream and reminded them not to neglect to drink. "It's no longer summer, but still the sun we give a little respect." He talked to the driver, he filled in a couple of boxes on a form, then jumped down beside Judith on the cracked tarmac. "Today is an easy job. Everybody will shop. Maybe they spend too much money, but is OK."

A pleasant way to spend the afternoon, strolling from hut to hut. Judith enjoyed watching the light strike the colours of the glassware, examining the jewellery in glass cases and admiring the intricacies of the Malta lace, *Bizzilla*. And always she was conscious of the man beside her, the smile in his watching eyes.

It was . . . unsettling. His eyes told her he desired her, but her clear and sensible head found it difficult to believe. Even middle-aged men tended to lose interest in middle-aged women. She had the bruises to prove it. If her ex-husband, Tom, a decade older than her, had succumbed to the tighter, younger flesh of Liza, why should she expect better from Giorgio, a decade younger?

The shopping over, Judith learned that the trip included first a visit to the magnificent Mosta Dome, and then a folk evening in Qormi.

She sensed his pleasure that he'd tricked her gently into spending longer with him than she'd meant. And felt herself smile.

By the midpoint in the evening most of his duties were discharged. Food had been eaten, *brojoli*, beef wrapped around mincemeat, and steaks of the local fish, *lampuki*, with spinach and bitter olives. Songs had been sung and dances had been danced. For the final hours the guests wound down with deliciously moist cakes and cold wine.

They sat on wooden benches in a dim corner of the courtyard with a tin table between them.

"Did you enjoy yourself?" His voice was low, obliging her to shut out other voices to hear.

She drew a little design in the condensation on her glass. "Oh, yes."

12

"I would like to meet you again. I would like very much." His voice was deep and intimate, his gaze intense.

"Yes," she repeated.

But, the next day, Richard frowned when she told him about her outing. He mopped the sweat from his pate and studied her carefully.

"What do you know about him?"

Surprised, she shrugged. "His name's Giorgio Zammit —"

Richard rolled his office chair over to hers, his forehead creasing over his black eyes. "Bus tours bloke?"

"Mm," she agreed, warily, realising from his tone that she wasn't going to like whatever he was about to say. "Why?"

He sighed, putting his hand over hers. "His wife lives in Sliema, too."

She recoiled. "No! He wouldn't ask me out if —"

Her uncle's round face was solemn and sympathetic. He hesitated, choosing his words. "*Some* Maltese men are attracted to British ladies for a specific reason, Judith. Maltese women are brought up strictly. And the majority of British women aren't."

Although reluctant to take the hint, she heard the uncertainty in her own voice. "I don't think that's it!"

"What better lover than a mature woman from a culture where women expected the freedom to take lovers?" He looked uncomfortable. "I think you're just a trifle older than him?"

She refused to voice the word *yes*. "I'm grateful, in other words?"

He squeezed her hand again. His reply was oblique. "I think you're wonderful. And I think you don't deserve to be hurt again."

All morning she toyed with pictures of Giorgio's smile and the warmth in his eyes. The curve of his eyebrow and the way his cheekbones made her want to touch his face. Obviously, the manner in which their paths crossed so often signalled contrivance on his part, but she was always glad to see him. She mulled over his motives. In the light of Richard's information, they seemed uncomfortably plain.

The moment he appeared beside her at the railings near The Chalet, she tackled him. "Giorgio, I doubt very much that you are a single man."

Meeting her gaze, he asked, "Why do you say this?"

Her heart contracted that he hadn't immediately burst out with a denial. "It seems unlikely that a man of your age has never married. But there's no divorce here, I know that. So unless your wife's dead, you're married."

He crossed himself at the mention of death. Then his fingertips tapped gently on the railing. "You are right. There is no divorce in our country. But some men live apart from their families. Many, many men. Shall we walk?"

They began along the broad, paved promenade between the busy road and the drop to the rocky beach.

Judith's heart was slithering in her chest. "So you do have a wife?"

14

Gravely, he nodded. "Johanna. And I have daughters, Alexia and Lydia. We are all very unhappy when we live together. It's better not. I have lived alone for fourteen years. Alexia is 19, she works in a chemist shop in Tower Road, training. Lydia is 17 and still does her education. I love my children very much. But I do not love their mother, and I have not loved her for a very long time. I doubt whether she ever love me, ever."

His emphatic tone and the glitter of his eyes moved her.

"So why marry you?"

He shrugged, an exaggerated, frustrated gesture that brought his shoulders up around his ears. "Many times I ask myself. Maybe her father thought I was best she could do."

"Giorgio," she'd said, carefully. "I *am* divorced. And I don't think we'd better go out together again."

"I am separate," he declared forcefully. But he made no attempt to detain her when she turned and returned to the office.

Two days later, he materialised at her side as she ate an apple on a green-painted bench facing the waves that were bigger today, bursting on the rocks. Despite her reservations, somehow she found herself joining another of his trips, this time on a ferry to Gozo, the largest of the neighbouring islands.

At the end of the excursion he halted her as she made to follow the tourists from the boat. "Tomorrow is my rest day. I spend a day on a beach. To help me enjoy this, will you be my company?" He thought for a moment, then amended, "My guest."

**15**

She failed to resist his charm. Once couldn't hurt.

They spent the day on the white sand of Anchor Bay at the north end of the island. Talking, laughing, swimming in a cooling sea barely ruffled by the breeze. That evening they ate in Rabat, in a small cellar restaurant aromatic with goat's cheese and herbs and lit by dancing light of red candles in wine bottles.

He drove her home in the early hours, the stars bright against a black sky. Parking outside her flat beside the slack night time sea, he cradled her face gently and kissed her, a deep, carnal kiss, a kiss of clear intent, a kiss that made her muscles melt. "Today we've made a good beginning. It's a big thing we begin."

A sudden bleak regret encompassed her heart. It was all very well to take pleasure from a single day to be enjoyed and allowed to sink into the past.

It had been so innocent.

Even if the air crackled. Even if his eyes burnt with hunger.

It could be glossed over. And one single kiss.

But now his words were forcing her to face facts, and she responded with a deliberate misconstruction. "You're right, it would be big, if we allowed it. But, although you say you've been separated for years, you take me to places far away from home."

He grew still. "I do not hide you."

"I think you do. I think your wife lives in Sliema."

He stared at her for several long moments. "I apologise," he said, at last. "Yes, is true, a little. Johanna and me have been separate for fourteen years, but I do

**16**

not make people talk of her by making a parade of my feeling for you. Why give her that pain? We will be always apart, but still we consider for each other, and for our daughters. They are good daughters and Johanna is a good mother. Also, my parents, they are unhappy their son cannot have a good marriage, and I try not to make them more unhappy. They are my parents. My Uncle Saviour and Aunt Cass, my cousins and their children, we all live in this big village, my parents would hurt to feel the family embarrassed by me. You live in Sliema, you know Sliema. People know other people."

"Difficult," she acknowledged, sighing. "I understand." But that didn't make it any easier. The street lights and the moonlight glittered together in the ripples of Sliema Creek and flecked Giorgio's eyes. "Perhaps it's impossible. I'm not sure I'm the right woman to be tidied away, a secret from your family." And she kissed his cheek, a fleeting farewell, hurrying from the car and safely through the entry door to the flats where he couldn't follow.

The next day he surprised her at the office a few minutes before she would normally take her lunch. He'd never visited the office before. Very solemn, he faced her over her desk. "Is *not* impossible. If you want, we promenade ourselves. We go now to Tony's Bar on The Strand, and eat at a table on the pavement where everyone in Sliema can see. Every day, if you want, we do it."

His eyes were almost black and her head spun with how much she wanted him. She could *not* let him make his life so uncomfortable, either for himself or for those he loved. Instead she allowed their love affair to begin. Discreet, if not quite secret.

He was, after all, separated from his wife.

In England, she would've thought nothing about going out with a separated man. The only difference was that Giorgio would never take the next logical step — to divorce.

Richard was brilliant, though he never approved. Richard, who married Erminia, a Maltese woman, when he'd been stationed on the island with the British Army in the sixties, at least understood. Probably too clearly.

"It's dangerous to go into these relationships half-heartedly," he counselled. "If your partner's Maltese and you want to live in Malta you're well advised to embrace the whole thing, race, religion — and marriage." He'd told her this as they worked together at polished maple desks, guiding foreign buyers through the labyrinth of acquiring property on the island. He tried to tell Giorgio the same over a palely gleaming Cisk beer at a pavement café overlooking the creek that bobbed with boats in blues and reds.

Giorgio just grinned. "We make our own rules."

But no, they didn't. They worked around those of others.

# CHAPTER
# TWO

The entry system intercom buzzed suddenly, jarring her out of her thoughts.

Disorientated, she reached quickly for the handset. "I thought you were never coming! Have you forgotten your key?"

A hesitation. "Is Charlie Galea. Can I speak with you?"

What on earth ...? Maybe Giorgio was ill. Or drunk! "Of course, Charlie. Come up." She made herself sound composed, and pressed the button to release the front door.

Charlie Galea was younger than Giorgio, thinner, taller. He lived with his wife and three small children in San Gwann, behind Gzira and Ta' Xbiex. She knew him a little, he was another recent addition to the diving fraternity.

He stepped through her pale green front door and into the entrance area that opened out into the other rooms, his eyes flickering around the white walls decorated with pastel watercolours.

He looked so drawn and ill at ease as she showed him into the sitting room. The poor lad was horribly uncomfortable. Probably Giorgio *was* drunk, and had sent gullible young Charlie Galea to make his excuses. Or perhaps to fetch Judith, so that Giorgio could sparkle his eyes at her and urge her to join the fun?

"Coffee?" she offered.

He shook his head. Cleared his throat. Then, unexpectedly, slid a hand across his eyes.

Silence.

Despite the temperature, Judith felt a chill slither around her. Giorgio being drunk would hardly make Charlie cry. Her lips tingled. "What, Charlie?"

The young man took a deep breath. "There was an accident, today. With Giorgio."

She sat forward, fists balling, heart pummelling her rib cage from the inside. "How bad?"

He nodded, sniffing. "Very bad. There was a jet ski —"

Her stomach tossed like a pancake. "Oh no!"

The story came tumbling out, torrents of words clumped together between Charlie's sobs. "There was plenty of sea for everyone. Anchored there was a cruiser, we see it before we go down.

"Under the water, we hear engines as we come up, but we are at the end of our air, messing about at three metres on the last of our tanks. We are well within the 50-metre zone and we send up our marker buoys already. We are safe to surface with caution." He wiped his face with his T-shirt.

"But there were two jet ski, put in the water from the cruiser, I think. They move so quick, right inside the reef. Giorgio, he surface first . . ."

Horrific images flashed into Judith's mind, Giorgio mown back under, his respirator torn from his mouth as the moaning beast of the jet ski bounced across the water, into the exclusion zone and right upon the surface marker buoy.

Her heart beating in her throat, she jumped to her feet. "He's alive?"

Charlie nodded. "But bad."

"I should have been there," she breathed. "Is he in St. Luke's?" The main hospital, at Gwardamanga.

He nodded again, coughing back his tears. "The helicopter take him."

Judith began to cast around furiously for shoes, her bag. "I must go —"

And suddenly Charlie was on his feet, his eyes enormous with apprehension. "They say no. They say no, *no*!"

Her movements slowed. Stilled. The world went quiet apart from a mosquito-like whining in her ears. She fell back, bonelessly, into her chair. "Who does?" she whispered. As if she didn't know.

"His wife. His mother. They ask the hospital to make sure you are kept out. You are not family, you not visit, they say."

"Nonsense!" she snorted, robustly. "They can't do that!"

But they could.

Until the accident, despite Giorgio's mother, Maria, walking out of the one meeting Giorgio tried to arrange, Judith hadn't quite appreciated the strength of his family's feelings. It hadn't mattered if his parents refused to acknowledge her. Their relationship could go on without them. Her existence shouldn't cause too much harm to Johanna, his wife, it had been so long since Johanna and Giorgio had lived together.

She'd had her rationale.

And now that disaster had struck, surely the family would realise that her place was with Giorgio?

Apparently not.

Giorgio was placed in intensive care, and Judith's pleas and demands for admittance availed her nothing but a variety of nurses advising her pleasantly, "I'm so sorry. Family only."

She called twice at his parents' house in an attempt to negotiate, willing to do anything, say anything, to make them understand and permit her to see him. But no one answered her knock.

She went to Cass.

Cass Zammit, Giorgio's aunt, was the only member of Giorgio's family who'd ever had any respect for their relationship, meeting them occasionally for quiet evenings well away from Sliema to eat pasta and drink red wine. Although she had her own children, Giorgio held a special spot in Cass's heart.

But even she was unable to help. "I dare not. I cannot," she declared. "It's too difficult at the moment. And if Saviour found out I'd interfered . . . !"

Her husband would be furious. Saviour was Agnello's brother.

"I'm sorry, Judith. But Maria and Agnello . . ." She hesitated. "They're adamant that it's your fault. You introduced him to diving, then abandoned him to an inexperienced partner. You could have kept him safe. They say it over and over, and tell Giorgio how you have let him down."

Judith couldn't even refute it. Since Charlie had broken the news the same thoughts had whirled through her head constantly. She should have found a way to stop Giorgio diving with another novice. Shouted or screamed or cried. *Made* him wait.

Damned well made him.

Giorgio had only just been certified for open water. Judith had more advanced certificates, and qualifications in first aid and rescue. Training and experience enough to limit the damage in bad situations.

"Just tell him that I love him." Responsibility and guilt felt liable to choke her. "Make sure you tell him, won't you, Cass? And that I never wanted him to dive without me. Try and make him listen."

"I'll tell him," Cass promised. She hesitated. "But I don't know if he will hear."

Helpless, Judith went through the motions of her life without really eating or sleeping. Empty days and endless nights were her harsh reality.

Richard was lovely, her rock on a suddenly heaving world. "You take what time off you need," he said. But she took none, because what would she do with it? Go hospital visiting? Hardly.

The *Times of Malta* printed the full story of this latest diving accident; the slow process of Charlie getting help, Giorgio airlifted to hospital as that first

"Golden Hour" when treatment to head injuries is most effective, filtered away. There was a new outcry against jet skis in letters to the editor, and diving clubs made statements both of caution and reassurance.

Judith winced at a counter outcry about novice divers. Was it fair to blame only the jet skier. Had the diver had adequate instruction? And supervision whilst experience was gained? Desperately sick in the heart, Judith collected the clippings.

She drove out to see Giorgio's partners, Anton Dimech and Gordon Cassar, at the large, low shed that housed the buses and the filled-to-bursting office of Sliema Z Bus Tours that backed up the kiosks in Sliema and Paceville that sold the majority of trips.

"Hello?" they said, as if surprised to see her.

She pulled herself up tall and drew all her people skills into play, pasting on a smile. She was a shareholder here, which surely gave her a little leverage in a negotiation. Private investment had been sought earlier in the year, expansion capital to buy two new buses. Purchase negotiations were obviously incomplete, but they still had her money.

"Good morning." She sat down and gripped her bag to prevent her hands from shaking. "I'm sorry to bother you at this awful time. You must be busier than ever in Giorgio's absence?" She waited out the following silence.

Gordon was the one to blink first. He was a small, pleasant man with coppery lights through untidy hair, and black-framed glasses. He smiled. "Of course, we

24

have plans to cope with the unexpected absence of a partner, you need not worry —"

Anton made a rapid gesture to hush the other man. "Madam, what is your enquiry?"

She swallowed, the quality of Anton's smile an uncomfortable reminder that he was used to being in control. He was the one the others deferred to, with his push and focus and faultless English. She cursed herself for not cornering Gordon on his own, the easier target. On his own she might have steered him into the channels of information she wished to investigate. "As a shareholder, I thought it was reasonable to ascertain —"

"Madam, we appreciate your investment. I can assure you that his absence will not affect our shareholders."

She was flustered by his cold courtesy.

"And how is Giorgio?" She hated to hear herself ask, she who'd shared a bed with Giorgio several times a week, and should now be beside him every day.

Anton cut off the reply Gordon had opened his mouth to make. "His family will have the most accurate news, Madam."

Her throat congested stickily, making it impossible to do more than poke out her chin against the humiliation of her reception, and nod her curtest goodbye.

She returned to the office to stare out at the traffic and the creek beyond. What else could she do? At least, there, she had Richard, his quiet support preventing her from racing in madness to St. Luke's Hospital and hurtling at the plate glass, or attempting to thread in through a door unlocked for a member of staff.

But she just had to wait.

It was weeks before she could persuade Cass to meet her in a café in St. Julian's, a tiny, front room of a place where Cass felt tucked away from curious eyes. A bead fly-curtain clicked softly in the doorway, and the serene young lady behind the little counter hummed under her breath as she put out trays of fresh *arancini*, balls of rice filled with cheese or bolognese sauce.

On the pale green table were two glass cups of capuccino.

"News?" Judith poked her teaspoon into her froth.

"He's out of intensive care." Cass had worked in England before her marriage, and her English was effortless. Cass lifted her cup elegantly, and pursed her lips to sip. Her dress was smart, her hair carefully "done".

"I read that in the paper." Judith leant forward eagerly, as if she could haul Cass's knowledge into herself by sheer proximity, her feelings, impressions, visions. "So how does he seem? When did you see him last? What are the changes? What do the doctors say?"

Sipping again, Cass raised her pencil-arched tan eyebrows sadly into hennaed hair. "Changes? *Everything* about Giorgio is changed. There is no energy, no smile, no laugh, no joke to make you smile, no endless conversation. It is a completely different Giorgio."

Hope sank and settled somewhat lower in Judith's stomach. "But he no longer needs intensive care?"

"He has stabilised," Cass acknowledged, sighing, shaking her head, then sipping again.

"And has he . . . has he asked for me?"

26

Another sigh. An aching silence. "He's not going to." Cass's voice was very kind. "If that had happened, don't you think I would've found a way to let you know? To leave a message at your office? Don't torture yourself."

Judith tried to lift her cup, but her hand was shaking, and her voice came out as a whine. "I must see him! I might not exist for his parents, but I *can't* just suddenly stop existing for *him*."

Compassionate tears stood in Cass's eyes. "I'm so sorry. But you do need to accept that Giorgio will never ask for you again."

# CHAPTER
# THREE

OK. Cass had confirmed it: he was out of intensive care.

Out from behind the locked doors.

She visited when siesta emptied the street, the Maltese summer sun blazing down to yellow the limestone buildings. Inside, the hospital corridors were cool and quiet. Judith stole along, following Cass's — reluctant, it had to be said — directions.

And there he was.

*Giorgio!*

He had a room of his own, his name written onto a tile on the door, she could see him through the doorway. He lay on his side, his back to her, hooked to a heartbreaking array of machines. But she recognised the way his hair lay at his nape and the gold of his skin.

The open window fluttered the yellow curtains, the bed a white island in the centre of the room. Two nurses and a woman in a white coat surrounded the bed, selecting from a trolley, talking soothingly to Giorgio in gentle Maltese.

She stepped slowly away. Giorgio was receiving necessary care. In ten minutes she'd return.

Ten minutes became twenty, then thirty before her heart hopped to see the nurses gliding the trolley up the corridor, passing her and moving on to a different white room and another patient. With a lift of her heart, she quickened her pace.

But then she saw them. The stocky Maltese couple barrelling towards Giorgio's door from the other direction. The woman's lips were set, eyes blazing.

Judith froze like a guilty child.

Furious words began to stream from the woman in rapid fire, her chest heaving beneath her sedate, navy, belted dress, her voice a frustrated hiss as a concession to the hush of the wards. "No! Get away! *Away*! Not you here, you, no!"

They'd met only once, but Judith had no trouble recognising her. She pitched her own voice low. "Mrs. Zammit, I was only —"

Maria Zammit thrust her short body between Judith and the door to Giorgio's room. "No! He not speak to you, you go. Leave." And then, as Judith hesitated. "*Now!* You never see my son. You English. Go England!"

"I love him," Judith tried, astounded by despair so intense that it seemed to suck away her oxygen. She glanced at Mr. Zammit, whose forehead was furrowed unhappily as he put his hand on his wife's arm and spoke to her in their own language.

Mrs. Zammit stood her ground. "Go! I call for the *ners*."

The ridiculous notion that a mere nurse would scare her away returned Judith to reality, she was tempted to fold her arms and challenge, "Ha! You do that!"

**29**

But then. Anger wasn't the only emotion in Maria Zammit. Judith hesitated. A muscle was tugging at the older woman's cheek and a tremor at her lip. "Go." The tic jumped more fiercely.

Judith was considerably the taller of the two, but Giorgio's mother didn't give an inch, evidently a tiger when it came to doing what she believed protected her family.

Family was important to Giorgio, too. Judith's conscience twinged because she, of all people, understood how he'd hate this confrontation. And his family was making his decisions for him, holding all the authority. If she wanted to get in to see him, she was going to have to think outside her usual box.

And Mrs. Zammit's outrage had given her a last-ditch bargaining tool. An all-or-nothing. She made her voice calm although her heartbeat was shaking her entire body. "I'll go away — after you let me see him. On my own."

Mrs. Zammit snorted. Her husband muttered something.

"If not, I'll just keep coming back."

A tear slowly escaped from one of Mrs. Zammit's dark eyes. She showed Judith gritted teeth. "You teach him to dive under the water. He nearly die. Is because of you! All know this."

Judith's face drained. "If I could change places with him, I would. Please, Mrs. Zammit."

Silence. Judith dug her nails into her palms, staring at Mrs. Zammit, willing her, willing her to comply. See sense. Judge the long-term benefit against a five-minute concession.

"You are not his wife," Mrs. Zammit pointed out unnecessarily.

"No. And I'll bet his wife doesn't visit him much, does she?"

Agnello Zammit made another remark, softly, palm up and shoulders shrugging. An older Giorgio. His voice went on, gentle, musical, Judith couldn't make out enough words to know whether he was arguing for or against her cause.

An angry glitter brightened Mrs. Zammit's eyes. "You go away? Stay away?"

Judith nodded, every muscle willing Giorgio's mother to concede.

Mrs. Zammit's lips thinned. "Five minute!" she allowed eventually, folding her arms. "He not talk to you. I know this."

Tears spilled out onto Judith's cheeks, and she wiped them away with her palms. Relief shook her voice. "Five minutes." And she stepped through the door.

Such quiet. A machine hissed and peeped. Wires. Tubes. White bedlinens, yellow curtains. Outside, the distant sounds of a vehicle straining up the hill.

Giorgio, on his side, didn't look up as she walked around the bed. She was shaken by the peculiar expression on his face, a twist to his lips that wasn't a smile.

For a moment she couldn't speak, shocked by his appearance. His face seemed to have softened and sagged, although he'd lost weight. He had a jowly, loose look that stepped him abruptly forward in years. She tried to catch his dark gaze, wanting him to focus on her face. "Giorgio?"

But, as Mrs. Zammit had forecast, Giorgio didn't reply. It was beyond belief that he'd ignore her — *her!* — like that. Impulsively, she took his bare arm, feeling the softness of the hair at his wrist. He must react to her touch, when such electricity used to crackle between them? "Darling!" she whispered. He twitched, as if to shrug her off.

Her hand on his golden skin was a little dry and lined, and she felt a pang at not making more of an effort. Lately, she hadn't been taking care of herself, not as she used to. Hand cream and moisturiser hadn't figured in her routine. Her mirror this morning had shown her a woman who had been attractive but wasn't bothering, her face bare of make-up and her hair grown out of style and sliding over one eye like a Disney dog's.

Giorgio's flesh felt hot and unresponsive. Even when Judith increased her grip slightly, he remained silent. His face still. The silver that had brushed his hair lately glinted in the light.

Mrs. Zammit looked in balefully through the glass aperture.

Judith wondered whether Johanna had been to see her husband, or had simply signed what forms were necessary to allow her to stay away. Such a waste, when all the time Judith herself was aching to be by Giorgio's side.

"I'm sorry you were so badly hurt," she murmured, voice catching on her grief. "I should've stopped you diving without me, it was too soon. I can't sleep for guilt. Forgive me." He still didn't look at her, but twitched more violently, as if he *really* wished she'd remove her hand but was too polite to say. Reluctantly, she dropped his wrist and backed off, her head flooding with images. Their love had grown behind closed doors, and the passion had been fierce. His lips at her throat, his body over hers . . .

Where had it all gone?

Mrs. Zammit opened the door sharply and entered the room, breaking the dream.

Slowly, reluctantly, Judith stepped out, passing silently between Giorgio's parents. The door closed heavily behind her.

Spinning, she fled. Numbly through long corridors. Down stone staircases of treads worn with age. Striding out into heat like the backwash from an open oven.

Cass materialised from behind parked cars, her face lined with anxiety. "Maria and Agnello came early, I had no time to warn you in case she spotted me. Did she . . .?"

"You don't have to worry." She'd been so thankful when Cass agreed to try and help her to see Giorgio that she'd tried not to think of what discovery of the flouting of Maria and Agnello Zammit's anti-Judith tendencies would mean for her.

Sagging against the wall on a surge of guilt, she closed her eyes. "I hadn't realised quite how . . . You were right, I should've stayed away. I'm sorry I hounded you into this, Cass."

Cass patted her shoulder. "I told you, you expect something that can't be there; the old Giorgio, his old feelings. Trust me — far better to have the memory."

Judith opened her eyes and gazed blankly at the china-blue sky. "But how can I just write him off?" Straightening slowly, she hugged Cass, although she knew Cass shrank at public embraces. "Thanks for helping me, even if it wasn't any use." She choked out a laugh. "But at least I know where I stand, now. That there's nothing left to wait around for."

# CHAPTER
# FOUR

In a very few days, Judith had her life all shut down ready to leave. It wasn't in her to obey Maria Zammit and "Go England!" But Malta just wasn't bearable now that she no longer had Giorgio, his smile, his love, the feeling of being alive in his arms.

Even though she'd loved her time here, adored the golden island set in the sparkling Mediterranean. The heat, the sea, the people. Even though Giorgio had once adored her. It was time to go.

On the flight back to England she was silent, ignoring the press against her knees of the seat in front, unable to bring herself to chat with the red-skinned tourist couple next to her who volubly mourned the end of their holiday. Instead, Judith dreamt out of the window, gazing at the clouds, the sea, mountains. Then, as they descended, at green and yellow fields and, eventually, the grey rectangles and roads that surrounded Gatwick airport.

It had to be bloody Gatwick, she thought. Luton, Stansted, East Midlands and Birmingham airports were all within an hour or so of Brinham, but the travel shop had only been able to get her bloody Gatwick on the bloody wrong side of London.

"'S tricky." The Maltese clerk's dark eyes had been sympathetic. He knew, she'd supposed, half of Sliema knew Giorgio. "Is short notice, is high season. Tricky."

"It'll have to be Gatwick, then." She'd sighed and tried to smile as she'd slipped her credit card onto the red and yellow plastic counter. She just must leave.

Once she and Giorgio had faced a list of problems threatening their happiness: Giorgio was younger than Judith, Giorgio was Maltese and Judith was English. Giorgio was Catholic, Judith was nothing in particular. Judith was divorced, Giorgio . . . well, Giorgio wasn't.

She closed her eyes, remembering his smile as he held her, kissed her, insisted that none of it mattered, it could all be managed, none of it was as important as they were.

And, in the end, he'd been proved right, in a way.

She fastened her seat belt over her sage trouser suit, chosen for the flight because it was loose and comfortable — although her entire wardrobe was fairly roomy, nowadays.

The plane went through an unhappy landing. The tourist couple became white and sweaty instead of red and sweaty as the aircraft yawed its way through bumpy air.

Watching England rushing up to meet her, Judith swallowed to equalise the pressure in her ears but felt no threat to her stomach contents, because she hadn't eaten. For the last two months weight had dropped away, her arms were like sticks on the blue plastic armrests.

The plane landed with a spine-jarring bump, engines howling into reverse. Finally, they were taxiing, stopping, passengers reaching up to empty their lockers.

The flight attendants flanked the exits to smile the passengers on their way.

Judith paused to prolong the last moments before she had to grapple with the realities of "coming home" to England. "Bumpy landing." And then, making it into a joke, "Ask the pilot if it's a plane or a yo-yo."

The flight attendants smothered grins and murmured about wind and turbulent air.

Judith strode from the plane, shuffled through passport control and into baggage reclaim, her jacket thrown over one shoulder, passing the waiting-at-the-carousel time thinking about being back in Brinham.

She conjured up the leafy, hilly market town in Northamptonshire. She'd lived there all her busy life, looking as if she were going to make a career of being a single woman until meeting and marrying Tom McAllister.

After a marriage of nine years and then a separation, and a few months into the new century, she'd quit England, convinced of the need to strike out, to go. She wished she was now as convinced about coming home.

Molly and Frankie were waiting when she battled out through the green channel dragging a stubborn trolley piled high with unmatched suitcases. Molly, her elder sister, much smaller than Judith and becoming plump, her black hair sporting Morticia Addams-like streaks of silver and spilling down the back of her red coat. Molly's husband, Frankie O'Malley, hands on hips, eyes impatient under his dome of a forehead.

"Here she is!" Molly, although sounding pleased, still somehow managed to frown.

Frankie fished out his car keys. "All right, Judith?"

Although Frankie took the trolley from her and Molly fell into step by her side, Judith noticed that there were no delighted smiles or hugs to welcome her home, no anxious enquiries. If she'd expected a demonstration of love, she was unlucky.

Once in the car and Frankie had navigated them through the rigours of the car park and the motorway approach, Molly turned within her seat belt. "So, you're home for good?"

"Whatever good is." From the rear seat, Judith craned back to look at the fat silver belly of a jet taking off over the M25, and almost wished she was on it.

"Where are you going to live? And what on?" Molly's eyes were full of elder-sister readiness to remedy Judith's problems by rectifying her decisions.

The plane above banked steeply, white now as its topside came into vision, and Judith fell into the younger-sister trap of self-justification. "I shall live in my house. Uncle Richard's selling some shares for me, so that'll get me by for some time to come. I can't expect his property agency to pay me now I'm not actually working in it." Richard was also selling her car for her, sub-letting her flat, and sending the last of her possessions on in crates.

Possessions. What did possessions matter? She'd lost Giorgio.

Her heart clenched.

A horror of sudden doubts sent sweat bursting across her forehead. Should she have left? Perhaps if she'd persisted, sneaking in to see him, talking to him, forcing herself to his attention, perhaps she could've eventually made his eyes brighten beneath his thick brush of hair, regard her with the old love . . .

Molly's voice sliced into her thoughts. It was an anxious voice. Molly was good at what was known in Northamptonshire as "whittling", or worrying too enthusiastically. "How are you going to live in your house? What about your tenant?"

Judith shrugged impatiently, wishing Molly would stop making her think of practicalities. Time enough for that. Time. Loads of time, now. "He'll have to go, I suppose."

"Can you just get rid of him, on whim?"

Frankie flicked on the indicator and swung into the outside lane, rushing up behind an old Metro and flashing his lights. "I think she can if it's for her own occupation. With notice. Might depend on the tenancy agreement. I'll find out if you want, Judith."

Judith yawned and wondered if they'd leave her alone if she pretended to sleep. They were like a pair of healthy fish nibbling on a weaker one, searching out her wound. She didn't need Frankie to find out the terms of a standard assured shorthold tenancy agreement for her, she was well aware of both her rights and her responsibilities. "I have to give him two months' notice,

**39**

but I'm sure he'll respond to a cash incentive to look for somewhere quicker than that. Melanie found him for me when the last tenants left, he's a mate of her husband. We've e-mailed, he seems a nice bloke." She didn't bother mentioning that she remembered him from her youth in Brinham. Remembered being fifteen when he was seventeen or eighteen, trying to get him to notice her. Lots of girls had wanted to be noticed by Adam Leblond.

Frankie snorted. "Being a 'nice bloke' don't mean much."

She let her head rest against the window. "Pity he's always been a good tenant: if only he'd been a bad one. Bad tenants only get notice of two weeks."

Molly swung around in her seat, aghast. "But you wouldn't have wanted a bad tenant, Judith! Friends of ours let to students, and they treated the house like a squat. Disgusting, honestly."

Judith felt her shoulders move on a silent laugh, but didn't risk offending Molly by pointing out that her remark had been an attempt at grim humour. How had she ended up with such a sister? Now Molly was being all earnest about how Judith hadn't been there to take control if things had gone wrong, and that she, Molly, wouldn't have wanted to take it on, and Frankie was just too busy. Tom might've been persuaded, of course, if he'd been in a good mood, but it was a bit much to ask him now Judith and him weren't married . . .

Frankie swerved into the middle lane to overtake — or should that be undertake? — on the wrong side,

40

making Judith's head tap uncomfortably against the glass. She shifted her position.

Molly grabbed the handle on the inside of the door as Frankie raced on to jink the car around a Land Rover. "Of course, you're welcome to our spare room for as long as it takes." She didn't sound exactly enthusiastic.

Judith shut her eyes. Molly and Frankie's spare room. Oh God. She'd tried not to think about it until now. Leaving the Giorgio-pain behind had been her priority, that last sight of Giorgio, so distant.

But now she considered Molly's spare room, a not-quite-a-double room with a single bed and a wardrobe full of old tennis rackets and one-man tents belonging to their son, Edward, remnants and reminders of his childhood that Molly refused to throw out. Edward was 33 now and lived in Scotland with a girl his parents scarcely knew. It was doubtful that he'd be off with the scouts any time soon.

Their house was one Frankie had built himself in the mid-eighties, steeply gabled and the window frames stained forest green. It always looked to Judith like part of a Tesco supermarket. A good big property, roomy, and, technically, with four bedrooms.

Of these, Molly and Frankie's enormous bedroom was the most impressive, with an en suite bathroom *plus* a dressing room. The other big room, over the double garage, was used as an office, and permanently strewn with paper and drawings of extensions. And then there was "Edward's room", which Molly kept as it had been when he left it to go to university in 1989, the bed covered with a marbled blue quilt and the grey carpet vacuumed every week. Judith would've liked to be offered Edward's room because it was pleasant and spacious and had a bathroom. But it seemed the modest spare room was as good an offer as she was going to get.

Maybe she ought to book into a B&B. The prospect seemed suddenly attractive.

Would Molly be offended — or relieved? She tried to envisage her life as a guest of her sister and brother-in-law. Was Molly still grumpy in the mornings? Would Frankie feel he couldn't relax and be himself with Judith there? Or, worse still, that he could? He might wear a gaping dressing gown and scratch sweaty bits of him.

In the spare room, she discovered, against her expectations, Molly had emptied the wardrobe. The furniture smelled of Lemon Pledge and the fresh peach bed linen of fabric conditioner. By the time all Judith's bags were in the room — carried ultra-carefully up the stairs, for God's sake don't mark the new wallpaper — the floor area had shrunk dramatically. Hemmed in by her possessions she felt a massive heave of homesickness for her own place. The comfortable rooms of her flat on The Strand, the balcony scorched by the sun and overlooking the rippling blue of Sliema Creek and across to Valletta. The double bed in the shaded bedroom at the back.

Bit late for that. Her flat had been abandoned along with the rest of her life in Malta. Uncle Richard or one of her capable cousins would have it sub-let in days. She yanked her thoughts away from Sliema, made an effort not to be ungracious. "Sorry to put you out like this, Moll. I'm disrupting your life, aren't I?"

"Oh well," shrugged Molly. But her curranty black eyes sharpened. "Of course, it was a bombshell, I'll be honest with you. A phone call yesterday — then today, you're here, bag and baggage."

She waited, her eyebrows raised. At Judith's silence, she reached behind herself and pushed the door closed. To signify that Judith could speak in confidence? Or that neither of them would be leaving the room until a measure of guts had been spilled?

With a sigh, Judith sank down on the bed.

Molly folded her arms and her face settled into lines that could almost have said *I could've told you something like this was going to happen.* "Is it that man you've been mixed up with? Gino?"

"Giorgio."

"*Jaw-joe*, then. Has it all ended?"

Judith tried to sound as if she'd considered, was summarising a prolonged deliberation rather than a snap decision to flee. Some degree of explanation was due to her sister, she supposed, for leaving her life, her job, the place that had been home for the past three years, to dump herself in Molly's home. "There doesn't seem much future for us."

Molly sighed — exasperation rather than sympathy. "All that business with his family, I suppose? Or did he find someone more his own age? I know you've never quite lost that angular, schoolgirl look that means you don't look your years, but a gap always seems more when it's the woman who's the oldest, doesn't it?"

She winced. "Neither of those things."

"Well, don't blame yourself —"

"But I think I am to blame. Look, Moll darling." Judith scrambled to her feet and slid a sisterly arm around the other woman. "I feel as if I'm putting you out enormously, why don't I book into a B&B for now, then perhaps rent somewhere for a few weeks until I can get my tenant out? I'll see him tomorrow and give him notice." She squeezed the cushiony shoulders. "I shouldn't have just dropped myself on you like this, you have your own life to get on with. I'm a disgrace, aren't I?" she joked.

Molly didn't seem to get jokes. "You're *welcome* here! I'll let you settle in." She swung out of the room, leaving Judith to flop back down onto the bed. Welcome? She automatically translated the word into Maltese. *Merhba*. Hmm. She shouldn't have presumed upon her sister's hospitality. But, with their mother ensconced in a care home now, an automatic return-to-family reflex had sent her to Molly.

At least, now she was "home", she'd be able to see more of Mum, pay surprise visits to. The Cottage retirement home. "Hello! I've called to see Wilma Morgan, I'm her daughter." Sit with her. Take her out. Talk. Try not to swear and make her mother tut. "Really, Judith, do we *have* to have that language all the time?"

And Judith not being able to resist, "Bloody right!" Or worse.

Making Wilma laugh in return. "Don't you think you're a little old to still be playing the rebellious child?"

She closed tired eyes. Immediately his face swam into focus. *Giorgio*. Her heart swelled and shrank sickeningly. *Giorgio*. She forced her eyes to open wide, wide, very wide. *Oh, Giorgio . . .*

After half-an-hour of unproductive staring at the ceiling, she rolled off Molly's spare bed. Better unpack sufficient clothes for a few days, she supposed, cardigans and fleeces included. Northamptonshire's summer was a different prospect to Malta's. Here the clouds were a pale grey blanket, no high blue sky, no heat clinging on the breeze or seeping up from the rock. Here she'd often need long sleeves, jeans and socks.

She threw open a case and yanked out a handful of underwear, stretchy, lacy, pretty. She opened one of the small drawers at the top of the oak chest set beside the window. Halted. The drawer was already full of underwear in neat piles, plain, white or beige, and definitely not hers.

She shut the drawer again, thoughtfully, and tucked her stuff into the empty one beside it.

Dinner was served formally in the cavernous dining room. Two Hepplewhite china cabinets and a dining suite for ten covered only a portion of the honey-coloured wool twist carpet. Judith was convinced that Frankie O'Malley earned enough to provide sufficient furniture to make the room gracious. It was like Molly, however, to not really see the point of furniture for furniture's sake. Not for her a couple of comfy recliners by the French doors, perhaps in bluebell leather, or plum, with a sexy little stereo and a bulbous lamp on a side table. Nor a jardinière to fill a corner, or a grandfather clock to chime companionably.

Theirs was a house that ached for loving touches.

Molly brushed aside Judith's offers to take them out for a meal or buy a takeaway. "You're our *guest*." Molly might sigh over the extra work even as she refused offers of help, but she would look after her guest with special meals and fresh towels. That was the way Molly was. "Also, Frankie will only complain if we were to go out, he likes home cooking." That was the way Frankie was.

"Does anyone else know you're home?"

Judith shook her head in response to Molly's question, and tried to feel some appetite for juicy lamb chops and pungent cabbage. "No, nobody. Yet."

"Not Thomas? Not Kieran?"

"No."

Frankie looked up from where he'd been silently engrossed in his meal, his attention caught by the sound of Tom's name. Frankie and Judith's ex-husband, Tom, each ran building firms in the town, occasionally combining forces to tackle larger jobs. They were mates, it was through her brother-in-law that Judith had met Tom fifteen years ago. Frankie displayed a fierce loyalty to his mates, to all things male, really. Wilma termed it being A Man's Man.

Frankie reached for extra peas. "He's very cut up, is old Tom. Had a hard time of it this last year."

"Because Exotic Liza left," supplied Molly, as if Judith might have somehow forgotten that his third wife had recently abandoned Tom.

Liza's name had once had the power to slice through Judith like a cutlass, not so much because she'd put paid to Judith's marriage, but because she'd shaken her self-belief. Liza had known that Tom was married — Tom had known that he was married — yet she hadn't let it stop her having a taste of his big, bullish body. Liza had been the classic "new model", younger, prettier, more desirable and, for all Judith knew, better in bed. But falling in love with Giorgio had so restored and healed Judith that it even made her grateful to Liza, because without Liza stealing her man she would never have found another.

"Careless with his wives, isn't he? Pam dies, me and Exotic Liza leave." Judith was scarcely even thinking about Tom, but actually coming to the agreeable realisation that she could ring Kieran tomorrow and speak to him, even meet him in person instead of relying on the wonders of e-mail to keep in touch. Kieran was home from university and working in Northampton now. He was probably right here in Brinham. This moment he could be playing squash at the sports centre or having a drink with his mates in one of the pubs Judith had known all her life, his boyish face quick to smile, his toffee-coloured eyes to twinkle.

47

Frankie shot her a severe look. "Tom took Liza's desertion very hard." He stabbed the meat from his cutlet. "He had no idea that she was seeing someone else."

Judith brought her mind back to the subject. "Not much fun, is it, to discover that the person you're married to is having sex with someone else? It rather blights the marriage."

Frankie pointed his knife. "You could've patched things up with Tom, if you'd wanted. He *was* prepared to give Liza up for you — it was you who chose to leave."

"True." She stopped pretending to eat. "I'm afraid I'm terribly unforgiving. After all, it only took me discovering his horrid little affair for him to offer to end it."

Frankie began enumerating Tom's problems on his stubby, grainy fingers. "That Liza, she took the Mercedes, she took all the money out of the savings accounts, she kept her credit cards, and she took . . ." He stopped, and snatched up his fork.

"What?"

Frankie shrugged.

Judith grinned suddenly, her cheeks stiff, as if wrenched into unaccustomed positions. Then laughed. "Has he been stashing away cash again, do you mean? Tucking it behind radiators and underneath drawers so the tax man can't find it?" She threw back her head. "Ha! Talk about hitting him where it hurts. Was it much?"

48

Frankie grunted. "Poor bastard's been left with nothing but the house."

"*Poor* bastard. Scraping by in a seven-bedroom palace."

"You can laugh!" Frankie flushed, his eyes glittering with irritation. He and Judith often became prickly with each other. "First he had to take out a mortgage to pay you off, and now Liza's snitched all the liquid assets and done a runner to France with her new bit of rough. He bought that house and spent a fortune doing it up, and, at sixty, he ought to be able to retire. Instead he's got to keep working just to put back what you women have taken out of him."

Pushing her chair back, Judith rose, any sympathy she might have felt for Tom flitting away. "Parasitical, aren't we? And all Tom ever wanted was a housekeeper/cook/gardener for his seven-bed palace, one who would also bring home a full month's salary and give him sex. I expect he would've preferred us all to die, like poor Pamela, bringing him in a nice fat insurance cheque."

"Liza never brought home no full month's salary!"

"Ah, but she doubled up on the sex."

Frankie began serving himself seconds. "All I'm saying is that you never *had* to leave him!"

Judith sighed, and smiled at her brother-in-law. "No. And I wouldn't have done if he hadn't been unfaithful. He did me a favour."

# CHAPTER
# FIVE

Morning. Judith woke to a silent Sunday, early daylight falling on her stack of suitcases and yesterday's clothes strewn over a chair upholstered in yellow damask. She sat up and raked her fingers through her hair. Two tasks today: take the first step towards reclaiming her house, and ring Kieran. Her tenant, being a mature man, might well be at home with the papers. Kieran, being an immature man, would likely be in bed until lunchtime. She'd approach the tenant.

It was a twenty-minute walk to Lavender Row at Judith's rapid pace. She must get a car sorted out, maybe one of those titchy, zippy little things, a Smart car or a Cinquecento.

But, in the meantime, the weather was dry and her smoke-grey fleece was warm, a walk would be good. It would get her out of Molly's house, too. Molly and Frankie had been bickering. She hoped they hadn't been bickering over her.

The sooner she was back in her own place, the better for all concerned. Apart, perhaps, for the tenant.

In her bag was a letter, hot off the computer in Frankie's office, giving the tenant notice. She'd printed on the smooth white envelope, *Adam Leblond*. Staring at the name, she was awash suddenly with memories of Brinham Grammar. Stiff navy blazers, tan leather satchels with doodles all over the inside (because doodles on the outside would get you detention and a sharp letter home). Logarithm books, sensible black shoes, white shirts and striped ties, echoing corridors, quadrangles at break time, hockey in the rain, the A stream, the smell of chalk dust and plimsolls, crisps from the tuck shop with little blue bags of salt in. Boys in the corridors and many of the lessons. Adam Leblond. It had always sounded like a good name for a pop star, a crooner with golden hair and a repertoire of dance steps. Still, she supposed, the name didn't sound bad on a fifty-something photographer.

As she walked, she absorbed her surroundings, the greenness of the fields glimpsed between the streets, the trees lining the roads, the flourishing gardens — some so "flourishing" that a machete and a flame gun would be required to get them under control. Weeds just didn't grow like that in Malta, it was a real contrast to the palm, cypress, twisted olive trees and grey-green spear-like agaves that dotted dry Maltese earth. Her eyes had become used to stone and sand-like soil, dust instead of mud.

She was bound to miss Malta.

Miss the constant, mighty presence of the sea, the unremitting glare of the sun. It would be different going back to Lavender Row. The houses there were terraced but what an estate agent might refer to as "villas", double fronted, the windows set into stone mullions, the rooms large and tall with ornate plasterwork, moulded picture rails and the high kind of skirting boards. Her house, number 18, had a gravelled area to the front, and a long strip of garden at the back.

She'd bought the house outright when she and Tom divided things up upon divorce. Divorce had brought to light the full extent of Tom's assets, although very few of them were liquid. In order to keep the house, the yard, the machinery and equipment, he had, as Frankie said, had to raise capital on his collateral to pay Judith off. She could have bought the house twice.

Once paid off, Judith had enjoyed furnishing her new home with plain carpets and chunky wood, relished the return to the pleasure of being independent.

Tom, in contrast, had growled and muttered and fought to remain in the seven-bed detached they'd shared in Victoria Gardens — all that housework! — because it was "an investment". Later, the value plummeted when an edge-of-town retail park was built on what had been a green belt of land behind it. Instead of looking out on hedges and fields, Tom now looked out on a row of leggy conifers doing an inadequate job of disguising a DIY shop's loading bay. For some reason, the planners had also allowed a nightclub to move into one of the industrial units, providing a noisy, technicolour finale to most Fridays and Saturdays for the nearby residents.

Someone ought to have pointed out to Tom that investments could go down as well as up.

Judith swung into Lavender Row where cars lined either side owing to the absence of driveways, and paused when she reached number 18. Neat. The front garden, a small strip, was gravelled, a dwarf acer in a cobalt blue pot in the middle. The front door was painted black.

She wrinkled her nose. Broken windows and rubbish piled in the garden would have suited her better, given her an excuse for early termination of the tenancy. Oh well.

Pressing the white button, she listened to the bell, and prepared to meet Adam Leblond once more. What would he be like, now? Fat? Bald? Grey?

But the man who answered her peal was none of these things. He was about the same age as Kieran and if he'd told her he *was* a member of a band, she would have believed him. Heavy metal, though, with his long hair and ripped jeans.

"Hey," he greeted her amiably. She knew, from Kieran, that "hey" was the new "hi". He pushed dark hair back over his shoulders, scratched his bare chest and tugged tattered jeans higher over his hips.

Judith glanced again at the house. It was definitely hers. "I'm looking for Adam Leblond."

"Yeah, upstairs. Do you want me to shout?"

She hesitated, checked her watch. It was eleven o'clock. "If you think it'll be all right. I'm Judith McAllister. I'm the landlord."

"Oh, right." He turned his face towards the stairs. *"Dad? Dad! Lady who owns the house is here!"* So this was Adam Leblond's son.

A pause, a muffled shout.

"Can you wait five minutes? He hasn't emerged yet."

"I'll come back —"

"No, come in." He pulled the door open further. The hall carpet, she'd left all the carpets, looked freshly vacuumed, otherwise the hall was empty. "I'm Caleb."

She wondered who Adam Leblond had produced this interesting young specimen with, whether any of the adoring legion of Brinham girls who'd pulled in their stomachs when Adam Leblond blew past on his dark green racing bike had been the lucky one. She'd hardly seen him since he'd left sixth form. He'd faded from her memory until Melanie's e-mail. *If you haven't got new tenants yet, would you let the house to a friend of Ian's? You might even remember him from school, he was two years ahead of us and his name's Adam Leblond.*

The name had sent a nostalgic shock through her, but, deeply involved with Giorgio, she hadn't spared the time to share those old emotions with Melanie. In any event her crush, secret and agonising, had been based on a solitary conversation about sweets outside the school gates.

*Sure,* she'd replied, glad enough not to have to get involved again with local agents. *If you and Ian recommend him, I'm sure he'll be ideal.*

She followed Caleb down the wide passageway to the kitchen with its side window overlooking the patio. Apart from an open bag of Hovis and a sprinkling of crumbs beside the toaster, the room was immaculate. She recalled e-mails from adam@adamleblond.co.uk seeking permission to decorate, and shrugging off her offer to pay towards materials. He'd evidently done a great job. White gloss gleamed on the woodwork, creamy yellow emulsion on the walls contrasted with blood red curtains, and the pine units were freshly coated. The worktops were uncluttered.

Caleb offered her a drink, taking down a thick, orange mug. "I would tell you to make yourself at home, but as it belongs to you . . ." He grinned. His eyes were grey and shone with humour in his tanned face.

She sat down at the kitchen table. "Do you live here?"

He slid two slices of white into the toaster. "On and off, while I'm deciding what to do with myself." He paused, as if struck. "Is it OK for me to stay here with Dad? It's not in contravention of the landlord's rules, is it? It's just for a while."

Blowing on her coffee, she tried to sound reassuring, but felt duplicitous. "I can't remember, to be honest with you. We have a standard assured shorthold tenancy agreement, there might be a clause that states Mr. Leblond should give me the opportunity to veto any long term guests or co-tenants." "Mr. Leblond" sounded overly formal, but she hardly felt that she knew him, and on the odd occasion they'd communicated he'd always signed himself with his full name.

"Oh. Right." Caleb pulled a conspiratorial face. "I don't want to screw things up for Dad, I'll push off to Mum's if I have to." So whoever Caleb's mother was, Adam Leblond didn't live with her.

Caleb reminded her of Kieran. She felt her lips curve into a small smile. That gangly, young man friendliness, the easy grin, the air of finding everything doable. "It doesn't matter now. As long as the house has been looked after."

He waved a dismissive hand. "Oh sure, you know what Dad's like."

"Not really. A friend arranged the tenancy while I lived abroad."

His eyes lit up. "Where have you been? I've just done my gap, Thailand, Cambodia and Australia. Dad had kittens if I didn't e-mail for a couple of days while I was in Cambodia. Isn't Australia so cool? *So* cool." He began to bombard her with stories about hostels and working in kitchens to pay his way, employing the vocabulary of his generation, *cool, crazy, wicked*. She wondered whether to tell him that she'd been around his age in the early seventies, when the same words had peppered her conversation. She kept waiting for him to throw in *groovy* or *fab*, to talk about living on a kibbutz, the icon of freedom in her late teens.

They were interrupted by the rapid rhythm of feet descending the stairs.

Caleb vacated his seat. "Here's Dad."

Adam Leblond jumped the final two steps and swung along the hall. He looked as if he'd come fresh from the shower, his hair combed damply back from a face pink from shaving. Brows drawn into straight lines, he looked as if he was always squinting into the distance. He was wirier than she remembered, quick of movement, flesh taut over his jaw and cheek bones. He wore a plain black T-shirt tucked into black trousers.

Caleb passed him in the doorway, carrying his toast with him. "See you later."

After a flash of a smile in his son's direction, Adam Leblond looked at Judith and frowned. "Sorry, I was reading in bed." His eyes were piercing, alive. He wasn't fat, his hair receded a bit at either side at the front. Faint diagonal lines on his forehead cut across horizontal ones when he frowned.

"It's me who should apologise. I should've phoned and made an appointment. I'm Judith McAllister." It wasn't worth reminding him that she had been Judith Morgan, in the fifth year when he'd been in the upper sixth. If he'd ever known her name, he would surely have forgotten by now. Automatically, she extended her hand.

He recoiled. Hesitated. Then withdrew his right hand abruptly from his pocket, displayed it for an instant before shoving it back. "I don't, really." He half-smiled.

"Oh . . ." Her heart hopped in shock at the glimpse of a hand with pink flesh closing over where his first three fingers ought to have been, a yawning gap between his little finger and thumb. Oh, poor Adam! She flushed hotly that she'd embarrassed him with her attempt to shake hands. "Sorry. I didn't know —"

Compassion for her discomfort flickered in his eyes, darker grey than his son's, one corner of his mouth lifting. "It's relatively recent. Are you here to inspect the house?"

"Not really."

He leaned back against the door jamb. "It's OK if you want to. I expect Caleb's room's a tip, but it's just clothes on the floor and stuff."

Caleb returned briefly into view, moving from the front room to the stairs, four compact discs clamped in his hand. "You were supposed to inform her that I was living here, Dad."

"Oh!" Adam Leblond flushed. "It didn't occur to me! It's only Caleb, he's my son, a guest —"

"I'm not really concerned."

"It's an oversight, it's not as if I'm sub-letting."

"It doesn't matter, now." Her face felt hotter and hotter. All they'd done so far was to make one another awkward, one apology countered with another. His obvious concern for his responsibilities as a tenant made her feel sheepish. She was here to chuck him out of his home, for God's sake. A deep breath. "Could we sit down?"

"Of course. In here." He led her into a relaxing room of subtle colours. Her grey-blue carpet was still on the floor, but he'd added inky damask curtains, a charcoal suite and ivory wallpaper. Everything in the room was functional; no occasional tables or ornaments cluttered the gaps. An Apple Mac computer, large, brand-new and what was customarily referred to as state-of-the-art, was hooked up in the same alcove where she used to have her rather more elderly PC.

Despite its sparsity the room was welcoming, lived in. A neat pile of glossy magazines stood on the floor beside one chair, and two empty beer cans beside the other. "Caleb," he explained, as he gathered the cans

58

into his left hand. "I'm sorry. You've caught me on the hop."

She flushed anew. "I shouldn't have called unannounced. But I came home yesterday, and I need to discuss something with you."

His tidying ceased. He straightened. Bright eyes suddenly wary. "You come home yesterday, you call on your tenant today? Sounds like a problem." They gazed at each other.

His lightning perception forced her into a blunter approach than she'd prepared for, but she made herself hold his grey gaze, speak calmly. "I'm afraid so." Fumbling, she extracted the envelope with his name on from her bag, and held it in both hands. "This is probably not what you want to hear, but I must give you notice. I shall need my house back." Her throat was dry.

Slowly, he took the envelope, and opened it awkwardly, holding it in his left hand while he slit the flap with the remaining finger on his right. Read the letter in silence. Folded the page up and studied her. "So I get two months? Two calendar months from today."

Wishing the news hadn't made him look so bleak, Judith shifted in her chair. If she hadn't been hoping to get him out without full notice, she would have sent the letter by registered post and been spared this interview. She cleared her throat. "To be honest — well, I'd really like you out sooner. If possible. I could offer an incentive —"

He laughed, grimly. "I've nowhere to go."

She pushed back her hair. It was annoying her. "Neither have I. And it's my house. I'm afraid I need it back."

He nodded, sinking into the armchair with the magazines beside it, and regarded her narrowly. "But under the tenancy agreement I have two months."

"Yes, you do. But you haven't precisely been sticking to the tenancy agreement, have you?" She glanced up, from where thumping rock music was filtering through the ceiling.

He did that half-smile again. It gathered the corners of his eyes into laughter lines and cut grooves at the sides of his mouth. It didn't seem to mean that he was finding things particularly funny. "I don't think a court would grant you early possession because I had my son to stay for a few weeks."

Court. She wouldn't take such a trivial matter to court, and he knew it. "I suppose not."

A silence. He frowned, pulling his bottom lip and gazing at the street outside. "The thing is, Mrs. McAllister," he began, slowly. "The thing is that I've been having an awkward time. I had an accident, and my marriage broke down. My wife got the house. The woman always gets the house, doesn't she? I hate solicitors and all the nasty procedure of trying to shoehorn the opposite party out, demanding shares of the equity, her solicitor insisting the dog belongs to her even if the dog thinks it belongs to me. So I left when my wife asked me to, making things easy for her because we have a long history and we're still friends. Foolish of me, on reflection, but I do tend to see myself as the guy who wears the white hat.

**60**

"I was relieved when Ian's wife, Melanie, said she knew of a nice rental, and now I'm happy and comfortable here.

"And then you come along and say, 'But it's *my* house!' And it is. But you're out of order — it's my home. Until the twenty-first of August, in law, this is my home. It's kept well, you've no grounds for eviction. You can examine every room if you want to, the empty beer cans are about the worst you're going to find. Sorry, but I don't feel too co-operative."

He twisted the letter over and over between the fingers of his good hand, the jerky movement the only sign of any agitation. "So if you've run home in a stress because you've had a row with your boss or been dumped by some man who doesn't realise when he's well off . . ." He threw down the letter. "Tough. I'm not inclined to roll over this time. Because the woman *always* gets the house, and I'm sick of it."

His tone was calm, but Judith could see anger in his eyes.

She clenched her hands. Her voice was low. "I'm sorry to even ask it of you."

"Don't be sorry. You've been refused."

"I can offer financial compensation for the inconvenience."

"*Inconvenience?* It's a flaming liberty!" He snapped his lips shut around his words as if regretting the letting of emotion. Then, more quietly, "It's not going to happen."

Her eyes began to burn. She blinked. He was right to be annoyed. She *was* out of order, she'd entered into an

**61**

agreement with him, and now she wanted to welch. He had every right to be cross and recalcitrant.

But, oh, her heart was sore and she didn't like living with Molly and Frank! She wanted to creep off with her own things, her own phone and computer, where she could decide whether the television went on and what to watch. Her own place to lick her wounds and recover. And this was her house!

She sucked in a big breath, and then let it out slowly, looking away for a moment to let her expression close. "Mr. Leblond, would you . . . would you consider just taking my word for it that I had a pressing reason to come home? That I'm in an emotional state that makes getting settled in Brinham and back on an even keel desirable? Without me going into detail?" She looked back at him, and noticed that he was watching her mouth.

Gently, he shook his head, as his eyes flicked back to hers. "Sorry, Mrs. McAllister." As his hair was drying it was lightening, becoming a silver-streaked version of the chestnut colour she remembered, sliding down at one side.

She closed her eyes for an instant, and swallowed. The ticking of the clock on the wall seemed suddenly very loud. She rose, hitching her bag onto her shoulder. "OK, you're right. It's a man." She saw a look of derision fleet across his face. "He hasn't exactly dumped me. But it doesn't look as if there's a future for us."

And, without warning, tears rose up and choked her.

# CHAPTER
## SIX

"Hell," he sighed.

There were no sobs, she was far past that. The tears just sprang silently from her eyes and poured down her cheeks. Judith opened her handbag and scrabbled for a travel pack of tissues. She'd used a whole rainforest of paper handkerchiefs in the last two months.

She pressed a wad of tissue against each eye in turn, and sniffed inelegantly. Another jerky breath, and her voice came out through a throat that felt stretched like wire. "I'm staying with my sister, but I need to be on my own. Or I wouldn't ask you to start looking for somewhere else immediately."

"I'm sorry," he repeated. But this time he sounded as if he might mean it. He hesitated. Asked gently, "You don't think you'd be better with your sister, for a while? Rather than being alone?"

Judith gave a strangled laugh through her tears. It was odd to be laughing and crying at the same time. It made her feel as if she might soon be flailing for whatever smidgen of control she had left. "She's driving me nuts. She makes me these meals. Proper square meals, nutritionally balanced. *Huge*. I don't even want to look at food, and she wants me to *eat*."

He laughed briefly. He'd forgotten to keep his hand out of sight, and she caught a glimpse of zig-zag lines across the palm like white lightning, new pink skin across the strange, shiny knuckles. "But you do look as if you need to put on at least a stone."

"I know, I'm a scarecrow." She wiped her eyes and sniffed again.

"Not as extreme as that. Perhaps a chicken carcass."

"Thanks a bunch." She tried a watery smile and he grinned suddenly, and winked.

But he didn't offer her the house back.

The Water Gardens were not so splendid now as when built in the late Victorian era. All the eight fountains of varying sizes were dry and the people of Brinham were left with just one algae-ridden, scalloped-edge pond. Either side, smaller ponds in the same design had long ago ceased to function, and were now flower-beds.

The parks department had planted up the waterless tiers of the fountains with French marigolds and catmint to clash gaily with the scarlet salvias and purple lobelia in the flower-beds below. The weedy grass around the beds and paths was mown and the benches thick with bright green paint, glossing over last year's *Baz luvs Katee* and *Northampton Town F.C.*

The park made a pocket of colour just off the town centre, somewhere for office workers to eat their sandwiches on hot days, gangs of teenagers to hang out once they'd exhausted their money at the shops, or the odd street-roamer to loll on a bench and drink special brew. Shoppers nipped through between town and the car park, a bare line in the grass where they cut diagonally across.

Judith had charged her British mobile phone the evening before and now found a vacant bench and pulled it from her bag to ring Kieran, pushing the little rubbery keys with mounting anticipation.

She got him straight away, raising his voice against the happy background clamour of a pub. "Hey!" he said. "I e-mailed you this morning, isn't this call costing you, like, loads?"

"Actually, I'm in the Water Gardens," she said, brightly, making her voice level and serene. "I'm home."

"Shut up, shut *up!*" she heard him yell into the escalating racket around him. Then, into the phone, "What, the Water Gardens in Brinham? You're in *Brinham*? How cool is that? I'm, like, in The Punch! Stay put!"

She folded the phone shut, and waited, her gaze on the old black iron arch that led to the lane threading between two hotels and into the town centre, her heart thrumming gently with anticipation. The Punch was a bar in the cellar of The Duke of Brinham Hotel on High Street. When she'd been a youngster it had been a popular venue for discos or parties. They'd tried to pretend it was The Cavern Club.

Judith had been Kieran's stepmother for the nine years from when he was seven until he was sixteen, really important years. Such a little mouse he'd been when she first knew him, an unlikely son for big, bullish Thomas McAllister. While Tom made her the subject of an exciting, conspicuous courtship, Kieran and Judith quietly clicked, the little boy who'd lost his mother, the woman who'd never had time for a relationship sufficiently lengthy to consider children.

Her gratitude to his mother, the unknown Pamela, was boundless. She felt guilty, as his father settled possessively on Judith for his second wife, to see Kieran dance with joy and demand to be allowed to call her "Mummy". Pamela's death gifted Judith a son, a dear little boy with an endless capacity for love.

Tom was a big cattle rancher of a man, gruffly kind to Judith and gratifyingly active in bed, but on her wedding day Judith probably loved Kieran more than she loved Tom. She loved Tom. But, oh, she did love Kieran!

She should have pushed harder for the adoption that would have given her parental rights. But whenever she brought the subject up, Tom merely pulled her into his arms and kissed her roughly. "He *is* your son, he more or less chose you himself. We don't need any fuss in the court." And so Judith settled down to the novel position of mother.

She loved it. Swimming lessons, football club, friends for tea, parties, school open evenings, new school uniform, bedtime stories. She took a five-year break from her career as a surveyor and invested herself in Kieran until he was safely settled in senior school.

Yes, *mother* had been more satisfying than *wife*. Constantly resisting being just another of Tom's possessions became wearing.

And when, after almost a decade of Judith being with Tom, Exotic Liza came on the scene, Judith was almost relieved. Tom's betrayal gave her back her freedom.

But then Tom tripped her up.

Because she might have thought twice about removing herself from a suddenly crowded marriage if she'd realised for just one instant that Tom would avenge himself in his enraged bitterness at her lack of forgiveness by roaring, "You can forget about keeping in touch with Kieran!" Would she ever forgive Tom for using highly-strung, gentle Kieran against her like that?

Sixteen or not, Kieran wept. Judith lost her head, screaming at Tom, "You overbearing arse! You never have his best interests at heart! No wonder the poor boy's scared of you!"

Her hasty words compounded the damage. If she'd kept calm and reasoned with Tom he might have rescinded his edict. She should have negotiated, cajoled if necessary. Tom, desperate to patch things up, was trying to force her to heel, she knew that.

Well, his clumsy strategy hadn't worked. Kieran, growing up fast, sneaked in meetings with her between school and home, meetings he didn't bother advertising to his father. And Judith certainly felt no compulsion to own up.

Tom's fury at Judith for refusing to pardon him his infidelity eased in time, of course, but Kieran had moved on to seventeen, then eighteen, and was well into the habit of being secretive with his father. Judith moved to Malta to work with Richard while Kieran was at Sheffield University, and had since funded his visits to her, as well as timing her visits home to coincide with his.

Thank God for e-mail.

And suddenly he was there, running into her view, multi-coloured trainers on jet-propelled feet, brown spikes of hair tossing over his forehead, eyes scanning the benches to find her. She sprang to her feet, her lips stretching effortlessly into a great grin of welcome. She faltered slightly when she realised he was towing along a slight, teenage girl in tight, turned up jeans who must, she realised with a spurt of irritation, be the fabled Bethan he'd talked endlessly about in every recent phone call and e-mail. But then Kieran let go of the girl and sprinted the final yards across the grass and Judith threw her arms open wide.

His long arms swept her completely off her feet. "Mum! Wow! This is so good, so cool! When did you get here? I didn't know you were coming!" He hugged her so tightly that she literally couldn't inflate her lungs, and when he let her go she had to cough for breath.

"Let me look at you," she gasped. "You look so well, darling! How are you? How's the new job? It's great to see you!" She wasn't a small woman, but her stepson gangled over her. His height contrasted with his boyish looks so that the impression was of a seven-foot-tall twelve-year-old.

With a final squeeze, Kieran let her loose. "Mum, you have to meet my Bethan." He swung around and hauled the slight girl forward. "Beth, this is my mum. My stepmother, I mean, Judith, who I talk about all the time, not Liza, obviously. God, this is so great! I can't believe I'm finally getting to introduce you guys!"

Bethan smiled shyly. "Hey." She looked as if she might still be at school, a tiny elf-child in an enormous hooded top, her hair artificially black and showing fair at her centre parting and above her fringe, as if someone had stood behind her and drawn a large T on her head. Silver studs ornamented her nose and lip, to go with teenage spots on her forehead. Kieran, Judith noticed suddenly, now had an eyebrow pierced.

Judith made herself smile and offer an enthusiastic, "Hey!" to Bethan, although she felt a swell of disappointment. Was it very mean of her to want Kieran to herself? She normally saw him only every few months, and had to fill the gaps with phone calls and e-mails that she sucked up whole into her memory to turn over and over until the next time.

Still, she was home now, and as Kieran was living with his father she'd have loads of time to get him on his own.

So she settled down to enjoy his company, his news, his excitement and enthusiasm for his new job, which was with the local water authority. But when two of Bethan's friends, as breakable-looking as her, wandered into the gardens on wooden-soled sandals, Judith grabbed the chance of Bethan leaping up to greet them. "I need to talk to you alone, Kieran." She swallowed against a suddenly closed throat. "Later, perhaps. Or tomorrow after work?"

The sparkle faded from Kieran's eyes as they searched hers, and he looked suddenly concerned. "I suppose there had to be a reason for you suddenly turning up. Hang on." And he ran across the grass to consult Bethan, who nodded, waved sketchily at Judith and turned to clomp off with her friends.

Kieran pulled her back for a kiss, a wide-open-mouthed kiss with visibly curling tongues. The friends watched casually. Judith looked away.

Then Kieran ran back, his hair blowing above his big brown eyes, his broad top lip creasing laterally as he beamed at her. He flung himself down on the bench. "What's up?"

Kieran was the only person from Brinham who knew all the truths, both wonderful and awful, about her affair with Giorgio. Kieran, with his English values, saw no reason why they shouldn't be together. Kieran thought Giorgio was too cool for words. Giorgio, who, until he met Judith, had always been happy to remain on the water's surface rather than underneath it, took Kieran night fishing, puttering along in a small fishing boat and shining a lamp into the water in search of squid. Then, afterwards, to drink in atmospheric little Maltese bars run by his friends.

And also on day trips when there were a couple of empty places on the bus, ensuring he got Kieran a seat close to the prettiest girls. Giorgio thought that every man deserved an attractive woman. It was the natural way of things. Judith could see his grin as he said it, feel the feather-light touches of his fingers skimming her spine, the tenderness as he called her *gojjella tieghi*. My jewel.

Kieran was going to be distressed about Giorgio.

Stroking his hands, she told him, quietly, simply, because she knew he was going to be hurt, and no amount of wrapping up of the truth would prevent that.

His light brown eyes widened with pain. "It happened two months ago? And you've only just told me?"

"It was hard to cope —"

Kieran swore, snatching back his hands to slap the bench with the flats of them. "And of course you *had* to cope all by yourself? That's what you've always got to do, isn't it? Keep it all in? Give up on him and come back to England, without even letting me know what happened. You weren't the only one to care about him! *I deserved to be told, if I wasn't going to see him again!*"

And then his shoulders began to shake, and Judith shared the last of her tissues with her son.

It was two hours before Kieran left to find Bethan.

Judith, exhausted by his anger and pain, trudged to the taxi rank and took a cab to visit her mother, in a care home on a tree-lined road out of town that looked as if it meant to go somewhere important, but had actually been superseded by the dual carriageway. Wilma had sold her own bungalow a year ago, when Molly helped her identify the tall, airy rooms of The Cottage retirement home as somewhere she thought she might be happy. And she would have twenty-four hour care.

It seemed early for lunch, when she arrived, yet it was obviously in full swing. She supposed meal times could be lengthy.

She opted to hang around in the no man's land inside the tall front doors while her mother enjoyed her meal in peace, deciding from the combination of smells that the residents were enjoying shepherd's pie, probably followed by apple crumble and custard. A few pages of an old copy of *The People's Friend* later, a cheerful carer whose tight uniform rode up in horizontal pleats above all the widest parts of her, popped her head around the corner. Her name badge, high up, near her shoulder, said Sandy. "She's ready, lovie, if you are. Shall I just tell her who it is?"

"I'd rather be a surprise." Judith followed the burly back up the wide corridor, past a room on her left where some residents were still eating, and into a sunny, pale green lounge with an aquarium and a television.

"As long as we don't get her too much all of a doo-dah, lovie, that's all I need to be sure of."

Obstinately, Judith ignored the note of warning in Sandy's voice. She wanted to see her mother's face shine with astonishment and delight at seeing her so unexpectedly.

From the doorway, Judith saw Wilma sitting in a high-backed chair, peering into her handbag.

Her hair looked so white and freshly washed in the sunlight, her face as soft and gently defined as bread dough, that Judith had to swallow before she spoke. "Hello, Mum! It's lovely to see you." She felt a beaming smile take hold of her face, even though her eyes burned hot.

Wilma jumped violently, and tipped her handbag upside down onto the floor. "*Judith*?" Her hand flew shakily to her chest, and her chin dropped. "Oh, Judith! Oh, darling. What on earth . . .?"

With a noise that might have been a gasp, a laugh or a sob, Wilma grabbed for Judith's hands, pulling on them until Judith pulled back to get her to her feet. Trembling with the effort of standing without a frame or stick, Wilma slid her stiff arms around her daughter, and leant heavily, breathing in uneven little gusts.

"Judith, oh, my girl! Come here . . . let me just look at you! My duck, when did you get here? Oh, what a fright! But how lovely . . . how lovely, how *lovely* . . . I can't believe I'm so lucky! I just can't, oh, I've gone as shaky as a lamb! Oh, I'd better sit down. Oh!"

Taking some of the weight, Judith helped her mother plump solidly down into her chair, then watched anxiously as she tunnelled clumsily up her sleeves for her hanky to catch some of her rolling tears. Guiltily, she began, "Perhaps I should've rung first —" when the carer, who'd paused to untangle a man's glasses chain from his buttons, cut across her in a loud, sing-song.

"Are we all right there, Wilma? Yes, darlin'? She was a big surprise, wasn't she? Have you got your breath all right, lovie, shall I get you a drink of water? Yes, all right, lovie, coming up."

Wilma managed to stop laughing and sniffling and blotting her tears, and called after her, "Thank you, just the job." Then she swung suddenly on Judith and pinched her arm. "You!"

"Ow!" Judith pulled her flesh out of the uncomfortable grip.

"You!" repeated Wilma, beaming, and, denied the arm, shaking Judith's shoulder. "Why didn't you let me *know* you were coming? I could've been looking forward to it for weeks! How long are you here for? Can you pick up my bag and my bits for me, duck? Just look at all my rubbish on the floor, now, what will people think?"

They were interrupted by the carer with the promised water, chiming loud, comforting phrases as she tucked the glass into Wilma's hand. Before she turned away, she studied her intently, then nodded to herself as if satisfied that Wilma was in no imminent danger of collapse. "All right then, Wilma, you just take your time now, lovie, and have a lovely visit with your daughter, and you just get her to ring that bell if you need another glass of water, all right, darlin'?"

Judith wished, now, that she'd done things differently, conscious that the carers had her mother to look after full-time, and didn't need her breezing in and getting her in such a "doo-dah" that it almost amounted to a funny turn.

Wilma took her large black handbag back and gripped excitedly onto Judith's sleeve, making it difficult for her to rise off her knees. "How long are you here for? Is everything all right? Is Richard all right, and his family?"

"I've come home." Judith smiled, gently, patting her mum's hand, and then freeing her sleeve so that she could get up and at least grab a footstool to perch on.

"Oh my *duck*," Wilma breathed in rapture. "Home for good? Are you back in Lavender Row? Have you seen our Molly?"

"I'm staying with her, until I've got my tenant out. In her spare room."

Wilma's smile faded. "She's a good girl, is Molly. What kind of a mood's her Frankie in?"

Shrugging, Judith pulled a face. "Never changes much, does he?"

"Frankie's Frankie," Wilma agreed, rolling her eyes.

The visit to her mother cheered her so much that Judith decided she might as well see Tom and get it over with, so took another taxi back through the town centre and uphill into an older sector of town. Past the grey hulk of the bus station, the market, coffee houses, print works, car parks, and, presently, past a white sign with *Thomas McAllister Building & Development* in red, arching over double gates to a yard, a cabin in the corner where a long-suffering clerk put up with Tom's eccentric work methods.

Little had changed there since the days of their marriage, she thought, gazing in at barrows, a dump truck, a skip, trestles, a scaffold tower.

But four streets away, at the house in the generously sized square called Victoria Gardens, it was a different matter. Liza had made her mark.

The extensive front garden of the gracious old house was all paved now, a big, ostentatious urn where the alpine garden used to be and the desert of drive flanked by ranked variegated box topiary balls. Judith had never cared much for variegated plants, which, after all, only made a virtue out of a virus. The low white wooden gates had been replaced by tall, spindly black wrought iron with golden spikes on top, an unhappy fit with the original ornate Victorian railings around the sunken gardens in the centre of the square.

She paused to gaze nostalgically at the sunken garden. It was kept up on an unofficial basis by residents who wanted the grass mown more often than the twice a summer the council thought necessary. Tall copper beeches glowed in the sunlight, and over a series of arches Russian Vine was a creamy riot. Mile-a-Minute, some people called it.

When she'd been married to Tom the residents had held Mile-a-Minute Sundays when they'd formed working parties to cut the vine hard back to prevent it from smothering the entire area, loud and happy occasions fuelled by glasses of wine and picnic lunches. Children, high on Mars Bars and Coca-Cola, would stuff the snaky clippings into black bags, screaming and racing and scaling stepladders no matter how often they were warned.

Judith turned away from the memory, and clanged through the fancy, golden-tipped gates.

It was an odd sensation to knock at the door of what used to be her home, especially since it was a different door now, with mock gothic hinges and an ornate black letter plate. She wondered what had happened to the gracious old one with the stained glass panel. Tom had probably sold it to a reclamation yard.

Tom, when he answered the door, looked stunned to see her. He also looked dishevelled, food spots on his shirt and hair on end. The contrast between him and Giorgio struck her like a slap. Tom looked slack and pale and all of his sixty years. A cynical person might say she'd done all right for herself, exchanging this husband showing definite signs of wear and tear, his hair leeched of colour, his face becoming pouchy, for Giorgio's dark good looks and fewer years on the clock. Giorgio's body had been more solid. Firmer beneath her hands. Tom's typically English appetites for the wrong food and too much beer had combined unhappily with the effects of gravity.

She arranged her features into a casual smile. "Hello Tom. You look as if I woke you from a Sunday nap."

The familiar parade of expressions flitted across Tom's lived-in face. Pleasure to see her, then anger. Lastly, resignation, because the anger had been futile, she'd left him anyway. "Judith! What are you doing here?"

"I came to tell you that I'm living in Brinham again, just so you'd know. I'd hate Frankie to surprise you with the news."

He blinked. Rubbed his hair back over his head. She was sure she'd woken him from a nap. Perhaps he wondered whether she was part of a dream.

"I was sorry to hear about Liza." She congratulated herself for actually sounding sorry, rather than smug at his comeuppance.

"Yes." He hesitated. "It was a bad time." Then, ungraciously, "Well. I suppose you can come in."

She stayed where she was. She'd never cared for a certain bluntness about Tom's manners.

After a second he sighed, and amended with overdone courtesy, "Why, Judith, how lovely to see you. Would you care to come in, perhaps for some refreshment?"

She grinned at his exaggerated air of indulging her. "A cup of tea would be very welcome."

"You know where the kitchen is." He closed the door behind her as she stepped into the big hall with the dogleg staircase.

She opened the door again and stepped back out onto the drive. "You don't change much, Tom."

"It was a joke!" he shouted after her as she strolled up the drive. "Judith!"

Her hand on the large gate latch, she halted. She'd overreacted. For God's sake, couldn't she take a bit of wry humour any more? She should turn back, have a civilised cuppa with this big bluff bloke who once was her husband.

But Tom yelled on. "You don't have to be like that . . . you stroppy, awkward mare! You always were flitty! Or we'd still be together!" Flitty, from Tom, was an insult usually reserved for exasperating (women) customers who changed their minds mid-job.

She stepped through the gate. "I might be stroppy and awkward, but deciding not to be married to you doesn't make me flitty. It makes me sensible."

# CHAPTER
# SEVEN

For two weeks, Judith stayed in Molly's spare room and tried to get the hang of living in Brinham again.

Brinham was a perfectly pleasant market town in an OK part of the country. The town centre had grown up in the era of dark red Victorian buildings with moulded brickwork and steep roofs, and what of that had been retained intact was still worth a second look. It wasn't beautiful, it wasn't ugly; it definitely had style.

Unfortunately, in the 70s it had been acceptable to demolish three streets of Victorian architecture and replace them with an enormous block of brown brick and dirty glass. The Norbury Centre, a development Judith had never cared for. It looked like something a five-year-old might make from Lego if Lego made only mud-brown bricks and long, narrow wired-glass windows. But now that the council had paved Market Square and the pedestrian arcade, installing olde worlde black lampposts that were handy for hanging baskets of vermilion petunias, the blemish of The Norbury was less conspicuous.

England, on the whole, she found a bit moist, but there were lovely days, too, with sunshine that caressed.

In Malta in the height of the summer the sunshine felt like being hit with a sheet of hot metal.

But it was odd and uncomfortable living with her sister and brother-in-law who, she sometimes suspected, only made the effort to converse when there was a witness. She spent most evenings reading in her room, which at least gave them their privacy to ignore each other.

In the O'Malley marriage it seemed rigor mortis had set in.

At the end of every day Frankie climbed out of the van with *Francis O'Malley Construction* on the side. Molly prepared a meal for him to come home to, a proper, cooked, two-course dinner from fresh ingredients. Then Frankie retired behind the paper and Molly sat before the television, watching without any change of expression soaps, dramas, reality shows and comedies. How on earth did she share a bed with someone she never spoke to?

Judith got out of the house as much as she could. She visited a hairdresser for fresh highlights — Sparkling Embers, long overdue — and to have her unbearable shagginess cut back into a new low-maintenance feathered style onto her shoulders. She liked it. It swished when she turned. She bought a small car, two years old and bruise-purple, she visited her mother in the care home, twice, taking her out in her new car to a coffee shop with yellow café lace and green gingham curtains.

"You're too thin by half," declared Wilma Morgan, struggling out of the car and patting her pearly grey perm. "I can't bear coffee in these places, it's nothing but froth and look at the price of the scones and you only get a dab of jam with them. I wish I knew what really made you come home. You never really *confide*, Judith. Is everything all right with Richard and family? Isn't it about time Richard retired? He might be my baby brother but he's knocking on." She smiled as Judith offered her arm, her jowls lifting and becoming part of her cheeks. "I wish you'd brought my wheelchair."

"You said you wanted to walk."

"Don't take any notice of me. I can't walk."

"Piggy back?" Judith turned, and crouched invitingly.

Wilma's chuckle was more of a wheeze. "Serve you right if I hopped on."

Judith saw Kieran several times a week, always Bethan by his side. She went to the pub with them — not The Punch, a bit too trendy these days. Just somewhere ordinary and multi-generational like The Prince or The Holly Tree. She asked Bethan's age when Bethan asked for a vodka shot, which made Kieran glare.

"Seventeen." Bethan pulled at the fronds of two-tone hair around her face.

Judith glanced at Kieran. "And you're twenty-two."

"I know that." He pulled his bottle of strong lager towards him. "There's no law against it, is there? You don't seem to worry about age gaps in your own relationships."

She stared down into her cold white wine, and suddenly didn't want it. Put it back on the table.

"Sorry," he mumbled.

"It's OK. Age gaps are all a question of perspective and . . ." She fumbled for a word. "— wisdom."

He frowned, and she knew he was searching for her meaning and suspecting her disapproval.

When she'd had enough of Kieran and Bethan's in-your-face conducting of their courtship, all those yawning kisses even if she were half-way through a sentence, she stepped out into the late evening purple darkness and left them to it.

It was drizzling. "Bloody weather," she muttered, turning up her collar. She was aware that it was foolish to wander the streets late at night on her own. This wasn't Malta where the world and his wife would be strolling in the comfortable evening temperatures along the promenade from Sliema to Spinola, without any sensation of threat. This was Brinham, which had its bad areas like most towns, and a sensible British personal safety code must be followed. It didn't pay to wander back streets with a handbag on show, late at night, alone.

Her phone beeped, and she fished it from her pocket.

A text message from Richard.

*Must speak, can u get 2 landline?*

She stared. It would be nearly midnight already in Malta. She returned, *Will be @ Molly's house 30 mins.*

And turned back towards the taxi rank.

# CHAPTER
# EIGHT

Molly had gone to bed.

Frankie was asleep in his chair, paper collapsed on his lap, glasses skewed, mouth open.

The house was still, dark except for a small reading lamp reflecting shinily on Frankie's head, and a long-life bulb that lit the stairs. Creeping quietly, Judith took the cordless phone from its stand in the hall to her room. The instant it rang, she depressed the key to ensure the others weren't disturbed.

Richard's voice filled her head, warm, friendly, reminding her sharply of Malta, the office, Erminia, her cousins. She pictured him at home with the doors and windows open to the night, stroking his smart little moustache, his feet bare on the tiles, Erminia reading a magazine in the background from the light of a lamp with a pink tasselled shade. "Molly said you were out with Kieran; sorry to have to bring you home early."

"No problem. What's up?"

"Business." He sighed. "Are you alone?"

She gripped the handset more tightly. "Yes." She could hear a tremor in her voice.

"It's bad news." Another sigh. "It's just that . . . well, Sliema Z Bus Tours have gone bust."

Bust. She examined the word. Bust? Bust. She couldn't, for a moment, see its relevance to Sliema Z Bus Tours. Or, of course, she *could*. But it couldn't be that. *That* would be too terrible. *That* would mean . . .

Her mouth went numb. She fought to remain calm. "What's happened?"

"I wrote to the directors advising them that you wished to sell your shares, and offering them the option, as we agreed. What I got back was a notice about insolvency, and the address of the Liquidator."

"Oh my God," she breathed.

"I didn't bother you at that stage, because I thought it was simply a mistake. It couldn't be insolvency, obviously. Probably something to do with structure, you know, because of Giorgio not being able to administer his own affairs. A technicality."

His voice began to echo in her ears. "But it isn't?"

"No." A hesitation. "A notice was among the mail at your apartment. They're in liquidation."

Blood thundered. Disbelief coloured her words. "That's ridiculous! Stupid! They're not in liquidation, I invested thirty thousand liri, they're negotiating to buy new buses. If they were in trouble they would've cancelled the expansion and simply used the money to trade out of their difficulties —"

"It's gone."

Wordlessly, she wiped sweat from her top lip and the base of her throat.

"Your money's gone. I've had a long talk with Anton and Gordon. I've been with them all evening. After you, and other private investors, took shares in exchange for

**84**

investment to fund the planned expansion, one of their drivers caused a fatal road accident. The company's insurance had lapsed."

Judith closed her eyes, very tightly. "That can't have taken all the money?"

Richard's voice was gentle. "More than. The Liquidator's selling the bits and pieces they owned, but the premises were rented and the other vehicles were leased. You know how these things are arranged. The Liquidator is making his usual enquiries about directorial negligence."

"Because the business is insolvent?"

"It's a complete house of cards. I'm sorry, Judith." A long silence. A slow breath, then he added, in a rush, "Anton says Giorgio was responsible for insurance matters."

"I see."

"I wish I could offer to return the money you invested in Richard Morgan Estate, but I don't think it's on at the moment." Richard Morgan Estate had bought into a new hotel development, a small one. And they'd been so bloody excited to be involved. And tie up their capital.

She scarcely slept. By early morning she was pacing the misty streets of Brinham, hoping the sun would burn the dampness off soon.

*Giorgio.*

A massive heave of sadness, her eyes boiling at the memory of the hospital, the tubes and beeping machines.

**85**

Cass had been right. How much better for her final memory to be Giorgio smiling, laughing, plunging his unbroken body into the sea, spending a raucous day on a fishing boat with his mates, drinking golden Cisk beer or bitter black espresso, eating unpeeled, sun-dried figs, *farkizzan*. Swaying with the movement of an impressive, modern, air-conditioned coach, eyes sparkling and hands gesticulating, captivating his passengers with tales of village festas, bareback donkey races, parades and *ghannejja* or folk singers. Ushering the tourists around ancient cities built of stone, catacombs and prehistoric temples, old film sets and bustling markets.

Had he realised then how close disaster loomed?

The impression Sliema Z Bus Tours gave was certainly one of prosperity, with the shiny cream coaches with rainbows on the side and an itinerary bursting with fun, history and culture. It didn't look, as Richard termed it, a house of cards, which one bit of mismanagement would send fluttering to the ground.

Had Giorgio known?

Surely he'd been comfortable that she'd see her investment again? That his seeking of private venture capital was legitimate? It must have been oversight or false economy that led to the vital insurance policy being allowed to lapse. She was fiercely certain it wasn't shady commerce.

Giorgio wouldn't have done that to her!

But, whichever, it had left her high and dry and she could hardly challenge him about it now.

There would be about two thousand pounds to come from the sale of her car, and although she had Adam

Leblond's rent, she had to allow for council tax, insurance etc out of it. It wasn't exactly an income.

Living for free at her sister's house could scarcely continue, she was the kind who felt an overwhelming need to pay her way. And at such time as she got her own house back she'd have electricity bills, gas, water, food . . . She sighed.

She'd have to damned well get a job.

And before too much longer.

Her feet took her into town where the market traders were setting up stalls and the butcher optimistically winding out his canopy to shade his window display from sunshine. A postman pushed a pram-like mail carrier up the street, pausing to force packets of letters through letter flaps set low in shop doors. Paperboys cycled on the pavement with baseball caps far back on heads of tightly cut hair, people hurried to work or sauntered to the newsagent.

Judith crossed Market Square into High Street. What kind of job should she be looking for? Before she went to Malta she'd worked long hours for big construction companies on sites like muddy, rumbling, cities. But she didn't want to go back to that, all the regs and permissions and head-in-the-clouds architects. The awful headaches of large projects. Things had changed, she'd have to get her head around updates and new conventions for things like glazing and insulation. And she'd have to overcome that male dominated world all over again.

No.

Girly, possibly, but she just couldn't hack it at the moment, too much pressure for someone whose emotions were all over the place.

A decent part-time job should be enough.

But something interesting. Not a shop, not a bank, not a big bland office, not a call centre, not a pub . . .

"Judith!"

She blinked herself out of her list of negatives. Tom stood across the High Street, shoulders hunched, a navy baseball cap pulled over his eyes. He waited for the lights to stop the traffic, then crossed to her pavement.

She regarded him with misgivings. She was *not* in the mood for more of Tom's grumpiness — "being in a mardy", as the local slang would have it.

But today Tom seemed quite genial. "Fancy a cuppa? There's a new caff up here, Hannah's Pantry, and they do a beautiful brew."

Others were already enjoying the fruits of Hannah's Pantry. It was panelled out in pine and served tea and coffee in mugs, with milk from a jug and sugar from a bowl and luscious homemade cakes from a glassed-in counter. The staff members were young, probably sixth formers, with one bulky woman — Hannah — in charge.

"Mornin' Tom." Hannah reached around her chest to pop toast from an enormous chrome toaster.

"Morning, Hannah."

"All right, Tom?" A tall young man did a squirt-and-wipe on a table.

"Hey, Tom." A diminutive girl rapidly set out a range of jams and marmalades, wiping each jar.

By the time that Tom had exchanged greetings with three staff and two customers, Judith had got the idea that he was a regular. They ordered coffee and toast and sat down at a pine table near the steamy windows. At the bottom of the glass the ghost of a smiley face from a previous layer of condensation beamed out.

Tom asked Judith about Malta. Judith told him a little of her life there but nothing about Giorgio, because apart from being just too weird to discuss him with her ex-husband, she simply didn't want to let Tom in. Giorgio was too precious, too special, too private to open to Tom's gruff brand of sympathy. Or, even, lack of sympathy.

"So what do you intend to do with yourself?" His large teeth crunched into toast made from thick, white bread and running with butter. Awake, washed and brushed, he looked considerably better than he had done when she'd seen him last.

She spread ginger marmalade, and took a bite, enjoying that particularly British combination of hot toast, cold conserve, and a slick of butter between the two. "A job's high on my list of priorities." She sipped her hot tea from the forest-green mug.

He grunted. "Back to the hard hat and wellies?"

"Hope not. I don't want to work full-time. Don't particularly want the stress of site meetings and trying to make architects understand why their pretty picture won't work on the ground. You know what that's like! I'll have to look around, think about what I can do."

**89**

He talked around his food. "I could look out for you."

She selected lemon curd to spread on her second slice of toast. Tom was already on his fourth. She crunched into the toast and the tart-sweet bite of the lemon. "Thanks, but I don't want to be in construction." And she didn't want to be involved too closely with Tom.

When breakfast was over she walked around three of the town's job agencies, gazing into windows to read the cards in the *P/time* columns. Nothing to take her fancy, the agencies all seemed to deal mostly with payroll, warehouse or driving. She could sign on at an agency for professional people, but then, surely, wouldn't they be offering her jobs within her profession?

All her life she'd decided what to do and then done it. This unsettled purposelessness was foreign.

She knew she wanted something different. Something . . . well, she didn't understand what. But different. For lack of anything else to do, she turned for Molly's house.

Her route took her close to Lavender Row. She slowed. No harm in calling in to see if Adam Leblond had begun the hunt for alternative accommodation. It might delay the return to the frigid life of Moll and Frankie for half-an-hour.

He was speaking on the phone when he answered the door, and gestured her into the house with a flash of his smile. She went in. In the sitting room the computer in the alcove displayed a screenful of thumbnail images and a cable attached a matt black camera. Silver photographer's cases stood nearby, paperwork was laid out neatly across the carpet. "Two minutes," he mouthed.

Then, into the phone, with restrained patience, "But that wasn't what you asked for. Of course I could have done the garden as well, but this is a bit after the event, isn't it? I can't rewind time." He listened for a minute. "Let me know tomorrow if you want me to schedule another shoot."

The moment he clicked the phone off and began, "Hello —" the phone rang again. He grimaced. "Sorry! But do you mind?"

"Go ahead." She picked up a glossy home magazine to flip through while he entered into another conversation, clamping the phone to his left ear with his shoulder and scribbling awkwardly with his right hand, the pen lodged between his thumb and the knuckle where his first finger used to be.

"Yes, I said I can. How many? What's the angle? Well, you must know the writer's . . . E-mail that to me, then."

He put down the phone, scribbled on for a few moments, then flung himself down on the sofa, shoving back his hair.

She closed the magazine. "Sorry. I really shouldn't turn up unannounced. I didn't think you'd be working on a Sunday."

He blew out his lips. "I shouldn't be. Unfortunately, I've just lost my assistant, so I have to deal with my paperwork myself. And the phone call was from a picture editor who can access her computer network from home. Probably sitting on the lawn with her laptop catching up on a few things while her kids play in the paddling pool."

"You work for magazines?"

"Mostly. Mags schedule features, then contact me to shoot the accompanying pix for them. A lot are case histories, you know, *I had an affair with the cannibal next door* sort of thing. I cover the Midlands for several titles. Very busy at the moment."

She felt like breathing a Kieran-like, "That's so cool!" But restricted herself instead to, "So you won't have had a minute to start looking for alternative accommodation?"

"No need." His calm eyes hardened. "Nowhere near August twenty-first. That's when you can run an inventory, inspect the property, give me back my key money, and I'll go."

Judith's stomach dipped.

Key money.

She'd forgotten she held his key money. The modest savings she'd thought she still had plummeted by about twenty-five per cent. Rats.

He grinned, suddenly, and all the grooves beside his mouth and eyes deepened. "Do you know you've got marmalade on your chin?"

She rose with a sigh to glare into the mirror over the fireplace. The cleft of her chin was decorated by a smear like a comma. "Bugger." She scrubbed at her chin with lick-and-tissue, succeeding in making the skin pink. "I had breakfast with my ex. His idea of fun not to tell me, I suppose."

"Breakfast with your ex? Civilised."

"Accidental meeting." She returned to her seat, her chin burning slightly and her cheeks burning a lot. "Then I went looking in job agency windows."

His eyes were interested. "You're looking for a job?"

She wrinkled her nose. "Economic necessity, like anyone. Something part-time, hopefully."

"What sort of thing? Because I'm desperate for someone like you to help me on a big shoot, tomorrow."

"Like me? What am I like?"

He gestured vaguely. "Personable, with a brain. I have a hassly day scheduled. Got to drive to a village near Coventry and take shots of a family with thirteen children, ranging from a new baby to twins of twenty. Nightmare trying to keep everyone happy at the best of times, let alone so many kids. And everything's more difficult since . . ." He indicated his damaged hand. "I had a brilliant assistant, Daria, a friend's daughter who came on shoots and did my routine phone calls and invoicing and stuff. Terrific. But she's just run off to Northumberland after a whirlwind holiday romance, leaving me stuck."

She glanced at equipment cases on the floor, open to display grey felt-lined compartments packed with cables and lenses. "Doesn't sound too difficult."

His face lit up. "So you'll give it a go? That's terrific!"

She was taken aback at this leap of faith. She'd actually meant it didn't sound too difficult so he ought not have trouble filling the vacancy. Did she want to be a photographer's assistant? How many people did it take to hold a camera? "Wouldn't you need someone full-time? And permanent?"

"Two days one week, four days the next, depending. I'll advertise for someone permanent, but in the meantime I've got tomorrow to get through. You'd be doing me a huge favour if you helped out. I pay by the day." The sum he mentioned seemed to Judith to be worthwhile.

"Oh. Um. Well, perhaps just while you advertise," she managed, eventually. "I have no relevant experience or qualifications."

Decisively, he pulled one of the metal cases towards him and picked up a lens in his left hand and a camera body in the right. "I don't expect you to, I can teach you what you need to know. Let's start by me telling you the names of things . . ."

At the end of two hours she was dizzy with changing lenses, taking equipment on and off tripods and putting the settings he wanted on the Nikon cameras.

"Earlyish start in the morning." Every item was now tidily back in its compartment. "Can you be here by seven? I need to get going about then. The shoot's not till ten, but you know what the traffic can be like at that time in the morning."

# CHAPTER
# NINE

"About" seven proved to be deceptively casual.

She was two minutes late, having found it difficult to wake after the sleeplessness of the night before, and arrived to find the gear loaded and Adam in the driving seat of his car, waiting. He started the engine as she plumped into the passenger seat.

"Indoor/outdoor shoot," he said, pulling away before she'd even got her seatbelt fastened. His right hand had some kind of aid around it that helped him grip the steering wheel, and the car had column gears so that his left hand didn't have to dip to a traditional gear stick and leave his right hand in charge of the wheel on its own.

"Is that significant?"

"It means we have to carry more equipment. We're heading for a village called Bulkington, north of Coventry. I know it's A14, M6, but can you look at the route from there, for me? The map book's under your seat."

Blearily, she found the page, and glanced at the network marked in blue, green, red, orange and white that denoted the country's roads. She yawned, and tried to focus, her head twice its usual weight. "Looks like you take the M69 off the M6, and it's just off that."

"Sounds easy enough. Find something on the radio that you want to listen to, then have another rummage through the biggest equipment case. Make sure you remember how to change memory cards, grip, tripod etc."

She dragged the case off the back seat with an inward sigh.

It would have been nice to relax the journey away. Not *sleep*, of course not, that would be an unprofessional way for a photographer's assistant to behave. And, also, she'd probably snore with her mouth open or something equally cringe-making.

But playing with memory cards wasn't interesting, and she yawned prodigiously all the way up the A14 as they progressed slowly through the morning traffic.

Eventually, he took pity. "How about a coffee stop?"

Another face-wrenching, eye-watering yawn. "Coffee would be brilliant. I'm sleepy."

"You don't say."

They bought coffee in big cardboard beakers and parked themselves outside the service station on a bench, the idea being that fresh air might wake Judith up. And, by the time she'd drained her cup, she was awake.

"Better get on." She looked at her watch. A proportion of the time Adam had built in for traffic hold ups had drained away.

Which proved to be a problem when they finally turned onto the M69 and Judith got the map out again to navigate them through the A roads. She could focus now on the multi-coloured strands that denoted the roads on which they travelled. She found Bulkington, close to the M69, with her finger.

Her heart sank. "Oh *hell!* We can't get off the M69, it's one of those places where the roads cross but there's no junction." And, as he sighed, she added, "Sorry," her face heating uncomfortably.

"Brilliant," he muttered. "OK, we can't turn on the motorway, so what's our best solution?"

He was obviously irritated, but at least he hadn't yanked the car onto the hard shoulder and snatched the map from her hands, as Tom would have done. Mortified, she studied the map with a degree of care that would have been useful in the first place. "At the next junction you can turn right onto the A5, then take the first right. The road curls back beneath the motorway."

"That doesn't sound too bad." But he flicked a glance at the dashboard clock, and moved purposefully into the outside lane. Just as they encountered the first signs indicating roadworks.

They were late arriving, but only by about 15 minutes. Judith had to ring ahead on Adam's mobile to apologise, still hot with embarrassment at making a silly, uncharacteristic mistake. "Don't you worry, dear, we won't be ready anyway," was the comforting response from Jillie Lasyencko, the mother of the impressive brood.

And she was right.

They arrived at the two council houses knocked together to find one of the eldest girls gone to the shop in a huff and the other not back after staying out all night. Jillie Lasyencko displayed a spectacular quantity of breast through her open dress as she fed the baby, there was a decided whiff of nappy, and a handful of the thirteen Lasyencko offspring raced around screeching in excitement. Having once been two dwellings, the house had two front doors and two back allowing plenty of permutations of racing in and out of the property.

"You're going to earn your stripes organising this crowd." Adam began to unload his gear from the car.

From this Judith assumed he was prepared to set up his equipment if she took charge of the personnel. "I'm not changing the nappy. I'll sort the rest."

"Fine. Smells don't show up on images." He grabbed cases in either hand, propped a tripod on his shoulder and took the path to the left front door.

If Judith had been tired before the shoot, she was going to be exhausted after. As Adam opened his cases, she grabbed the two oldest-looking Lasyenckos available, one male, one female, both gothic. "You look like the guys with the authority. How do I go about organising the tinies so we can get this photo shoot underway?"

The male sighed. "Yeah. Us as usual." But he turned the older half of the family with practised ease to subduing the younger half, combing hair, washing faces and doing up top buttons or hair ribbons, snapping out instructions. The twins returned sheepishly from their sulks and high jinks respectively and disappeared upstairs to get ready. The baby burped without decorating his blue outfit or his mother's black-and-violet dress, Jillie thrust her breasts away, and Pete Lasyencko, the man of the house, emerged from the lavatory with the *Daily Express*.

And they were set for a shoot in the vast sitting room that had been made from most of the ground floor of one of the original houses.

Adam took Judith aside. "I normally do my best to coordinate everyone so that we don't have horrible colour clashes on the page. But we need to work fast while we have their attention. So do your best — and at least get that girl with the cochineal hair to stand away from the lad with the blue plume. Blast, that tall boy's got a black eye, look. Turn him three-quarters on so it's hidden. Pull the curtains and we'll work entirely with flash, bloody sun beams into this room from all angles." And so it went on, Adam reeling off what he wanted, what he envisaged and how he was going to get it, and Judith fielding toddlers as they made a break for freedom and getting teenaged girls to pause in their chewing and *smile*!

While he worked, Judith noticed, Adam managed to forget about keeping his damaged hand out of sight. He used it as he needed it, and adapted over what he had to.

Adam managed the Herculean task of completing the shoot before everyone got totally cheesed off, with a mixture of his charm and Judith's bullying.

Then they had to get all the gear back in the car, trying to avoid too much "help" from over enthusiastic and sticky young hands. But, eventually, they were able to shut themselves back in the car and drive away.

And when Judith woke up, she was in Lavender Row.

Groaning, she flexed her stiff neck. Her mouth was dry, her eyes were gritty, and her hair was flattened over one eye. "Are we home?"

"Yes, wake up. I'll show you how I download the pix." Adam threw the splint from his hand into the centre console, apparently as fresh as he had been at seven this morning. "And then run you through the paperwork."

"Paperwork?" She trailed indoors behind him.

He pushed into the sitting room. "My assistant does most of my paperwork. And some phone calls. It's in the day rate, OK? I need an invoice for the month, so you mark the days you work in that black diary, and at the end of the month type an invoice on the computer, print it out and put it on that pile."

She blinked at her temporary assistant status being so casually extended. "But you'll be advertising, soon?"

"Yes, yes. Now, downloading the images isn't rocket science, but it does have to be done correctly or you can lose the work or mess up the settings on the camera . . ."

And when she finally left, after he'd shown her how to download and organise the images, explained his computer system and then carried his camera stuff upstairs while she raised invoices and posted them to the appropriate spreadsheet — the paperwork was a doddle because Adam was organised and everything was up to date — it was turned six o'clock. She was now going on shoots with him on Tuesday (a donkey sanctuary), Friday (girl who'd done well in *Pop Idol* revisiting her old school), and Thursday and Friday of next week (a couple who'd married each other three times and a windmill turned sumptuous dwelling).

"Just until I advertise," as he repeated.

So she ought to be able to keep the wolf from the door while she looked around for something else.

Although it didn't alter the fact that she'd still lost a rather substantial nest egg.

And Giorgio.

Weary from her busy day, pain swept through her anew, making her limbs weighty and slow. She drove home in a fog of misery. And then, groan, groan, she discovered that Molly and Frankie were engaged in a teeth-clenched row. Just when all she wanted to do was flop down. Creeping upstairs, she showered, shut herself away in her room with her radio and book and tried to ignore increasingly unignorable shouts and slams. Eventually, she put on her shoes and slipped back out of the front door.

Not having an abundance of places to go, she opted for visiting her mother.

One of the carers in a lilac overall showed Judith to Wilma's pink-and-white room, where she'd sought the comfort of Coronation Street. "Hello, dear," said Wilma uncertainly, rocking her tubular aluminium walking stick on its three grey rubber feet. "I'd forgotten you were coming. I haven't put my lipstick on."

Judith kissed her mother's soft cheek. "You haven't forgotten, Mum. There was nothing arranged. I just thought I'd like to see you. Is that OK?" She sat down in an orange plastic chair, massaging an ache above her left eye. Sleep was beckoning madly, but it wasn't going to happen for a couple of hours chez O'Malley.

"Of course! It's lovely to see you." Wilma agitated her stick some more, and sucked her teeth. "What shall we talk about? I haven't really had a chance to think of anything to say."

How odd that her mother should need notice to gather together the ingredients of a conversation with her daughter. Had Judith been very self-absorbed not to notice how her mother's world had shrunk? She must make more effort. "I've got a temporary job." It would probably be easier for Wilma if Judith began the conversational ball rolling. "I'm a temporary photographer's assistant."

Wilma laughed. "A temporary assistant? You? Does your employer realise that you'll be bossing everyone about in no time?"

Settling in the chair, Judith got herself comfortable. "That doesn't sound like me at all! Anyway, it's just one bloke. The one who rents my house, Adam Leblond, he was two years above me and Mel at school. It's just till he gets someone more suitable. What's new with you?"

Wilma gave the matter some thought. She wore no powder, and her skin looked duller than usual. "Nice lunch, today," she offered. "Beans."

"Green beans?"

"Yes, I don't like baked beans. And a chop and new potatoes. Very fresh and tasty. They look after us lovely, here."

"That's good." Judith cast around for more material for discussion. "Have you read your paper today?"

"Most of it. And done the crossword, the crossword's my favourite, I always leave it till last. And the problem page." Wilma explained how she and her friends at The Cottage all bought different newspapers and passed them around during the day. Florrie had read out a problem from a magazine today, ever so racy, and only from a girl of seventeen. They'd all giggled and been embarrassed.

Despite her good intentions, Judith's mind began to wander. Giorgio in a stark white hospital room, his gaze not meeting hers. Sliema Z Bus Tours in liquidation.

Wilma grasped Judith's wrist gently, regaining her attention. "Today there was one from a woman who was awfully worried about her daughter."

She blinked. "Sorry?"

"A problem, m'duck, on the problem page."

Like many people, Judith only skimmed problem pages for the snigger-worthy and the salacious. "Oh?"

Wilma went on, adjusting her glasses that had the fancy designs up the side and flexing her fingers on the handle of her stick. "She's middle-aged, the daughter, and a very competent person — on the outside. But she's thin as a rake and awfully upset. Something horrible's obviously happened, but she hasn't told the mother what it is. Which is quite all right. The daughter

**103**

has always bottled up her problems and solved them herself, right from when she was a tiny girl. But it doesn't stop the mother worrying."

Hot tears pricked Judith's eyes.

Wilma shuffled in her seat so that she could lean forward and take both of Judith's hands in her cool fingers, leaving the stick standing alone on its three feet. The light overhead reflected on the lenses of her spectacles, making her expression particularly earnest. "But she will get over things, duck. However horrible whatever it is that's happened. It's just that the road to recovery is uphill all the way."

# CHAPTER
# TEN

Judith had cried off Moll's traditional Yorkshire pud meal (and the traditional washing up that followed). Things had calmed down in the O'Malley household in recent days, but still Judith liked to be out as much as possible. Moll had refused point blank to talk things over, putting on a smile. "We're fine, don't worry about us."

The Sunday stroll took Judith through a park, where she watched a football match, and to Hannah's Pantry, where she drank latte, and she managed to keep occupied until lunchtime. She was determined to get in touch with her old friends and get back in the swim of her English life. But Sunday lunchtime probably wasn't the moment for dropping in, when roasts would be out of the oven for carving and gravy thickening on the hob.

The rain, which until then had stayed in the bruised clouds, began after she'd left the town centre on the way to the riverbank to have lunch at the coffee shop and watch the narrowboats. Big splats on the pavement to begin with, then faster, heavier, heavier, and cheered on by thunder. In seconds the rain was soaking her hair and bouncing up from the pavement and onto her bare ankles.

She changed direction rapidly into her old neighbourhood — Leicester Road, the shop on the corner of Senwick Street, The Wells, where the May trees would have been decked with deep pink blossom a couple of months ago — and then Lavender Row. Her jeans were sticking coldly to her thighs as she turned the corner.

She knew that Adam was away for the weekend, but she had her key. Thunder rolled, lightning flashed, and rain hissed from a smoke-grey sky, stinging her scalp and her face. Adam surely wouldn't mind if she sheltered from the storm.

From this direction number 18 was out of sight around an elbow. As she neared, she frowned over the clamour of noise riding over even the sound of the rain. It sounded almost like a fairground with pounding music, shrieks, bellows, howls of laughter, girlish cries. A woman under a golf umbrella stopped and shook her head. "It's been going on all night. All night! My husband wanted to call the police, but you don't want any retribution, do you? It might be our windows, next." Pulling her thin blue mac more tightly around her, she scurried on her way.

Judith listened. Thump-thump-thump-roar. Squeal.

She rounded the bend.

Almost every sliding sash window was open at number 18, and several had been smashed, letting curtains flutter out into the rain. Empty cans and bottles lay in the tiny frontage and glass was spattered in with the gravel.

"My *house!*" she breathed.

Dispensing with the formality of ringing the bell, she flew through the front door, pulling up short at a pool of vomit and a plump girl sprawled at the bottom of the stairs who looked suspiciously as if the vomit might belong to her.

To avoid the mess, she picked her way past the girl and stamped upstairs. The house seemed to be shaking with the beat of the music and people bellowing to be heard over it. Cigarettes had been ground out on the carpet and the mixture of stenches made her want to gag.

The bathroom door was locked. In the smallest bedroom two young men smoked joints and examined one of Adam's silver cases of camera equipment, clumsily, cans of beer between their feet.

She moved swiftly on to the second room, evidently now Caleb's and decorated with posters and a litter of dropped clothes. There, a girl cried blue mascara noisily down her face while a lad slept crosswise on the bed. The room at the front that used to be hers — presumably now Adam's — hosted at least three couples on the bed or the floor, one of which was awake and naked. "For God's *sake!*" she protested, as she backed out hastily. "This is my bloody *bedroom!*"

Then a shock of splintering glass. She whirled and ran downstairs again, hurdling the vomit to get down the hall.

**107**

In the kitchen, eyes wide, hair tumbled around his face, Caleb's lips were moving as he gazed from the broken glass in the back door to the broken glass in the door to the hall. Judith was almost upon him before she could distinguish the words over the music.

"My old man will go mental. My old man will go mental." Joint in one hand, vodka bottle in the other, he chanted the words like a mantra, shock stretching his face. Behind him, a lad with a short, square haircut was thumping on the cupboard doors with a fist, globs of blood flying from his lacerated arms. Presumably it was a similar action on the glass panels that had destroyed them.

"Stop that!" Judith bellowed through the broken pane, fury coursing hotter and hotter through her body. "That glass was original!"

Swaying, Caleb turned his gaze and frowned as if trying to place her.

A new sound broke through the music from the sitting room, sharp, staccato, metallic. Judith hurried in to find a bare-chested youth hitting the cast iron fire surround with a poker, and giggling as the inset tiles starred and shattered. A girl was retching into the seat of an armchair. Two men were having a beer-spitting competition, roaring with laughter as they spattered her back, and the computer. A further dozen or so people were comatose.

Judith felt a bellow of anger swelling in her chest, but self-preservation stopped her attempting to disarm the poker-wielder. She contented herself with tearing the plug of the booming stereo out of its wall socket instead.

Her ears rang in blessed relief at the silence.

She stamped her way back to Caleb, who was still wearing an expression of comical dismay. "This is my *home*," she snapped. "I'm calling the police!"

"They've trashed Dad's house," he told her sadly.

"No, they've trashed *my* house. Wait till I see your father!"

Caleb rocked on his heels. "Grandma's ill. Dad's gone to Bedford to see her." Shakily, he drew on the fat roach between his fingers, which had gone out anyway. "Back on Sunday."

"Today."

"Sunday."

"Sunday's today!" She wanted to shake him, preferably by the throat.

Caleb's eyes grew rounder. "Holy crap. He'll go mental."

"That'll be two of us!"

Should she call the police? It was the sensible option for several reasons. An aggressive party reveller fuelled by God-knows-what might turn on her as she tried to clear the house. Officialese, in the form of a crime report with statements could very well prove to be necessary.

And on the off chance that some stupid young idiot had died during the revels, the police could deal with it instead of her.

But then . . . She studied Caleb, wide-eyed and pasty white. Caleb might get arrested. Charged. She'd be responsible for getting him a police record. The house stunk of dope, he and most of his unattractive mates were off their faces. The government might've seen fit to downgrade grass, but she wasn't sure she wanted to put their reaction to the test when damage to property was involved.

And how would she feel if it were Kieran?

She was saved from further heart-searching by the banging of the front door as it slammed back against the hall wall. And, slowly, in stalked Adam. "Shitty *death*," he spat. Judith watched his progress up the hall as he carefully skirted the girl at the bottom of the stairs and the evidence of her excesses, peering into the sitting room, wincing, and heading inexorably for Caleb.

Father and son stared at each other. The square-cut man who'd been thumping the units advanced, fists clenched, but Adam shoved him irritably in the chest, and, with a stagger, he ricocheted harmlessly through the back door.

Adam had eyes only for his son. "Are you all right?"

Caleb nodded, and swayed. "Sorry, Dad. They, like, got completely out of hand." For an instant, he looked as if he might burst into tears.

Then Adam spotted Judith. Eyes crackled like a winter sea in a moment of infuriated pride. "Oh, *hell!*" Each stared at the other. "I take responsibility. I'll get it cleared up," he ground out.

She folded her arms. "You bet."

It took till mid-afternoon just to empty the house of unwanted bodies.

**110**

Showing some inventiveness, Judith thought, Adam filled a plant-sprayer with icy water and travelled around squirting the slack faces of the unconscious. "Come on! Up you get, son, on your way." Squirt. "Wake up, wake up! You must leave. You! *Hey, you!* Wakey, wakey!" Squirt, squi-irt. "Time to go."

Grunts, snarls or squeals greeted his efforts and he was equally impervious to each. "Out, now! *Now*, I said! On your feet and get out."

The bathroom door remained obstinately locked, he had to kick his way in to where a waxen girl was out cold on the floor, the room a filthy mess around her where her stomach had rejected its contents.

Judith swore in outrage at the sight of her snow-white suite so defiled. If there was one thing she hated it was a dirty bathroom.

Caleb lurched about, gathering cans and bottles into plastic sacks, imbibing plain water at his father's behest. Periodically, Adam grasped his son's face and stared into his eyes, satisfying himself that Caleb was in no immediate danger from any of the poisons he'd put into his body.

Judith patrolled the clean-up operation with hands on hips at this insult to her home, (even if it wasn't, strictly speaking, *her* home at the moment). Adam swept up the glass then borrowed a wet/dry cleaner from a friend and scoured the carpets, improving the situation but failing to return the carpets to their state before cigarette burns and unsavoury stains.

Gradually, the smell of carpet cleaner and bleach began to overpower tobacco, beer and vomit. A glazier

**111**

made the appropriate emergency repairs to the windows and doors. Caleb was finally permitted to haul himself upstairs to collapse atop his duvet.

Slowly, Adam returned to the kitchen, where Judith waited.

"Is Caleb going to be OK?"

"I think so," he said, flatly. "I need him to live, so that I can kill him. And when I've done that I'm going to resurrect him and kill him again."

Despite her anger, she almost smiled. It hadn't escaped her that his first words to Caleb had been, "Are you all right?" rather than a screamed, "What the hell have you done?" which she was sure would have been Tom's reaction had Kieran put him in a similar position.

With curt movements, Adam made coffee and set out a biscuit tin.

They sat down facing one another at the pine kitchen table.

Adam passed his good hand over his eyes. As so often his damaged right hand was out of the way, in his pocket or beneath the table. He looked exhausted. "So now you have perfectly good grounds for eviction," he offered, bitterly.

"In anyone's book," she agreed.

He nodded. "Can I have seven days, Judith?"

"Yes, you can use the time to do the repairs. I should think the key money might just about cover it."

# CHAPTER
# ELEVEN

So she found herself in the odd position of working for Adam at the same time as chucking him out of the house, each of them adopting the policy of speaking only as necessary, getting through the week without friendly chats or exchanges of jokes.

Adam moved out of 18 Lavender Row at the end of it, all his possessions in a hire van.

On the Monday, Judith moved back in.

The insurance company had yet to stump up for the tiles and the fire surround to be refinished, some of the carpets to be replaced and for the bathroom door to be repaired, but the house was habitable.

Her furniture arrived from the storage unit, the cottage suite in shades of blue and lilac, the bed with the carved wooden headboard, the maple wardrobes and the dressing table with the mirror. The phone line had been returned to her name.

The proud possessor of a landline again, she was suddenly overtaken by a desire to ring Cass and pass the number on.

First she got down to the jobs of arranging the furniture and making tea for the deliverymen, trying to squash it to the back of her mind. But, at the first opportunity, she nipped into town and bought a phone with built-in answering machine.

Safely installed, the shiny grey plastic set seemed to taunt her, waiting to see how long she'd hold out before looking up Cass's number. That wasn't all there was to it, though. Judith must be careful. If Saviour knew Judith was calling his wife, Cass's life would be made difficult.

She dialled.

The first time, Saviour answered, but Judith had prepared the voice of a confused tourist. "Oh, dear. Is this the Park Hotel?"

She heard Saviour's deep chuckle. "You call the wrong number."

"Oh, I'm so sorry!"

"Is OK."

But, in the evening, when she tried again, she heard Cass's high voice. "Cass, it's Judith," she whispered. "Can you talk?"

Cass sounded tense. "Saviour's not here, if that's what you mean. But I have nothing to tell you."

Judith felt ridiculous disappointment slinking through her. What had she expected? A miracle? "No change at all?" Her voice was hoarse.

"He won't suddenly begin asking for you. You know that, Judith."

"Can I . . ." Judith had to clear her throat. "Can I give you my new phone number?"

"Of course." Cass's voice was sad, weighed down by the words she didn't speak. *If you think there's any point.*

Judith felt her breath desert her and could scarcely get the numbers out.

After the call she heeled her hands fiercely into her eyes, holding back the scalding tears.

The tears wouldn't be held. They burst from her eyes and flooded down her cheeks, ran into her mouth, burned the inside of her nose and filled her throat.

Two hours later, her entire head aching, she came to a decision.

She would cry no more for Giorgio.

It was pointless now, wasting energy that she was going to need to build a new life that didn't include him.

She had to accept that she would never again see laughter in his dark, dark eyes, or desire as he reached for her. There would be no phone calls to interrupt meetings with long-wooed clients, no waves from the windows of buses returning after a day trip.

No waking in the morning to find he'd kicked off the sheet and was spooned around her, sharing her pillow.

No whispers, no laughter, no hanging entangled beneath the waves.

"That was then, and this is now," she told herself aloud, treading up the stairs. "This is Brinham, this is England, this is my life. I'm going to finish unpacking my cases. Because I live here, now." She blinked away a fresh burning.

Three cases left to unpack, and she could ring Richard tomorrow and ask him to ship the things that had been too bulky to bring, a few small items of furniture, several pictures. She was fond of watercolours of the island by local artists. Giorgio had bought her two, the ferry crossing Marsamxett Harbour to the bastions of Valletta, and the promenade along Tower Road, The Chalet projecting starkly into the sea. Where they'd met.

She emptied the first two cases, enough stuff to fill a wardrobe and spill over into the spare, and then began on the third, a grey giant filled with what she'd judged she wouldn't need much. She stood for a painful minute clutching the neoprene of her wetsuit, the rubber mask and fins, breathing in the familiar smell, remembering long sunny days when she and Giorgio dropped together into the quiet and cool green-blue depths.

Then she bundled it quickly into the built-in cupboard in the box room. She wouldn't need it. She wouldn't go under the waves again.

There were no shoots in the next week. It was blessedly peaceful now that she'd winkled Adam out of the house and given Molly and Frankie their spare room back. She had time to . . .

Almost anything.

Time was not a shortage.

Time to think, time to grieve, time to be freshly aware of what she'd lost. Time to wish she'd never left Malta, time to realise that it was probably for the best.

Brooding made the time go slowly and left her unable to sleep, to eat, so she threw herself into activity.

The garden looked a good project; she watched garden makeover programmes and thought the physical

**116**

work might be just what she needed. She got only as far as cutting the long, narrow lawn, which was growing strongly. It took ages with the lawn mower, and even longer to neaten the edges with the clippers. And the raw smell of cut grass made her sneeze and her eyes run. Enough to remind her how much she hated gardening.

So she abandoned the garden and rang The Cottage retirement home to say that she was coming to take her mother out. Even so, Wilma was flustered at her appearance and Judith couldn't decide whether it was with pleasure to have an unexpected outing, or irritation that she'd miss *Neighbours* and *The Natural World*.

Judith whizzed her in the car into the neighbouring county of Buckinghamshire to shop in Milton Keynes.

On the ice-smooth floors of the shopping mall the wheelchair bowled along. Wilma folding her arms over the handbag in her lap. "It would be lovely to go outside to the market, wouldn't it, duck?" So Judith manhandled the heavy chair through the glass doors and into the market place, where the chair moved like a bent supermarket trolley through mud.

But Wilma was content as they wheeled past stalls of fruit or cleaning fluids or jeans. At the end of its last row Judith was thankful to manhandle the chair back into the mall.

Wilma's eye fell immediately on a nearby kiosk. "That frozen yoghurt looks lovely! And they've got peach!"

Judith chose strawberry, and finished first, licking her spoon and her fingers. "That was a good idea of yours, Mum."

Wilma laughed, still trying to manoeuvre the tiny blue spoon. "It's all on my chin and my hands! Have you got a tissue, Judith? Then we can go and look for my new bag."

But after they'd rolled around the mall from department store to department store for what seemed to be hours, Wilma sighed. "They're jolly expensive and I don't like any so much as my old one. And you must be getting awfully tired, heaving me about." She sounded suddenly dreary.

Judith squeezed her shoulder and sighed inwardly. The shopping trip seemed to be more a trial than a treat. She cursed herself again for not appreciating her mother's world. Molly would have known, Molly always knew how to handle their mother. "Is this all a bit much, Mum? Would you rather I took you home?"

Wilma considered. "But we shouldn't leave without having a cup of tea first, should we? And a scone, with lots of jam. John Lewis does *lovely* scones."

Two scones later they set off home, Judith reminding herself that she really must stop pouncing on her mother on whim, interrupting Wilma's routine and not giving enough thought to whether she'd actually enjoy what Judith decreed a treat.

Later in the week, Judith met Kieran for dinner, accompanied, naturally, by Bethan, taking Molly with her because Frankie was at work.

**118**

The insurance company paid up and she chose a new carpet.

She was glad that next week she'd have her part-time job to occupy her mind. She hadn't begun scouring the sits vac ads yet because helping Adam wasn't demanding, was generally interesting and quite often fun. Hopefully, the froideur between them would soon thaw.

Being a full-time lady of leisure would surely have confirmed her in the flea-jump mental responses from which she was suffering, flitting from thought to thought.

Because, however much she'd yearned to be on her own, now that she was she felt unlike the self she'd always known, it was like hearing a familiar song with the words changed.

She searched around for occupation.

And phoned Melanie.

Melanie had been Judith's friend since school. At Brinham Grammar she'd been an absolute knock-out, the one that all the lads fancied rotten, with a lush figure, clear skin that tanned rapidly in the days when a deep tan was considered a desirable sign of health, and a sultry brown gaze.

She'd peaked early, unfortunately. Her beauty became overblown, her busty body overweight, the one people always said, "Shame, because she's got a lovely smile," about.

But so far as Judith was concerned Melanie was still Melanie, a ready grin, a dry wit, and a sympathetic nature.

**119**

Melanie was enchanted to hear from Judith and demanded a girls' night out that very night, organising tickets on-line to see a play about murder and betrayal at the modern Derngate Theatre in Northampton, and booking a table in a wine bar afterwards.

And it was so *wonderful* to see Melanie again, to be yanked into a big, squashy hug, Melanie's cry of delight ringing in her ears, "Judith, how I've missed you! How fantastic that you're home!"

Judith felt unexpectedly choked. "Oh Mel, I've missed you, too! I wish we hadn't bothered with the play, now. I just want to go somewhere and talk our heads off."

Ian, Melanie's husband, waited outside in the car, sportingly prepared to undertake chauffeuring duties to allow for a decent session at the wine bar. His eyes twinkled through his big, silver-framed glasses at his wife and her friend squashed in the back seat of his Punto so they could talk without drawing breath all the way to Northampton.

But the play was good, although they agreed that they preferred the old Royal Theatre next-door, joined on to the Derngate now, and the pantomimes there when they were kids. The ice-creams had seemed bigger and the performances magical.

After the curtain, Melanie threaded them through the streets to a wine bar with a primrose frontage and a grapevine painted across the windows. "So," said Melanie, pouring big glasses of deeply red wine. "Poor old Adam blotted his copy book, did he, and you had to throw him out?"

Judith felt a flush heat her cheeks. "His son, Caleb, had a party and trashed the place. Adam instantly agreed to leave. Hard luck on Adam, I realise, but it's good to have my own place back."

"And it's your house, of course. But, yes, hard luck on Adam. And he's had enough bad luck lately." Frowning slightly, Melanie fanned her face with a beer mat.

The flush deepened. "I know he's a friend of yours."

Melanie's ready smile burst across her face. "A good friend of Ian's, really, but yes, Adam's lovely. He's moving into a new place this weekend, a flat."

Judith knew that. She sipped her wine. But she hadn't felt able to ask him where he was staying prior to the flat becoming available. Felt guilty that in leaping at the opportunity to reclaim her house afforded by righteous wrath she hadn't much cared where he went. "Been staying with friends, I suppose?"

Melanie fanned herself harder. "Shelley, his wife. They were never what you'd actually call *devoted*, you know. But they're fond of each other. I don't know if she ever actually wanted him to leave. She certainly misses him."

"So why did he go?"

A shrug of Melanie's rounded shoulders. "Who knows what goes on in a marriage?" She blotted her face with a tissue. "Do you remember Adam, from school? A bit of a star attraction in the sixth form. Too much sought after to bother with us fifth years."

Judith let her lips curve up in a tiny smile. "I think I spoke to him once."

★   ★   ★

At the weekend, Adam came to call.

When she opened the door, his smile was polite but his eyes were wary. "Are you safe to be spoken to, yet? Or still likely to erupt?" His brows drew down intently.

She shrugged. "Depends what you have to say."

"A Judith answer." He turned and beckoned. Caleb stepped into view. "Don't be shy," he said. "This is your conversation, not mine."

Gingerly, Caleb edged closer.

His thick, dark hair looked combed, his jeans were unripped and his T-shirt bore no offensive slogan. Judith could imagine Adam instructing, "Make yourself presentable."

"Hello, Mrs. McAllister."

She folded her arms. "Hello, Caleb."

Caleb eyed her, apprehensively. "Would it be OK if we came in for a minute?"

She stood back and let them troop past and into the sitting room, having trouble keeping a straight face at the deep sigh Caleb vented as he trudged back to the scene of his recent crime.

In the sitting room, Caleb and Adam waited to be invited before they sat down, and Caleb kept his eyes averted from the still-damaged fire surround. "I've come to, like, apologise."

Judith, seating herself across from him, raised her eyebrows. "Only *like* apologise? Something similar to an apology, but in actual fact something else?"

Adam coughed.

Caleb looked bewildered. Hesitated. "No, I *have* come to apologise."

"Go on then."

He scratched his head and stared at her. "Um, sorry," he said, sounding baffled.

"What for?"

"For, like, trashing your house. No!" Before she could open her mouth. "Not *like*; I *am* sorry for trashing your house. I thought it'd be cool to have a party while Dad was away, but it got completely out of hand. People turned up that I'd never met, and they were seriously out there. Know what I mean?"

Judith frowned. "Not really. Everybody's out there, aren't they? Except we three, I mean, because we're in here."

He stared at her again. "I meant that they were . . . they went mad. Smashing stuff up, and everything. And I think some people had too much to drink."

Judith assumed a look of horrified amazement. "Really? I wonder how that happened?"

Silence. Then, softly, Adam. "Caleb!"

Caleb heaved another huge, mournful sigh. "Yeah, OK. *Everyone* had lakes of stuff to drink, and most people were stoned, too. There's no excuse. I shouldn't have had a party here, it was totally out of order and I'm totally sorry."

For the first time, she smiled. "Thank you."

He looked slightly relieved, but still shifted uncomfortably in his seat. "Dad thought . . . no, *I* thought that I might do something, you know, something to help you out. To make up."

Beside him, Adam caught Judith's eye, and nodded slightly.

She cast around for a job that she could reasonably expect him to accomplish without taxing him unduly or placing herself or her property in too much jeopardy. "How are you at cutting grass?"

"I expect I could do it," he admitted cautiously.

"Shall we find out?"

Judith and Adam took to the patio bench while he began, a bench that had been green wrought iron with white slats last time Judith saw it, but was now all black, which she rather liked. Adam had been the perfect tenant; he'd decorated everything in sight, kept the house immaculate, then, precisely when she wanted to evict him, had made it possible by fouling up so comprehensively. Or, at least, having a son who fouled up on his behalf.

Her conscience twinged afresh.

Once settled on the bench where they had a good view of Caleb trying the lawn mower's pull-cord starter, they swatted gnats and drank tall glasses of orange juice, rediscovering rapidly the easy companionship that had developed prior to Caleb's party.

"I kept thinking you were going to giggle."

Judith sniffed. "I wasn't aware that anything about the episode was funny."

He swung around accusingly. "Your eyes were laughing."

She shrugged, and sipped at her juice. "Perhaps," she admitted, her lips curling. "A teeny bit."

**124**

Adam grinned briefly. Then touched the back of her hand. "And now Caleb's made his apology, it's time for me to offer my thanks. Thank you for not involving the police. I'm sure you must've considered it, I wouldn't have blamed you. But I am grateful that you didn't. Caleb's wayward enough, he doesn't need a police record, however minor."

"Really *out there*, is he?"

Adam laughed, eyes gleaming silver in the sun, and she thought, objectively, what a very attractive man he was, especially with his day's growth of beard to emphasise the angle of his lean jaw. Then he sobered, groaned, and sighed. "You've been brilliant, and now I have to give you some really bad news, and you're going to hate us all over again. And you'll be right to hate us, because it's something really annoying." He put down his glass on the floor, and leant forward on the bench to look into her face.

His expression was one of concern and apprehension. In fact, he looked a lot like Caleb had in the sitting room. "Go on, get it over with," she said, resignedly.

He hesitated. "You're really going to hate it."

"You're scaring me."

He ran his hand over his hair. "After the party I noticed something was missing from the smallest bedroom."

She felt herself relax. Why should he think this would make her hate him again? "Camera equipment? I'm afraid there were two lads messing around with it, but I wasn't in the mood to attempt a rescue at the time. It's

**125**

up to you if you want to take it further, I could give a reasonable description of the hoolies involved."

But he was shaking his head. "No. Although my equipment *was* rather mauled about by those disrespectful bastards. I'd love to get my hands on them —"

He broke off, glancing down as if tripped by a sudden and unwelcome reminder of the state of one of those hands.

He gathered himself. "But there was something else I kept in there, and I think it must still be in your house, somewhere."

He blew out a breath. "I'm afraid it was Fingers. My snake."

# CHAPTER
# TWELVE

For a moment she didn't absorb the full import of his words. "You called your snake *Fingers?*" Her eyes flicked involuntarily to his hands. The left one was clasped around the right, keeping the damage, as so often, out of sight.

He smiled, faintly. "Caleb's idea of a joke. He bought Fingers for me after I lost mine, and at first I thought I'd take him straight back to the exotic pet shop where Caleb got him. But then I began reading the book about keeping corn snakes, and I got interested. In fact, I got to like him."

All at once, Judith felt a funny sensation in the pit of her stomach; a pulse began behind her eyes and her neck to sweat. "I hate snakes! Is he dangerous? Is he poisonous? Is he *big?*"

"He's harmless, honestly! He's not poisonous, he's a couple of feet long. Not much longer, anyway. He's still young, his markings haven't changed into stripes, yet. But I'll get him back, I promise. Just don't go around spraying wasp killer or whatever, trying to gas him."

Judith felt her toes curling off the floor as if the snake might be slithering towards her. "That would harm him, would it?"

He nodded earnestly. "Of course. Snakes are alive, they breathe air, drink water and like sunshine, just like us."

"They're not like us at all! A *snake*, yuk! A *snake* in my house. And this is what you term *annoying*?" She hadn't even liked the eels she'd come across on dives, and eels weren't snakes. They were fish, even if, occasionally, they had a bit of attitude.

"I'm really sorry, Judith. But it's not his fault he's a snake. If you'll just give me a chance to find him . . ."

She shuddered, thinking words she didn't like, such as *slither* and *coil*. "Snakes are green and slimy."

His half-smile tipped one corner of his mouth. "Not Fingers. Autumn colours. Rather pretty. And snakes aren't slimy."

She shucked this minor point off. "Where could he be hiding?"

"Well, I've already checked my stuff, inside my sofa and chairs, for instance. So I'm thinking now about under your floorboards, or behind the fire. Under the kitchen units . . ."

"Fantastic."

"Sorry."

"*Bloody* fantastic!"

"Bloody sorry."

She glared. If Adam had once been the perfect tenant, those days were certainly over. "Don't you laugh at me, Adam Leblond!"

"Never, Judith," he declared, firmly. "Never in a million years." But he looked the other way so she couldn't see his face.

128

He didn't find Fingers that day. Caleb finished the lawn and left with an air of virtuous relief, while Adam systematically took the house apart upstairs. "Good job you haven't had the new carpet down," he panted as he pulled the existing carpet off its gripper and began to lever up the floorboards.

"Yes, good job." She pulled a face. "How on earth would the snake get down there?"

He flashed his torch into the hollow he'd just exposed. "They can squeeze their way into seemingly impossible places."

Judith backed away. "I don't know whether to feel safer here or in the sitting room. I don't want Fingers jumping out at me."

He snorted a laugh, his eyes gleaming as he looked up at her. "Snakes aren't well known for jumping."

The hunt for Fingers drew to a close at about 9pm. Adam was sheepish. "Can I come back tomorrow to do the same demolition job on the downstairs?"

She groaned. "I suppose I've no choice. It's either that or walk around scared to death in case he appears. He just better not slither into bed with me, that's all!"

"He wouldn't dare."

Judith spent a jumpy and wakeful night, remembering Giorgio telling her the legend of how Malta had no poisonous snakes after St. Paul didn't die after a viper bit him.

And Fingers wasn't poisonous, either. It didn't seem to make much difference. She didn't like snakes.

Where was Fingers? Snakes were nocturnal, weren't they? Adam had told her they fed on rodents, so unless she had a colony of mice beneath the floorboards Fingers would by now be getting hungry. Looking for food. Coming out from hiding. *Slithering* out. *Coiling* up.

She tucked the duvet firmly around her shoulders, and left the light on.

Judith was more than ready to quit the house when Adam appeared the next morning. She felt unsettled and nervous, examining every patch of carpet before stepping on it as she moved around the house. She dropped the spare key into his palm. "I'm going to have lunch with my stepson, and, no doubt, his ever-present girlfriend. If you find your scaly, slimy friend you can lock up after you when you leave."

Handbag, fleece, out into the street, glancing up at a cotton wool sky with blue patches.

He stood on the top step, watching her unlock her car. "Snakes aren't slimy. Did Fingers try to slither into bed with you?"

A horror wriggled up her body. "No!"

He swung the keys slowly. "He's a gentleman."

She made it her business to stay out of the house all day.

First she had lunch with Kieran and, for once, not Bethan. Kieran didn't seem in a very good mood. He hardly smiled at all, and was more interested in gazing morosely at other people in the pub than in holding a conversation.

"Have you and Bethan had words?" Judith tried, gently.

130

"No!" Horrified, as if she'd asked a rude question.

Hmm, OK, not her business. Maybe Bethan was out with her mates and Kieran was possessive and wanted her always with him. Tom had been the same irksome way. "How's your dad?"

A snort. "Much as ever. Loud, opinionated and critical."

"That does sound a bit like him."

After lunch, she went to see her mother, who wasn't in a much better mood, mainly, it seemed, because Mrs. Yeats, who sat in the chair opposite Wilma in the lounge, had just received a walking frame of a slightly different design to everyone else's.

"Why does it matter?" Judith was unable to enter into her mother's dissatisfaction.

"If it were anyone but that smug cat," Wilma responded, obscurely, tapping discontentedly on her own walking frame.

Judith tried to bring up other subjects, Kieran, Molly, Brinham and the new benches they were putting in the market square, but she was aware of her mother's gaze on Mrs. Yeats's walking frame, throughout.

Rather than risking a doleful hat-trick by finding her sister in a bad mood, too, Judith guiltily knocked Molly off her intended visiting list and spent the last couple of hours of the afternoon roaming around The Norbury Centre. Odd to shop on a Sunday after Malta's Sunday-closing policy. She bought two new pairs of jeans, one black, one indigo, and a host of items that seemed distinctly lacking in her house — bin bags, a washing up brush, spray polish, dusters, cling film, a basket of multi-coloured pegs, pens, and a turquoise can opener.

Then, hoping that by that time Fingers would be safely corralled, she made for home.

Adam's BMW that he insisted was only just getting into its stride at ten years old was still parked in Lavender Row. She sighed. Honestly, this having space to herself business was not working today.

"Hello-o?" She managed the key with one hand while straining the fingers of the other to grasp six carrier bags, and staggered into the hall. She'd be glad when the carpet was replaced. She didn't like that bit at the bottom of the stairs where there seemed to be the lingering of an unpleasant smell. She stepped over it. "Adam?"

He appeared from the sitting room, hands in pockets, smile sketchy, his shoulders hunched. "I need to talk to you."

She dropped her bags. "What, now? Can't you find that bloody snake?"

Standing back, he indicated a glass tank on the floor near the sofa, and a red-and-russet shape in a corner half under a piece of wood. "Under the kitchen units. Come sit down."

She turned her eyes hurriedly from the tank. *Coiled.* Urrrgh. "So what have you done this time?"

His voice was very gentle. "Sit down, Judith."

She remained on her feet. "What's happened?"

"Please."

132

Flopping down onto the sofa, she groaned. Adam looked as grim as a wet weekend. "Some new disaster created by Leblond and son? Lost your tarantula, or arranged a rave for next Saturday?"

He waitcd, very still, very grave, his eyes fixed on hers. She tailed off. His voice became low, and very soft. "I'm really sorry. But there's some bad news."

The hairs on the back of her neck prickled up. She had an absurd desire to stroke them flat with her hand. "What?"

He hesitated. "Someone's left a message on your answering machine. I didn't answer when the phone rang, of course. But the machine kicked in. And I heard the message."

Her heart flopped. "And how do you know what kind of news it is?"

His face twisted. "It wasn't difficult to recognise as bad news."

She turned her head and regarded the phone. New and shiny, palest grey. The *message waiting* light blinking red on the base. She swallowed. Rose shakily. Her heartbeat seemed to be in her eyes. Her throat. Her head. Vaguely, she was aware of Adam leaving the room, the sound of water whooshing into the kettle.

With an effort, she pressed the *play* button.

"*You have one new message.*" Difficult to breathe, waiting for the time, the date, the tone. A second's silence, then gentle crying. And Cass's voice. "Judith, I ring to give you news. This morning . . . this morning, Giorgio died. They think a clot blocked his heart. He felt nothing, of course, he died very suddenly, with his mama beside him." Cass began to sob. "May he sleep peacefully." Click. "*End of message. You have no more messages.*"

Dimly, beyond the rushing in her ears, she became aware of Adam's return, the shifting of the sofa as he lowered himself onto the cushion, the clunk as he deposited coffee on the low table. The pungent smell hit the back of her throat. She reached out and pressed *play* again. And again. Then he gently stayed her hand.

He gave her the hot mug, china, she noticed, she was glad he'd used the china mugs, she preferred them to the pot ones. He'd given her the white one with roses, and taken pale blue with birds for himself. They were Albert china, she'd bought them as seconds from a shop in London's Piccadilly. He held his left hand over hers on the mug until he was certain she was holding on securely.

Then he was silent. Sipping from his own mug, watching her over the rim as she tried to drink.

"You were close?" he asked eventually.

She nodded. Despite the hot fluid, her teeth chattered, clicking on the rim of the mug. He slipped off the denim shirt he wore over his T-shirt and dropped it around her shoulders, but even this warmth he tried to lend her seemed to simply drain away, leaving her shivering so hard it felt as if the sofa was vibrating.

"Was he . . ." He hesitated. "Was he the one?"

She nodded, again. Nodding too hard, like a child.

He breathed out a sigh and ran his hand over his hair. "So this is a terrible shock."

For several moments she couldn't speak, couldn't swallow, couldn't breathe. It was as if a huge sob had turned to concrete in her throat. *Giorgio! Oh Giorgio, Giorgio.* Her eyes closed against dancing dots, red and black. Gradually, the sensation receded and her airway cleared.

She lifted her eyes to his. "This wasn't entirely unanticipated." She dragged in a deep, quivering breath. "Giorgio was in a coma."

# CHAPTER
# THIRTEEN

The words revolved around the silent room.

Outside, youngsters called to one another, a dog barked, a woman laughed.

She could almost feel Adam's shock.

"The doctors had classified him as in a persistent vegetative state." She could give him chapter and verse on coma and PVS, how it's decided what constitutes what, which expert disagrees with which. The way the victim could twitch, grimace, groan without stimulus, but react not at all when stimulus was given. She'd read up on it. A lot. Exhaustively. Absorbed the results of this test case, that campaign, what the Pope said about how victims must be cared for. "He had an accident, three months ago."

Three months since Giorgio had been air-lifted to St. Luke's Hospital from the dive site at Ghar Lapsi. Since Charlie Galea had turned up at her flat because he knew she had to be told what Giorgio's parents wouldn't.

All the if only's came crashing back. If only, if only, if only . . . If only she'd been Giorgio's diving buddy that day, would it have been different? Could she have kept him from harm? *Surely she could have?*

She made herself take another of those long breaths. "He was in a scuba diving accident. He surfaced, and a jet ski hit him. There was a surface marker buoy to warn that there were divers down. But some jet skiers are menaces. They aren't licensed, they just buy the damned machine and hurl themselves about without bothering about safety rules."

"I'm sorry." His voice echoed with compassion.

"You'd think you'd be safe from them at Ghar Lapsi, it's a steep descent to the sea, it would be murder to carry a bloody jet ski down the steps. It's not as if it were Mellieha Bay, a proper beach, where surface water sports are common. Accidents there are not unheard of, there was a girl killed last year.

"But some hooray had sailed his gin palace out from the yacht marina and anchored off Ghar Lapsi. They sometimes carry jet skis on the huge boats. The hoorays came pounding in towards shore, wanted to see the caves, I suppose. *Ghar* means cave. Probably had no idea it was a dive site or that they shouldn't come within the arm of rocks. Morons."

She stared into her now empty coffee cup. "I went to see him. Giorgio. Before I came home." She drew in a quavering breath. "Giorgio had gone. The damage where the ski hit his head was too much. He was a husk, just the machine keeping him breathing. His eyes were lifeless, I knew he'd gone. His family had been told that he wouldn't recover.

"I couldn't bear to stay on the island."

"I'm sorry." His hand was warm on her arm. The good hand.

137

She jumped up to pace the room. "Before he met me, Giorgio didn't dive. If not for me, he would never have had the accident. Would still be alive. Alive and breathing, laughing and smiling —" And then she was crying, dry, painful sobs that scourged her throat and pleated her chest.

Warm arms threaded around her and her head fell forward onto Adam's shoulder, as she groaned the questions that those left behind have always asked. "*Why?* Why him? Why did he have to surface right there, right that instant? A few seconds more, a few seconds less. That's all he needed! And if *I'd* been there I would have realised what was happening, known from the engine sound under the water how close it was and how quickly it was approaching! *I should have been there!*"

The room grew dark around her.

Adam left her mainly alone to cry out her anguish in the depths of the sofa, returning only occasionally with a glass of water to ease her aching throat and a fat kitchen roll to absorb her tears.

He squatted down beside her. "Shall I fetch someone to be with you? Your mother?"

She blew her nose. "Too old and frail."

"Your sister?"

"Molly's wonderful, but I'm not sure I can bear her particular brand of sympathy, at the moment."

He hesitated. "Then I'll stay. I'd feel like hell, going home and leaving you like this."

"I've stopped crying. I'll be all right." But even as the words left her lips, her face crumpled anew.

He made a deep noise of concern. "I'll sleep down here, just so you're not alone in the house, tonight. It would be wrong to abandon you."

She blew her nose for the millionth time. A heap of damp tissues was building on the carpet at her feet. Went attractively with a red nose and swollen eyes, no doubt. "I'll be OK. I'm going to get drunk. Obliterate the pain."

"Good idea." He shrugged off his jacket, pulled the curtains and switched on a light. "What have you got?"

She'd expected him to try to dissuade her rather than join in with gusto, but led him through to the kitchen where they found a bottle of whisky in the fridge and two bottles of red wine in the under-stairs cupboard. He also discovered a tin of biscuits that Molly had given as a welcome-back-into-your-home gift, and cajoled her into nibbling her way through two shortcakes. Then they began on the whisky, sloshing the twinkling amber brew into cut glass tumblers that were heavy at the base, fragile at the rim. Side-by-side on the sofa, they propped their feet on the coffee table.

Judith tossed back her first glassful and squeaked a gasp at the scorching in her throat.

"You unman me. I shall have to do the same." Adam copied her, then had to wipe his eyes on the back of his hand.

She poured refills, and sniffed. "Life is sometimes very crappy."

"Absolutely."

Judith blew her nose. "He didn't deserve to die. He had a lot of life left."

Adam had kicked his shoes off, his feet were alongside hers on the table, encased in black ribbed socks without holes or pulls. It occurred to her that he was a comfortable person to be in proximity to; nothing about him was worn or stale.

"If only I'd never introduced him to diving. I should have been with him that day, I could've —"

His eyes were intent. "Did you make him happy? Were you good together?"

She had a vision of Giorgio's face, the smile that felt only for her, the way his dark eyes became darker as he pulled her into his arms. She nodded, biting her lip.

"Then don't 'if only'. Pointless. If you loved each other, be glad. You can't change anything now."

It wasn't bad advice. But so difficult to follow! Sombrely, she sipped her whisky.

She wasn't sleepy. She was hollowed out and exhausted, aching with sorrow, but felt as if she'd never sleep again. Adam yawned occasionally, but Judith just drank steadily, watching the room turn to blurs, feeling her brain sloshing gently within her skull, hearing her voice stretching and contracting as her tongue struggled to cope with S and other difficult letters, and she told him about the last time she'd seen Giorgio in his hospital room and the confrontation outside it with Maria Zammit.

Her ears were hearing slowly, making Adam's voice thin and distant. "Why wouldn't Giorgio's family let you into the hospital?"

**140**

She sighed. "I didn't exist, to them. Giorgio's been separated from his wife for fourteen years, but there's no divorce in Malta."

"Ah. Uncomfortable."

"It was their coping mechanism to acknowledge only Giorgio's wife, it was all about surface respectability. Maria, Giorgio's mother, was particularly good at it. When Giorgio invited his parents to dinner and then produced me, Maria simply walked out. Agnello shook his head and asked Giorgio why he had to hurt his mother like that — he had a wife, till death, not till the marriage becomes difficult. Giorgio didn't want to cause any more pain to his family than necessary, so we carried on our relationship discreetly."

Adam shook his head as if trying to clear it. "He let you be treated like a dirty secret?"

She ran her tongue reflectively along the hard, thin rim of her glass. A dirty secret. "You could look at it like that, I suppose, although Giorgio said a secret affair was simply impossible in Malta. I was angry, in the beginning. But if we'd tried to force the issue, what would we have achieved? We would have been together, but Giorgio would've been estranged from his family. Possibly including his children — I couldn't be responsible for that. We had to go along with the charade."

"Really?" Adam pulled a face as if the idea were sour.

"Don't be too judgmental, his family were acting on what they believed in. In their eyes I was a despicable interloper. They're not alone in their attitudes, my own mother wasn't thrilled when I left Tom. She considers that marriage is for life and she was very tight-lipped about me ending things."

He opened his eyes wide. "You're confusing me. I'd forgotten you were married."

"I like to forget it, too." She explained about her marriage, Tom and Exotic Liza, and Kieran.

"Tom must be stupid," he commented, swirling whisky unsteadily in the depths of his crystal glass. "But at least you have someone else to blame for the break up of your marriage."

She wriggled to get more comfortable, slanting herself into the corner to face him. He was in jeans today and his chestnut hair, faded to grey in the wings above his ears, fell over his eye, making him look very laid back. She remembered that he knew one or two things about separation. "How about you? What was your downfall?" She'd drunk far too much to worry about impertinence.

He glugged some whisky, and reopened the biscuit tin. He'd been feeding her biscuits to put something inside her stomach other than booze. After the shortcake, she'd eaten two bourbon, two custard creams and a digestive. Because he shook the tin at her she chose a ginger nut and a chocolate chip cookie, but once she had one in either hand couldn't imagine herself eating them.

"Shelley and I were married for a long time. Since I was twenty-four. But . . ." He shrugged. "We were very good friends — are still. It turned out not to be enough." He gesticulated towards her with his chocolate digestive. "It wasn't the love you've talked about, you and Giorgio. There was a lot of affection, and when she brought the subject of marriage up I believed it was logical. And I'd be able to sleep with her every night, which, frankly, *was* appealing. I suppose I mistook affection for love."

He creased his brow. "Or it probably was love, but not the right sort, the deep sort."

She sniffed, and blew her nose again. Her throat felt as if it were lined with hay and her eyes with sand. "But she must've thought she loved you, or she wouldn't have wanted marriage."

His eyes slid sideways, fastening themselves on her through a narrowing slit between his lids. "Not necessarily. I think girls in those days operated on a fixed programme. If they went out with someone for a certain length of time, they got engaged. They got the sparkly ring and the party, they were the centre of attention."

It was true, that had been the norm. What was it about herself that had made her fall outside this *fixed programme*?

"And she's always joked that it was because *Shelley Leblond* sounded glamorous, big improvement on Shelley Dobben, which sounded like a cart horse."

"Funny thing to joke about."

He shrugged. "She's artistic. An interior designer. Things like that are important to her."

Tired of their sticky presence in her hand, Judith ate the biscuits slowly. Crumbs worked their way in between the buttons of her grey-green blouse and she tried to flick them out with her fingers. Stopped when she realised he was watching. The crumbs tickled. "So did one of you find someone else?"

He drew his eyes back up to her face. "No. But when I had my accident, Shelley found the whole thing very difficult."

Judith shook her spinning head. "How?"

His eyes narrowed. "She has a problem with ugliness."

# CHAPTER
# FOURTEEN

In those few, carefully chosen words, Judith got a glimpse of his pain and felt a dart of anger towards the unknown Shelley Dobben Leblond.

"She couldn't bear the sight of my hand. And as for touching her — forget it!" He laughed, mirthlessly. "The occupational therapist warned me that I might need to 'rethink my position in the marital bed', and 'get used to doing things with the left hand that had always been done with the right'. Fat chance of that, as it turned out. Shelley didn't want me anywhere near her."

Judith put down her whisky, suddenly getting that threatening feeling in the back of her throat that told her to slow down. She enunciated carefully. "That's not nice. Not supportive." She struggled for what she was trying to say. "Not wife-like."

"At least she was honest. Better that she told me candidly that she didn't want to sleep with me any more. Can you imagine how humiliating it would have been to realise she was suffering in silence? Pitying me? Gritting her teeth but shrinking inside?"

She frowned, and admitted, "That doesn't sound very nice, either. But it's still big of you to be so . . . understanding."

"Realistic."

He went to make coffee, leaving her in a hazy brooding on the vagaries of fortune until he returned with two mugs for each of them, fragrant and steaming.

"Two mugs at a time seems a good idea. Saves getting up again. Wonder why I never thought of it." She began her first mug. "So how did you hurt your hand? Lawn mower? Power saw?"

He shook his head.

"You're a photographer, I bet you were in a war and had to try and toss a grenade out of a vehicle, careening across the desert, caught in cross fire?"

He raised his eyebrows. "You know I'm not that brave or glam kind of photographer. It was a stupid, freak accident." Picking up his coffee, he half-closed his eyes. "I was helping Shelley. She'd taken on this huge first floor room, where they'd knocked the walls out to create "a space". All wooden floors and Swedish furniture that didn't match. She asked me to take pix. I often did, so that she had a portfolio to show to clients.

"Nice house, well-heeled customers. And they were keen to get their place into one of the glossy home magazines, so they engaged me to shoot some stuff for them, too, then they were going to approach someone to write it up." He paused to sip his drink.

"The *space* had French doors opening to a first floor sundeck. They wanted photos of the family toasting one another with champagne, on the deck. I was absorbed in what I was doing, trying to get the bloody woman to shut up so I could get a photo of her not mouthing like a fish, and then someone let these dogs out." He shook

146

his head at the memory. "Rottweilers, they were, half dog half monster. They came flying in, baying for blood, straight at me."

He surprised her with a sudden smile. "Major heart attack time! I shot backwards. The wooden rails weren't up to twelve stone of Adam in a panic, and gave way."

He drained his cup. "There was a conservatory underneath. I fell through it."

"Oh my God."

"It just *exploded*, shattering into my palm and fingers — sliced into me like razors. And my back, my neck." He pulled down his collar to show her a white curve from just below his ear. "But those were relatively superficial, and healed OK. It was the hand that really suffered."

She reached for his hand to examine the cross-hatching of thin, white scars and the tiny dots of stitches on the palm.

He took it back, and pushed it into his pocket. "I didn't realise how badly hurt I was, at first. I was all gashed to buggery and I could see the fingers weren't exactly intact. So off we went to Northampton General, Shelley driving and me with my hand held up in the air and towels soaking up the blood."

He finished the first coffee and poured whisky into the second. It seemed to Judith that some object was being defeated, but she'd always enjoyed coffee with a tot in, so followed suit.

"What I noticed immediately was that I'd lost a lot of movement, and what I did have sent sort of electric shocks searing up my arm. It was nerve damage causing the awful pain, but it turned out I had *everything-damage* — tendon, muscle, tissue, artery. I had microsurgery, nerve repair, tendon grafts. But the whole thing was just slashed from my fingers down to the heel of my hand. Chopped up. Then I got a deep infection that resisted antibiotics. The fingers never worked and pretty soon began to wither — that's from the nerve damage. Looked really strange, as if they belonged to a corpse, sort of pale blue." He smiled thinly.

"Quite quickly I realised that it was about as good as it was going to get. I'd have greater use of the hand without the useless, immobile fingers getting in my way."

"That's horrific."

Looking down at his coffee, he shrugged. "Much worse things happen to people. Being in and out of hospital brings that firmly home to you. For everyone who loses a finger there are others who lose an arm. There's even amputee humour: the patient says, 'Doctor, doctor, I can't feel my legs!' And the doctor says, 'That's because I've cut off your arms!'" He snorted.

Judith wiped her face with the back of her hand, not knowing if she were shedding tears for Adam or tears for Giorgio. They just seemed to well up endlessly of their own accord. "So Shelley couldn't cope with the amputation?"

He shook his head. "She'd turn white at the very word. Couldn't cope with any of it, gave up completely once she realised the fingers were never going to *be better*. The disfigurement made her skin crawl. That was pretty painful, too."

Judith tried to imagine if it had been Giorgio who'd suffered like Adam. Put herself in the place of a woman who loved beauty and couldn't bear mutilation near her. Failed. Surely love should have transcended the loss of a few fingers? "When you compare it to what happened to Giorgio —"

"Yes!" His eyes were bleak. "In comparison with death it's pretty minor. And that kind of illuminates the quality of her feelings." He jettisoned his mug roughly onto the table, and it rattled around in a circle, almost spilling the remaining contents. "Finishing the marriage was a similar process to deciding on the amputation. A clean end. Cut away the rotting stuff. No point hanging onto something that's never going to work again. Shelley cares for me a lot, but there's a gulf between *a lot* and *enough*, and you can't bridge it artificially."

"So that's why you always hide your hand away," she thought aloud.

His head whipped around as he fastened a scorching glare on her. "I don't do any such thing! My occupational therapist says people who don't hide their damage feel better about themselves." Then he immediately contradicted himself. "It's emotionally quite difficult to have it on display. Some people like to have a good stare and some people avert their eyes. I don't know which is worse."

"What about prostheses?"

"I didn't like the idea. There are quite a few of us who'd rather put up with the loss of limb than wear

**149**

artificial replacements. I do exercises to assist with strength and symmetry, I have one or two gadgets and aids, and I apply the problem-solving strategies I've been taught by the occupational therapist. I make the best of things."

Judith remembered observing him. "Like using your left hand for everything?"

"Not everything. I can write with my right hand — untidily. I can drive — although it's better if the car's modified — and I can play the violin, with a bit of adapting to my bowing. I tend not to wear too many buttons, but use my left hand for those I do. I use my left hand for the computer mouse, to hold a spoon, and clean my teeth. And one or two other things you won't want to discuss."

She managed a watery smile. "Yet you've done all the decorating here since you lost your fingers?"

"I have this gizmo to help hold things like paintbrushes." His response was short, as if he'd had enough of the subject. He was probably only allowing it to give her something to focus on other than Giorgio. It would be fairer to let him go to sleep. But something inside her quailed at the thought of being completely alone with her grief. It might swallow her up.

He yawned again, and turned the subject. "Kieran's a step, isn't he? Have you got kids of your own?"

"The time was never right. Your Caleb seems such a lovely lad. I know I was furious at him about the party, but it was bad judgement rather than malice. He's very pleasant and personable. A live wire."

"Live wire," he repeated dryly. "Polite-speak for Caleb ricocheting from one disaster to another. As you say, there's no malice in him, but from the moment he could crawl he's been getting into strife. A big shock for us after his brother, Matthias, who was a golden child, bright but with common sense."

Judith smiled. "I didn't realise you had another. Tell me about Matthias — fabulous names your kids have, by the way."

Hunkering down more comfortably on the sofa, Adam folded his arms. "Shelley's choices; I wanted Patrick and Mark. But what can you do against a woman who gets up out of her hospital bed and visits the registrar herself?"

"Did she do that?"

"Yes, she did." His smile was caustic. "Patrick and Mark are their middle names."

She absorbed the idea of someone who didn't view the names bestowed upon shared children as joint decisions.

He let his head tilt back. His jaw-line was a firm sweep. "I indulged her too much. Laughed at the more outrageous pieces of selfishness and quite admired her for doing what it took to get her own way. She got used to it."

It was deep into the night, now. Judith would have ended the conversation, found Adam a quilt and crept away upstairs so he could sleep. But Adam, now he'd begun, seemed in the mood to talk and talk.

"My mother mutters darkly that Caleb takes after Shelley. Does that mean Matthias takes after me? I'd

**151**

like to think so, but Matthias is impressive. He's intelligent, motivated, good-looking, and engaged to the most amazing girl. Davina. The Divine Davina."

Because he'd shut his eyes as he talked, Judith could study him properly. The tightness of the skin across his cheekbones under the fans of his lashes, the burst of deep laugh lines at the corners of his eyes, the cleft in his chin. Where many men, like Tom, sagged and slackened with age, somehow Adam seemed to have tautened and become wirier. "How is she amazing?"

"Apart from being frighteningly clever and hard working, she's as gorgeous as Lara Croft." One of Adam's eyes opened slightly to look at her. "Honestly, she's a goddess."

"Personality?"

"Definitely personality-plus; cheerful, interesting, caring. They're going to have the most phenomenal children."

"But is Caleb more fun?"

The eye shut again. "Certainly less predictable." He gave several huge yawns. "My boys are like the tale about the chap with two really good friends. The chap gets drunk and ends up in jail, and one friend gets him a solicitor and hides the escapade from his wife. But the other friend is beside him in the cell, saying, '*Damn that was fun!*'" He yawned again.

A little like Adam getting drunk with her tonight. "I ought to go up and let you sleep."

"Will you be able to sleep, if you go to bed?"

She shook her head.

He smiled. He had a really nice smile. It could be gentle or sympathetic, and, sometimes, wicked. "Sleep's overrated. I can sleep any time. I'll stay with you a little longer." He pulled himself more upright. "You and I went to the same school, didn't we?"

It took her by surprise that he realised. Maybe Melanie had told him. "I believe we did."

"I recognised you the instant I walked into the kitchen when you first called. Judith Morgan. We had a conversation once outside the school gates about Polos and if they'd rot your teeth."

He remembered all that! She would never have admitted it herself, in case it led him to suspect the gigantic crush she'd had on him. Weakly, she offered, "I still like Polos."

"Me, too, the mint ones are my favourite. And the fruit, of course. I'm not keen on the butterscotch or the citrus."

"New fangled inventions."

"Absolutely. And the spearmint, with those flecks, they look as if they're made of washing powder."

His eyes drooped again. "You always insisted on being called Judith; the guys from your year used to sing out, 'Hey Jude!' after you, and you'd get sniffy."

Her own eyelids were feeling heavy. Maybe she ought to go up to bed after all and leave him to what was left of the night. "Paul McCartney sang it so much better."

And despite everything, despite the heavy, gluey despair in her heart, despite the gallons of scalding tears waiting behind her eyes for the moment when she stopped thinking about other things and thought again about Giorgio, she couldn't help feeling pleased that someone had noticed and remembered these things about her.

"I always thought it was kind of a shame," he murmured, drowsily. "I thought it would be nice to call you Jude. The name conjures up someone who dares to be different, fun. Interesting."

She wasn't altogether sure what to say to that.

# CHAPTER
# FIFTEEN

Morning. Early. Judith opened her eyes to the sun-filled sitting room and discovered that eventually, last night, she'd fallen asleep, her legs curled and cramped and her head on the sofa arm.

Her face felt creased, her mouth and eyes dry.

Adam was asleep at the other end of the sofa, feet still on the table, arms folded, head propped against the upholstered wing of the sofa as if he'd just dropped off for five minutes during Grandstand.

He'd stayed, she remembered, because of Giorgio.

*Giorgio.*

Sickness clutched her, but her eyes were too dry for tears.

Her mind had held the knowledge of his death cradled complete while she slept, ready to give it back to her now with sickening clarity. Giorgio was dead, and very soon would be committed to the ground of the island he'd loved.

The floor heaving like the deck of a boat beneath her feet, she went to the computer in the alcove and left it to start up while she visited the bathroom, brushed her teeth and showered. Sliding into an enveloping cotton robe, she returned quietly to the computer. Adam slept on.

The World Wide Web was a wonderful thing, she acknowledged, contemplating the elegant web-site of *The Times of Malta*. *The Times* could be accessed as easily in Brinham as in Sliema.

Clicking on the correct link, she watched the social and personal page flicking onto her screen. She scrolled down and, even though she was expecting it, Giorgio's name leapt out and stopped her breath.

ZAMMIT. On July 27, at St. Luke's Hospital, GIORGIO, aged 42, passed away suddenly, comforted by the rites of Holy Church. He leaves to mourn his irreparable loss his wife Johanna née Grech, his daughters Alexia and Lydia, his parents Agnello and Maria, sister Josephine and her husband Paul Gauci, his uncles, aunts, nephews, nieces and friends. — R.I.P. The funeral leaves St. Luke's Hospital on Tuesday July 29 at 1.30p.m. for Stella Maris parish church, Sliema, where Mass praesente cadavere will be said at 2.30p.m., followed by interment in the family grave at the Santa Maria Addolorata Cemetery. Family flowers only.

She'd guessed that Maria and Agnello would place the obituary in *The Times* as well as in the Maltese papers, *In-Nazzjon* or *L-Orizzont*. Giorgio had been a businessman, his death would need declaiming in both of the island's languages. She stared at the formal words.

**156**

Adam stirred, and she realised he was awake.

She had to clear her throat, concentrate to make herself speak. "Obituary." She nodded at the screen. "I must go."

He frowned for a moment. "To the funeral?"

"I have to be with him."

He didn't precisely try to dissuade her, but he rubbed his unshaven chin, making it rasp. "Somebody ought to go with you. I volunteer, if you can't scare up anyone better. You'll need an ally. The family will shut you out. Feelings will be running high. A mother and father have lost their son, children have lost their father. The wife will act with wounded dignity and ignore you."

It was an uncomfortable picture. "You're right," she said, mechanically, "what was I thinking? But thank you. You've been really kind, Adam, especially considering that I threw you out of your home."

"You're having a rough time."

The doorbell shrilled. They raised their eyebrows at each other.

"Half-past seven?" An unusual hour for visitors. Judith pushed the chair away from the computer.

Adam stood up, winced, and lifted a protesting hand to his head. The right hand. He must be feeling rough. "Do you want me to answer it?"

"I'll do it." At the front door Judith squinted out over the chain, pain lancing across her eyes at an attack from the cruel morning sun.

The figure on the step snapped, "It's me."

"Molly?" She unchained the door. "What are you . . .? I mean, come in."

Molly's Lexus was pulled up at the kerb, very gold in the early sunlight. Judith frowned as she made out solid shapes crouching on the back seat. Suitcases?

"Can I stay for a bit?" asked Molly, calmly, taking off her cardigan and smoothing her hair. "I've left Frankie." She took in Judith in her robe and bare feet, and Adam with his slept-in his clothes. "Who's *he*?"

The morning grew hazy with heat. Judith stood the door to the garden open, and filled the kettle.

After making room for Molly's things by removing all the clothes that she'd just stowed in the spare wardrobe, she occupied herself with small chores, wondering about her sister and feeling nauseous and headachy. It was a long time since she'd been drunk enough to have a hangover and the whole unpleasant process had not improved.

The computer hummed gently, the 3-D design on the screensaver rolling slowly through its contortions. She didn't need to click the mouse and let Giorgio's obituary beam again from the screen and jolt her with fresh pain. It was there, but she hadn't quite brought herself to remove it. In fact, she could almost have lit candles around it, an illumination in a plastic shrine.

The sounds of Molly moving purposefully about in the spare room filtered through the house; the wardrobe door opening, shutting, opening, shutting, the drawers of the chest groaning in and out.

It was a kind of inverted déjà vu. A few short weeks ago she'd shut herself in Molly's spare room to unpack her life methodically from her suitcases. And now here was Molly, returning the favour.

Judith stepped out onto the patio, the flagstones warm beneath her bare feet, looking up the long narrow garden at the lawn, and Adam beyond it, cutting back some shrub that grew in an enormous spray of cerise flowers against the ochre tones of the back wall. He had far too much alcohol in his system to drive straight home and she'd brushed away his offers to walk the three miles or so to his new place, or to call a cab.

He'd kept her company when she needed someone to be with. She wasn't going to heave him out prematurely just because her sister was taking her turn to have a crisis.

"Coffee? Tea?" she called.

He shaded his eyes to look back at her. "Tea would be nectar."

Borrowing his pragmatic approach of the evening before, she made two mugs and took him them both.

He grinned appreciatively. "The only thing better than a cup of tea is two cups."

Back in the kitchen, she jumped to find Molly waiting.

Molly was composed, neat in black trousers and a cherry red short-sleeved jumper, her hair brushed loose and shiny over her shoulders. "Sorry that I didn't feel like talking straight away."

Judith slid her arm around her sister, looking down at the pale face. "That's all right. How are you doing?"

"OK." Molly didn't look OK. She looked glum. "I'll get the coffee on, shall I?"

She was going to take over, Judith could see, putting herself in charge of the kettle was the first step. She wondered whether to form some kind of protest, but realising that a) Molly probably needed something to do, and b) Judith didn't enjoy chores enough to hog them, refrained, as Molly busily poured the steaming water from the kettle into the mugs.

Feeling slightly less nauseous in the fresh air, Judith carried their drinks out to the bench.

"So." She made herself concentrate on Molly. "Tell me what happened. Do I have to go round and smash his face in?"

Molly didn't bother to smile. "As long as I don't have to stay with him any more, I don't care what happens." Her entire body was loose, still.

A silence.

"Look." Judith linked the soft arm and drew her sister closer. "I don't want to compromise your privacy, but I think you're going to have to give me a few hints. He hasn't been knocking you about, has he?"

A head shake.

"Having an affair?"

"No."

Judith waited.

Eventually, Molly sighed. "I just can't bear him any more, ruling the roost like a Victorian, treating me like a skivvy. Never showing me any affection, thinking it's fine to ogle other women and ignore me. He even told me that I bored him, and he wouldn't . . ." She blinked

160

fiercely. "He wouldn't be able to *do it* if we tried, because I don't arouse him. So I packed."

Judith gave Molly's arm a sympathetic squeeze. "Good for you." What else could she say? Frankie had always ruled the roost, and always treated Molly like a skivvy. Equality had come in the seventies without Frankie ever taking out his subscription.

But saying that he couldn't get an erection for her, well that was just nasty.

It was difficult, given recent history, to protest about Molly landing herself in Judith's newly acquired space, but this wasn't a great moment to be landed upon. She was sympathetic, of course she was sympathetic, she loved Moll to death. But it was tough to "be there" for her just at this exact moment, when all she wanted to do was sit in the sunshine and think of Giorgio.

Her eyes were beginning to burn ominously, as if her tears were preparing to flood out again.

Molly nodded in Adam's direction. "When's he going?"

"When he's not so full of booze."

With a quavering sigh, Molly put her hand over her eyes. "Honestly Judith, you can't know what Frankie's like! He's so grumpy all the time . . ."

Judith watched Adam, how he squinted against the bright light.

"— dictatorial, criticising and carping . . ."

He had his back to them, his cowboy legs planted firm against the earth as he worked his way methodically over the shrub, snipping off a leggy branch and snip, snip, snipping it into smaller pieces into a garden refuse sack. He seemed to be able to work the secateurs OK with his right hand, he'd slipped it into some kind of protective splint, leaving his thumb and finger free to lever against a projection where his fingers used to be. Probably the "gizmo" he'd talked about.

He'd been so kind last night. Had seemed to instantly understand the depth and futility of her pain, amplified because her grief would forever go unacknowledged by Giorgio's family.

*Oh Giorgio! Will it always hurt this much?*

"— and he should've found someone else years ago if he's found me unexciting for such a long time. Shouldn't he? Judith?" Molly waited.

Stricken, Judith turned. "I'm sorry Moll, I didn't —"

Molly's face flooded dull crimson and her eyes blazed. "I'm sorry if I *interrupted something* with my obviously inopportune appearance, but is it too much to ask that you stop lusting after the gardener just long enough to attend to my woes for a change? Honestly, it's different when it's you, isn't it? Talk about selfish."

Misery closed in. Judith had to swallow hard before she could speak. "I'm not 'lusting after' Adam. He stayed last night because . . ." She breathed in. "— because Giorgio died yesterday."

A silence. Shock dragged down Molly's jaw. "Don't be stupid," she denied uncertainly. "How could he?"

Wearily, Judith let her head tip back. "Do you want me to show you the obituary? He had an accident, he was in a coma, which is why I came home. And now he's been released."

And then Molly was crying, and Judith let her fall into her arms. "I'm sorry," Molly wept. "I'm sorry, I didn't know! But please don't ask me to go back to Frankie, Judith. It's been horrible, hardly speaking, sleeping in the spare room."

*That explained the underwear.* "Of course not." Judith closed her eyes as her sister cried in great soaking gulps.

She shouldn't have come home.

She couldn't give much support to her sister's unhappiness or her mother's frailty. Tomorrow, she should be standing on the rock that was Malta as Giorgio Zammit became part of it forever, there to see his grave. How, from green, leafy Brinham, could she feel close to him? Sense him in the yellow stone and blue sea of the place he'd lived, the place they'd loved, feel proof that he'd existed?

In Malta she would have been able to talk to his friends about him, Charlie, Carmelo, even Anton and Gordon, bring him back to life in their stories, his sense of humour and his gentleness.

Perhaps, in time, she would be able to overlay the inner vision that haunted her, of Giorgio, helpless and empty, like a big baby in a white gown on a white hospital bed with his head bandaged and his life lived for him by a handful of tubes.

Even as she patted Molly's heaving back, making comforting noises, framing soothing sentences, other words were forming in her head.

*I can go back.*

# CHAPTER
# SIXTEEN

Judith sat on the clifftop at Ghar Lapsi and stared at the glittering sea.

She'd driven there straight from Malta International Airport and made no attempt to see the funeral cortège set out from the imposing buildings of St. Luke's Hospital, nor to slip into the church to hear the mass said for the repose of Giorgio's soul or skulk among the mourners at the cemetery.

Instead, she watched the delicate movements of the sea where they'd dived together and been happy, and remembered loving a man with a joyful heart. Even if he'd proved to be a bit butterfingered with insurance premiums.

The cliff top — more of a broad shelf, really, as a second cliff rose behind her — was scrubby, but she found a slab of rock and sank down. It was quiet up here, she'd positioned herself away from the restaurant with its tables on the terrace, the concrete pathways, the steps to the sea. She could gaze down into the bay sheltered by its arm of rock and not be bothered by the tourists or the fishermen.

Having learnt respect for the power of summer sunshine she'd brought a big bottle of water in her bag, and wore a black straw hat.

The sea was ultra blue, the waves shattering the sun's reflection into smithereens of blinding light. Insignificant waves today, sighing against the dark craggy rocks with little spray. There might be divers down, a slight choppiness like that wouldn't affect them. It was when there was a swell that the currents were treacherous. Divers died, dragged out past the reef with its sponges and coral, or trapped, slapped about somewhere in the underwater cavern system.

The sea was mighty.

But today was a beautiful day for a dive. The light would be filtering through chinks in the rock and into the caves, rainbow wrasse, rays and moray would flit through weed swaying with the motion of the sea. Divers would fin through the near-silent, turquoise world in pairs, communicating with occasional gestures and signals.

Out to sea, looking closer than it was, the dark shape of the tiny island of Filfla, a nature reserve and possibly, depending on what you believed, the home of two-tailed lizards. A couple of fishing boats surged across the waves perhaps half-a-mile out. The rest of the sea within eyeshot was empty.

Except, on the horizon to the left, purple through the heat haze, the oil rigs some moron had allowed to wait there for their next job. Resolutely, she ignored their spikiness.

**165**

It was probably how it had looked the day Giorgio was injured, the squatting presence of Filfla and one or two boats. One, at least. One that carried jet skis.

It was almost evening by the time she roused and rose stiffly from the rock, her eyes burning from the salty breeze. She could have stayed all night, watching the sun set and the sky turn shrimp pink, purple, then black. But she needed the loo.

After the public toilets she retrieved the hire car from the car park and drove towards Tarxien and the Santa Maria Addolorata cemetery. In the residential areas the buildings were turning tawny as the sun angled low, the forest of television aerials glinting above.

Tiredness crept up on her. The day had begun early, she'd only just made her flight because the southbound M1 was closed owing to a chemical spillage. Tight with anxiety she'd had to find a way onto the M11 and then M25 and pass London to the east.

She'd left without telling anybody.

No doubt she'd catch hell from Molly. Molly didn't understand that Judith had to do things her own way. And if that way included booking a flight and leaving for Malta before Molly was awake . . . She could almost hear her elder sister's scandalised complaints. "Fancy just going off like that without telling a soul! Leaving me a note to say make yourself at home and there's plenty of food! What a way to treat a guest! That's just like you, Judith . . ."

What was surprising was that Molly should expect her to be anything other. Who else would she be like?

She left the car outside the black, wrought iron cemetery gates that were patterned to echo the gothic stone arches beyond. The flower stalls in the car park were being closed up, the stallholders calling to one another as they worked. A pretty girl flashed a smile as Judith asked her if she'd sell her a single white orchid. "Of course, Madam."

The hilly cemetery was still except for the grumble of nearby traffic and the rushing of the wind. Funerals were over for the day and the dust had settled. There was no rolling grass here as in an English cemetery, just clumps of trees among the broad paved walks between the mausoleums and graves with sculpted figures that terraced the hillside. Having only been to Addolorata once before, she'd forgotten how big it was.

She followed a couple up a succession of pathways that led, eventually, to recent graves.

There was nothing there to indicate any connection with Giorgio. Elaborate wreaths, yes, but the names were wrong — Borg, Debono, Gatt. Her heart began to thud in panic as she walked up and down.

Where was he?

And then she remembered the words "family grave" in the newspaper, and relief seeped in. Methodically, she returned to the older area, and continued to walk the paths. It was quite a place to cover and it took her some time, her nails digging into her palms and her legs feeling as if they belonged to someone else. She passed between the ranks of marble, the occasional black to punctuate the pale grey, plots arranged close together like terraced houses and some edged with wrought iron

**167**

or with posts and chains. She'd thought that fresh flowers would give her the clue to a recent burial, but many of the graves were graced with sprays, along with candles burning in glass lanterns.

The gates would close at dusk and she began to fear that she'd have to leave or be shut in. But then a significant burst of colour caught her eye, and she made her way between the stone crosses and exquisitely carved saints to a blaze of fresh flowers that spilled onto the graves on either side.

And on the head of the plot, beside a mourning angel carved from marble, were the words she was looking for. *Zammit Familja.*

The grave had been closed, gravediggers obviously prompt in hot countries. The floral tributes arranged before a series of marble plaques angled and ranked like pictures on a shelf, with the names of the Zammit family already passed inscribed beneath small oval photos.

Reality hit her like one of Sliema Z Bus's buses: Giorgio was down there. Because Giorgio was dead. Separated from her now by six feet of soil and stone. And suddenly it was all too bald, too raw and real. Instead of the comfort she'd searched for, the resting-place was a place of horror.

Forget the twinkling eyes, it seemed to say, no more laughing mouth and hungry lips. No more searching hands. It's all ended down here with a box thrust into the ground, and Giorgio trapped inside it.

She closed her eyes and struggled to remember that this was better, better a proper death than to be a shell of a man at a hospital, a mockery and an insult.

**168**

"I knew you wouldn't be long."

Judith staggered in shock on the sloping path as she spun around. "Cass!" In a black dress overlaid with lace fluttering in the evening breeze, Cass clutched a white handkerchief. She'd aged ten years in the last months. Her eyes, washed with too many tears, were pink rimmed in the deepening folds of her face.

Cass stepped closer, crossing herself. "They don't know I'm here," she said. "I pretended I'd left some medication at home that I needed. I knew you'd be around. I watched Maria watching for you all day. She was so very relieved when you didn't come. Thank you for letting the family mourn."

Judith had lifted her arms to drag Cass into a fierce embrace, but now she let them drift down again to her sides. She was being thanked for not inflicting herself.

It was a queer thought, and one that made her feel strange and distant. She hadn't fainted since she was a teenager, but now she felt hot and empty, her ears ringing. Her voice emerged reedily. "But I'm mourning, too."

Cass's smile was thin. "I know. *I* know, believe me, I know how it was between you. But they don't care. They want him for themselves." She made a gesture as if clutching something to her heart.

"I loved him."

Cass took out a brown leather purse and extracted a small item that glinted gold. Giorgio's crucifix, that he'd worn against his skin. She wiped wet cheeks with her handkerchief, then closed Judith's fingers around the gold. Her hands were cold. "And he loved you.

Only his body is here. You have his heart. Take it with you." She turned and walked away, leaving Judith beside Giorgio's grave alone, feeling the gold warming in her hand.

It was three days later when Judith pulled up outside her house in Lavender Row. She'd spent a couple of days with Uncle Richard, it calmed her to be with him. His wife, the lovely Erminia, had smiled her big, warm smile and was serenely unmoved that Judith was unwilling to join in dinners with her cousins Raymond, Lino and Rosaire and their families. Molly and her mother should be so restful, she thought, struggling to open with one hand the tall front door.

Then Molly was bustling to meet her in the hall to offer a quick hug. "I can't believe you've been all that way to go to a funeral."

Judith didn't bother explaining that she'd been "all that way" *not* to go to a funeral. It was too complex. She was just grateful that Molly wasn't launching into a session of sighs over Judith's strange ways.

Molly clasped her hands. "I've done some shopping, there's a casserole in the oven, you'll be hungry."

"Um, thanks." Casserole sounded stodgy and worthy, very Molly, and unappetising even though she hadn't eaten much recently. She thought longingly of an empty house and a full wine bottle. It didn't sound healthy, but it did sound attractive.

In the kitchen, she found white wine in the fridge and red below the stairs. Excellent. She opened the white. "Wine, Molly?"

170

Molly looked surprised. "Oh, no, thank you." As if drinking wine were naughty.

Judith poured herself a big glass, one of those enormous glasses meant to be quarter-filled with red wine to allow for breathing. She filled it. It took almost half the bottle. On the kitchen table lay her mail, on top a white envelope with *Jude* written large and untidy across the front. She opened it.

Jude,

Your ferocious sister grudgingly told me you'd be home tonight. You evidently decided you didn't want company on your odyssey, but you know where I am if you need anything.

Don't forget to eat.

Look after yourself.

Don't get drunk alone (ring me).

Good old Adam. "What's in the casserole?"

Molly smiled, on solid ground. "Chicken, leeks, carrots and potatoes." She reached swiftly for a bowl and took the casserole out of the oven with mitts — Judith was sure there had been no oven mitts in the house when she left for Malta.

She accepted one ladle from the fragrant casserole. It steamed in the blue bowl she reached down. Judith breathed it in. "Lemon?"

Molly looked pleased. "And thyme."

Judith began to eat, because if she didn't make an effort she'd soon be as thin as a witch.

171

Halfway through the modest portion, Molly asked in a small voice, "Can I stay?"

Judith laid down her fork, and patted her sister's soft shoulder. "Of course you can! You'll need somewhere until you decide what you're going to do."

Eyes reddening, expression relieved, Molly turned away to reach for a phone pad — Judith didn't think there had been one of those before, either — and tore off a message for her. "Kieran's coming round in a while. Desperate to talk to you about something, apparently."

Immediately, Judith set the wine aside.

# CHAPTER
# SEVENTEEN

"Can we stay?"

Kieran and Bethan sat together like a pair of cuddly toys on Judith's sofa, hands clasped tightly. Their cheeks were hollow, eyes shadowed. Molly had ostentatiously taken herself off to her room, although slowly, perhaps hoping for an invitation to stay and be part of the solemn meeting. Judith would have changed places with her like a shot, gladly leaving her sister to deal with what was very obviously going to be a problem.

"Stay here?" repeated Judith, thoughtfully. That would fill her house right up and deprive her of the peace to mourn that she craved. She'd even have to ask Molly to move from the spare double room to the box room. She'd be able to hear Kieran and Bethan through the wall. Giggling, making the unmistakable sounds of sex. Embarrassing her, unembarrassed themselves.

There would be a morning and evening queue for the bathroom.

The television on non-stop. Music at headache volume.

She was too fragile for this. OK, fragility aside, too *middle-aged* and probably too curmudgeonly. "Why?"

Bethan looked down at her trainers, oversized things that had once been white. "I'm not getting on with my parents."

"Why?" Her voice was calm as she looked from Kieran to Bethan and back.

They gazed at each other. Kieran whispered to Bethan, "Be best to explain."

Bethan's eyes filled with tears as he slid an arm around her narrow back. She nodded. "Tell her, then."

The caramel flecks in Kieran's eyes were very bright. "We're going to have a baby."

Oh. No.

Frozen, Judith stared at him. Had to force herself to remain calm. No good would come of yelling, "Oh you *stupid, stupid little buggers!*" however much it was her first instinct.

She spoke out of stiff lips. "So you told Bethan's parents, and they were furious?"

Two shaken heads.

She thought again. "You haven't told them? You've just assumed that they'll be furious?"

Two nodded heads.

"You don't know what they're like," added Kieran, earnestly. "They're awful. They'll murder Bethan when they find out."

"She's going to tell them!" squealed Bethan, leaping to her feet in panic. "We can't stay, I can't bear it if she goes and tells them!"

Kieran jumped to his feet, too, uncertain, his complexion very white against the bright red bead on the ring he wore in his eyebrow. "I won't let her!"

Judith sat still. Leaping to the feet took energy she couldn't summon. And, oh God, a new great sadness to add to the one she carried already. Obviously, pregnancy outside marriage didn't mean the same shame or economic difficulties that it had when she was seventeen.

But what would happen to their youth? They were hardly more than babies themselves, it was too soon to give their lives over to parenthood and putting themselves last all the time. "Sit down," she suggested, without raising her voice. "I *can't* tell Bethan's parents — as I don't know who they are or where they live. And I think we three need to talk some more. Could you please sit down? You're giving me neck ache, and dramatic outbursts simply won't help anyone."

Deflated, Kieran and Bethan sank back onto the sofa.

At the end of a torturous hour, Judith had established that Bethan was eleven weeks pregnant, had both done a test and seen a doctor, and felt unable to tell her parents, especially as they didn't even know that she was going out with anyone.

"Why not?" Judith demanded, blankly astonished at this information.

Bethan leant forward earnestly, as if urging Judith onto her side. "It's one of their rules that I can't go out with anyone more than two years older than me." Then she launched into a tangled explanation about the deceptions and subterfuges she'd felt obliged to employ so that they wouldn't realise she'd broken that rule. "They have loads of rules. Loads and loads."

"Rules to do with wellbeing and safety, I expect."

Bethan fixed Judith with big, tragic eyes. "You don't understand."

Sympathy twisted in Judith's chest. At least she understood that Bethan was young to give her life over to bringing up a baby. She made her voice gentle. "On the contrary. I think I understand all too well." She thought furiously for several minutes, caught in the age-old parental obligation of wanting to act in a way most likely to benefit the kids. The clock ticked, and Kieran and Bethan held hands and stared at the carpet.

Eventually, Judith offered, "I'm prepared to consider letting you stay here if you ring your parents and tell them where you are."

With a smirk of relief, Bethan jumped up once more and started for the door. "I'll ring from my mobile."

The poor thing must think Judith was simple.

Rubbing her forehead wearily, Judith disabused her of this notion. "What, *pretend* to speak to your parents? And then declare that they don't mind a bit that you're moving in with an unknown woman for no particular reason? I don't think so! Ring them from this phone, and they can speak to me as well."

Silence. Slowly, Bethan sank down again, making no effort to make the call.

Kieran looked at Judith pleadingly. "You don't know how awful they are!"

**176**

Judith's patience began to stretch. "For minding that she's ballsing up the life they gave her for the sake of a condom or a pill she could get free from the doctor? That she's kept you a secret because you're precisely the person they've asked her not to go out with? That she's lied to them, fabricated a tarradiddle of outings with friends and mangled their trust? Forced a grandchild upon them in the most difficult of circumstances, robbing them of all the joy a grandchild ought to bring?" Her voice rose in volume.

"And how are you to know whether they're awful? You've never met them!"

Kieran looked stricken. Bethan went deadly quiet.

Judith looked from one of them to the other. She felt furious for all the reasons she'd just outlined. But also because they were making her deal with this when she had so much else to deal with. And still she had hanging over her the task of telling Kieran that Giorgio was dead, it not being news she cared to break over the phone. An inappropriate time now, and it couldn't even be considered a priority.

She could do no more for the life that had gone out of the world. The life coming into it took precedence. She forced herself to concentrate on that difficulty. "Does your father know, Kieran?"

Kieran looked horrified. "No!"

Taking a deep breath, she focused on limiting the damage, making her voice sensible, reasonable. "You've made a bad job of this, and now you're preparing to make it even worse for your parents by running away, adding more crushing fears to the ones they'll have already." She shook her head at Bethan. "Your poor parents!"

Bethan began to sniffle.

They sat in silence for some time while Judith frowned. "I'll come with you both," she offered, heavily, in the end. "Because you do have to tell your parents. You have to grow up tonight and learn to think of someone other than yourselves. If you're bringing a child into the world you'll find you do a lot of that. Stop manufacturing reasons to feel hard-done-by, and bloody well face reality."

It wasn't a textbook counselling session, Judith was certain the counsellor wasn't meant to yell and swear. But it got Bethan and Kieran into her car.

Bethan lived in a nice new part of town in a detached house, overlarge for its plot but not actually big. The bricks were yellow, the roof tiles red, the window frames had been stained with a too red mahogany, and would soon need doing again.

Hannah and Nick Sutherland looked bewildered and suspicious at the party descending on them. Hannah was small and mousy with blonde streaks that might have once brightened her up a bit but had now almost grown out. Nick was chunky, with thinning brown hair.

They stared from Bethan to Kieran to Judith.

In the silence, Judith wondered whether the youngsters actually expected her to do the breaking of the news, and wished she'd established earlier that it was their job.

But then, with a noise like an elephant's sneeze, Bethan burst into tears and threw herself into her mother's arms. "Mum, I'm so sorry. You're going to be so sad and angry!"

She was right.

It was a long evening. Nick and Hannah Sutherland, as predicted, were both sad and angry. Also horrified, hurt, gutted, disappointed; the list of their emotions was long.

Judith did what she could to keep everyone calm and focused on the problem rather than on their anger. And, eventually, to reassure them. "You probably can't see it now, but Kieran is a lovely boy. Immature, of course."

"I'm not!"

She smiled at her stepson. Ex-stepson. "You are! Or you would've wanted a girlfriend your own age, you wouldn't have allowed yourself to be kept a secret, and you would've made damned sure that you didn't impregnate her! *And*," as an afterthought, "you wouldn't be scared to tell your father."

Then she gave Hannah and Nick, stunned and flabbergasted, poor souls, her telephone number, "In case I can be of any help to you," and prepared to take herself off home with a parting, "If you want me to see your father with you, Kieran, ring me. But I think I may have done all I can do to help, tonight." She was very tired. She'd been up about twenty hours, and hadn't slept much prior to that.

Kieran sent furiously after her, "It's nothing to do with you!" And then, contradicting himself, "Don't go!"

Judith turned back to press three kisses on his forehead. "You know I'll always be on your side, darling. But I think you and Bethan need to talk to Bethan's parents, now. And I think you ought to tell your father."

In her car, she suddenly became aware of the crucifix touching the skin below her throat. She fished it out of her shirt, held it, kissed it, closed her eyes very tightly. Anyone watching might think she was engaged in private prayer. But she just wanted it against her lips because it had lain so long against Giorgio's flesh.

How she needed to be alone! If only Moll would be in bed when she got home, then she could get back to that bottle of wine.

But it wasn't to be. Although it was midnight Molly was waiting up for her, buttoned up in a pink candlewick dressing gown that didn't suit her and looked as if it should have been cut up for dusters years ago. Not that Judith ever cut things up for dusters, but Moll did.

"Hot chocolate?" offered Molly. The drinking chocolate powder was in the cups, ready.

Judith retrieved her huge glass of wine and drank half of it quickly so that no one could expect her to do anything else responsible for a few hours. "Not for me, thanks."

Because she knew something was up, and even though she was aware that Tom ought to know first,

180

Judith told her sister about the impending fatherhood of Kieran.

Molly curled up tightly in the chair, her voice small. "You've got a lot on your plate, haven't you?"

She quelled the desire to thank her for noticing. "Quite, yes."

"I ought not stay."

Molly looked so forlorn that Judith felt her heart melt. For a big sister, Molly took some surprising detours into the territory of little sister, looking for help and comfort and, chiefly, support. "Of course you must stay, as a temporary measure." She took her sister's cold little hand in hers. "But it won't work, darling, not long-term. You can't slide into my life. You won't like it when I want to read for hours, or stay on the computer all day. Or invite Adam round to get drunk." His face flashed into her mind, his half-smile, the concern in his eyes. Adam was the one person who'd offered her unselfish support during her intense grief.

She caught a grimace flashing over Molly's face. "You see! You don't like my friends. You'll warn me about Kieran and grumble about Adam or Melanie, you'll expect me to consider you, your likes and tastes. Well, that's OK for a fortnight or so, but it'll soon get old. You need to sort out your life."

Molly sniffed. "Me? If anyone needs a life sorting it's you —"

"No!" Judith interrupted, firmly. "You've got no basis for that remark. I think your disapproval of me must be habitual. If you examine the situation, you'll see that, actually, my life is sorted. I live alone in this

**181**

house from choice. There's no mortgage, so my income is enough to get me by."

She let her voice soften. "I don't need to sort out my life, Molly. I need to recover. To grieve. To adjust.

"But you're in a different place. You need either to attempt to save your marriage, or to make the decision to abandon it. You need discussions with Frankie so that you can make those decisions, see solicitors if necessary. Limbo isn't the place for you — it's my province. Because Giorgio's gone. And I've been left behind."

# PART TWO

# The Road Gets Steep

# CHAPTER
# EIGHTEEN

"Why have you got the hump with me?"

Judith watched Adam as he drove through the centre of Ashby-de-la-Zouch, his eyes on the road, face giving nothing away. Although only mid-afternoon, winter's early dusk was turning the world purple and making brighter the Christmas lights that surely should be taken down now. It was the end of January.

"I haven't got the hump with you. I just asked why you see Tom's happiness as your concern."

"Same reason you see Shelley's as yours, I suppose."

He shook his head, his mouth quirking up at one side, as it did when something wasn't really amusing him. "We're still friendly, but that's as far as it goes. She's no longer my concern; she's able to run her own life. As Tom is."

Judith turned away to look through the steamy glass into the bow window of a shop full of intriguing glass decanters. She would have liked to mooch around the centre of Ashby, but it seemed that Adam wasn't in the mood for one of their impromptu stops after a photo shoot.

In the last seven months — could it really be seven months *since Giorgio*, as she'd begun to think of it? —

she'd become used to zipping all over Northamptonshire and the surrounding counties with Adam. It was now second nature for her to take responsibility for certain things on a shoot, especially the fiddly stuff, leaving him free to talk to his subjects or prowl around considering light and angles.

The work suited her, sporadic, varied, enough to harness some of her energy and intelligence but not so much as to tie her down to routines and regular hours. After Giorgio's death, a shock she hadn't quite been prepared for, Adam had offered her more hours and a permanent job, as if sensing her desperate need to be occupied, to have a structure to her life.

Somehow she'd never moved on. Adam was so easy to get on with he was now a firm part of her life.

She'd become attuned to his quiet directions. "Jude, gold umbrella, please. We need warmer skin tones." He'd refer to her, jokingly as his umbrella girl. She was au fait with his admin — OK, she'd reorganised it — and took over the phone calls that made him cross, typically wheedling usable addresses from picture desks or chasing up late payments from accounts departments.

People skills, she thought, yawning. Adam had loads, but didn't always bother to harness them. Especially when it came to editorial assistants. The subjects of his photographs, on the other hand — victims, as he termed them — got the full benefit of his charm, and that's how they were persuaded to change clothes and jewellery for the fourth time, or shunt enormous amounts of furniture in and out of their rooms to suit his shots.

As well as their working relationship, she and Adam had created a mutual aid society, from which Judith was certain she profited most.

Oh, the relief, for instance, that he'd taken over her rampaging garden! A more than fair exchange for her undertaking his household correspondence and bill payment, tasks that she could perform in minutes but irritated Adam like an attack of scabies. Adam serviced Wilma's wheelchair, Judith ironed Adam's dress shirt, tied his bow tie and fastened his cuff links when he had to go — scowling — to some magazine's awards evening, a networking opportunity that couldn't be missed. The list of exchanged favours was long and complicated.

And she didn't want to jeopardise friendship, working relationship, or mutual aid society, with a falling out over nothing.

"I feel bad for Tom," she temporised. "He's lonely, and he realises that his relationship with Kieran is bad. I feel guilty that Kieran came to me, putting me in the position of colluding with Tom's son against him." Then, because she could seldom resist winding him up, "You don't mind if I care about Kieran, do you, if I'm not allowed to feel bad about Tom?"

He flicked her a wry glance. "I completely understand you caring for Kieran." His attention returned to the jammed traffic, the red brake lights blurred by the rain. "But hasn't Tom got a more recent wife to feel bad for him?"

She grinned. "No good, though, is she? She ran off with a toy boy and got her own life."

Suddenly they were clear of the centre, and Adam put his foot down. "Haven't *you* got your own life?"

She studied him as she swayed with the rhythm of the car, curious at his irritation. "Look, I'm sorry Tom rang my mobile during the photo shoot. I forgot to turn it off, and I know that annoys you. I tried to get rid of him, but he didn't want to be got rid of. That's why I agreed to meet him tonight".

Adam took the road for the motorway, and shrugged.

After her usual stint in front of Adam's computer, swapping his mouse from left to right, then home for a shower and a meal, Judith met Tom in a pub. It was too odd to visit the home where they used to sleep together and where Tom later slept with Liza. Nor did she wish Tom to call at Lavender Row, because then she wouldn't have the option of leaving if things got tricky.

Tom hadn't liked this decision. He had old-fashioned views of pubs: they were for guffawing over dodgy jokes, pint in hand. So far as heart-to-hearts were concerned, they lacked privacy.

Over the past few months Tom had taken each and every opportunity to coax Judith to petition Molly to return to his poor old mate Frankie who was, by Tom's account, utterly miserable since he'd failed to persuade Molly to give their marriage another go. Better Frankie be miserable separated than Molly be miserable married, in Judith's opinion, and she invariably gave Tom short shrift on the subject. But today Tom had agreed to leave the subject of Molly and Frankie alone — because he wished to confide his worries over Kieran.

Which was uncomfortable for Judith, who was deliberately keeping Kieran's secrets.

She was no saint, but she was generally straight with people, and Tom's unease only increased her sense of duplicity.

From a wine-red velvet banquette, she faced him across the smoky atmosphere of The Holly Tree, he on a stool, crouching like a bullfrog. He drank the three halves of John Smiths that he believed was the limit to keep him safe from the breathalyser, and regarded her from beneath whitening eyebrows that seemed to beetle more busily each time she saw him. "I don't know what to do with my son, I really don't."

Judith sipped her grapefruit juice. It had a gin in it. She didn't trust the breathalyser to concur with human judgement on safe limits, so it would be her only alcoholic drink of the evening. "Do you have to do anything with him? He's twenty-two."

Tom snorted. "But he's my son, living in my house! I ask why he's so damned miserable, and he gets all defensive."

"Perhaps he doesn't wish to be asked?"

"But he's living in my house."

Judith sighed. "That doesn't mean he can't run his own life."

Tom, as always, simply ignored opinions that didn't chime with his. "Do *you* know what's the matter with him?"

Judith dropped her eyes. *Yes,* said her inward desire to confess.

> He's got his girlfriend pregnant, a young girlfriend you know nothing about. Her name's Bethan Sutherland and she's a seventeen-year-old schoolgirl. Her parents hate him for spoiling her life, but when they try to keep Kieran away from her, Bethan threatens to run away. Neither Kieran nor Bethan want to be parents, they're screwing up their courage to have the baby adopted, but feel wretched at the idea. Kieran's hushing this up, he's never really stopped being scared of you. He'd like to move to his own place, but he knows he's not good with money and has trouble running a car and a mobile phone, let alone a flat. So he's stuck with you. I'm resisting his hints to let him live with me. That *would* cause you pain — but Kieran believes in your bluff exterior and thinks you have no feelings . . .

"Why would I know?" she parried, instead.

"He's always confided in you."

He drank the last of his final half of bitter, and glared at the glass as if it had betrayed him by being empty, frown lines deepening to furrows. "You were the one who did the lion's share of bringing him up. Pity you couldn't have stayed and seen the job through." As so often, he brought anger to what had been a perfectly amicable situation. His eyes lifted accusingly. "You act

190

so goodie-goodie, with your cross and chain and your sincere expression. But you gave up on us too easily!"

Judith pushed aside her empty glass. The trick in dealing with Tom when he turned unreasonable was to remain calm. "I know you long ago excused yourself. Having your cake and eating it was a mistake rather than a divorcing offence, in your opinion. But it's not the case, Tom, not for this cake."

He glared, persisting, "No one made you go, I didn't want it, Kieran didn't want it, it was your choice! Sometimes things go wrong in a marriage and you have to be strong and —"

She rose and stretched, unhurriedly. "Night, Tom."

He did a big, exaggerated tut-and-sigh, throwing his thick, rough hands into the air. "Don't be so sensitive! I was only saying."

He watched her as she felt for her car keys. And he sighed like a gust of wind, his shoulders dropping. "Judith . . . people keep telling me they see Kieran out around town. With a girl. And she's pregnant."

Her heart accelerated.

He turned his face to her, pain and anxiety in every furrow. "Why don't I know what's going on?"

"You need to ask him," she suggested, gently, her heart going out to a man who found it difficult to express any emotion but anger.

His eyes narrowed. "You know, don't you?"

"Ask him."

A great sadness swept over his face. "Why didn't you tell me?"

She sank back into her seat, and covered his big, rough hand with hers. "Ask him." She hesitated before adding, "Ask him as if you want to help. Try not to shout."

He snatched his hand from under hers with a growl, and Judith thought, with despair, that a mushroom cloud was going to appear over Brinham now that Tom knew about the baby.

A funny day, she mused, striding back to the market square where she'd parked the car. Adam being difficult, then Tom being . . . Tom. She thought longingly of the peace and quiet of Lavender Row. Molly was out so she could have a long, hot bath and read her book in peace.

Except, when she drew up outside her house, she found Caleb and Matthias Leblond waiting on her garden wall, hunched into a thick army parka (Caleb) and a red Marmot Alpinist jacket (Matthias). They slid from the red brick and onto their feet with matching grins as she climbed from her little car.

"Seen Dad?" Caleb, the last person she'd associate with peace or quiet, huffed into the chilly air and watched his breath turn white.

"I was hoping for a last chat about the wedding photos," added Matthias, "but we can't find him." Matthias was completely calm about his wedding, even now when the great day was less than two weeks away. Not for him half-meant jokes about only having one woman for the rest of his life, or not wanting to hear another word about bouquets, bridesmaids and black cars. Judith had never met a bridegroom so willing.

Caleb, as usual, looked crumpled and bemused as if he'd come from a heavy weekend at a rock festival. The upper section of his dark hair was pulled into a tail at the top of his head and his jeans were slashed. In contrast, Matthias, with his sharply short tawny hair and ironed denims, looked as if he'd just stepped from a *Next* catalogue.

She locked the car with the remote. "I saw him at a shoot today, and left him at his flat after I downloaded the pix."

Caleb's forehead furrowed gently. "Wonder where he's gone?"

Huddling further into her coat against a wind that felt as if it were slicing her to shreds, Judith frowned. "Is his mobile off?"

Matthias nodded. He really was a terribly good-looking man; he had Adam's cheekbones. "Mobile off, answering machine picking up at his flat."

"Maybe he's with a woman?" Caleb grinned, lewdly.

Matthias shrugged. "Possible, I suppose."

"He's such a gent he's bound to turn the phone off during —"

"Have you tried your mother's house?" Judith interrupted, making for the front door. The street was too chilly for her. No fan of cold weather at any time, this first winter back in England was proving particularly unbearable, even after the purchase of an enormous duvet-thickness coat in emerald green that Adam laughed at and called her cocoon.

Caleb allowed himself to be distracted from prurient speculation. "He's not there."

Both young men hovered as Judith wriggled the key into the lock. She grinned at their transparently hopeful expressions. "Coffee?"

"Brilliant!"

"Cool!"

They jumped up the two steps and crowded into the warmth behind her, full of young man energy. "Tot in the coffee?" suggested Caleb, extracting a half-bottle of whisky from one of the many pockets of his parka.

Judith tutted in mock disapproval as she slid it from his hand. "You're a lot like your father."

Once coffee mugs were steaming fragrantly on the low table, Judith pressed play on the answering machine as she dropped into a chair.

*You have two messages. First message,* "Oh, Mum! Aren't you there?"

She rolled her eyes. "I can't be here all the time, Kieran."

The second began with a lot of clicking and beeping. And then Adam's voice, measured and deep. "Jude, I tried your mobile, but it went straight to voicemail. I'm at the hospital. Bethan's in labour and panicking like mad. Kieran's gone to bits and has asked me to try and locate you. Bethan's parents are being hostile. I'll hang around till you get here."

She snatched her mobile phone from her pocket. A blank screen. She must have forgotten to put it back on after the shoot.

"So that's where Dad is!" Caleb sounded pleased to have the mystery solved.

Matthias looked interested. "Who's Bethan? Does Dad mean your Kieran, Judith?"

But Judith, a sudden victim to the shakes, was handing back the whisky and hunting down the emerald green cocoon.

She whizzed through the frosty evening to where the blocky grey shapes of the hospital buildings huddled at the edge of town. At least there were parking spaces available at this time of night, she thought, reversing raggedly into one. Parking was murder during the day, and if you ever found a space it cost you three quid.

Gathering her bag, she fumbled to lock up. How strung up Kieran would be with excitement and nerves! Amazing to think of him as a father. Her son! What would that make her? A step-grandma. An ex-step-grandma? She'd never hankered to be any such thing, but it was difficult not to be moved at the thought of Kieran's baby.

Adam was waiting in the lobby of the maternity building. He met her as she dashed into the serene, cloying warmth and antiseptic smell of hospital. "He rang my flat, trying to find you —"

"My phone was still off from the shoot —"

They stopped. Judith laughed, dragging off her coat, far too warm for the powerful central heating. Adam looked as if he was dealing with things with his usual calm, but she felt like a fizzy drink that had just been shaken, ready to explode in a fountain of bubbles. "You're a saint, Adam, thanks for being with him. Is he in the delivery room?"

**195**

"Bethan's parents have been doing their best to exclude him, but he's hanging in there. I expect he'll be out looking for you any time now." His eyes looked dark in the night-time lighting. "He rang my place, trying to find you, Jude. Both he and Bethan were in a state, so I offered to drive them to the hospital, as I was only a few minutes away."

She clenched her hands. "You are kind. Crikey, this is exciting, isn't it? Although I still feel for poor Tom . . . Anyway, I hope the baby will bring joy, and perhaps the tension between Kieran and the Sutherlands will fade as they realise they all have the same baby to love. I think Bethan and Kieran will keep it once they've had it in their arms, don't you? How could they not? And maybe Nick and Hannah Sutherland will realise that Kieran's not such a bad lad."

Adam picked up his jacket. He looked tired, strained, she thought, noticing the deep lines beside his eyes and mouth. Maybe he was feeling under the weather? It would explain his crankiness this afternoon, and the sudden hug he gave her. He was not a casual embracer, they didn't kiss cheeks when they met or link arms if they were walking. She wasn't certain whether he'd always been reserved, or whether it was Shelley's disgust for his maimed hand that made him so unsure how welcome was his touch.

"Matthias and Caleb were looking for you," she called after him. "Matthias wants to talk about the wedding photos."

He raised a hand to show that he'd heard.

**196**

It was very still, after he'd gone. Still and almost silent. She caught a bustling midwife who promised to tell Kieran that she was there, then settled herself on a blue plastic chair to examine the lobby. Dim lighting. A broad green line leading from the front door to guide labouring women to the sanctuary of the delivery suites, a silent understanding that brains sometimes turn to custard under the onslaught of childbirth and following a floor plan might be too difficult.

Twelve blue chairs, the hard kind that bit into the buttocks until they found bone.

Periods of silence punctuated by doors swishing open, the faint groan of a woman. Another, crying jaggedly. The drinks machine gurgling. The glad sound of the wail of a newborn.

A half-hour passed slowly.

And another.

Where was Kieran? He'd asked for her, why didn't he come? And, now she had time to think about it, why had he asked for her? Surely the place for her was at home, on tenterhooks for news? If Bethan had only just gone into labour it might be twenty-four hours before the baby arrived.

She looked up at the sound of voices. The Sutherlands! Nick's arms around Hannah. Her heart leapt with anticipatory joy as she hopped up. "Any news?" She was appalled to hear herself adopt un-Judith-like hushed-but-soppily-thrilled tones.

The couple sank into seats. They didn't look as if they were coping well with the strain.

Nick glanced up at Judith. The only colour in his face was the blue of his eyes and the purple shadows below. He hesitated. "I'm afraid the news is bad. You'd better sit down."

Bad. Bad? Dread formed in her chest, ice cold and solid.

Her knees weakened and she sat, heavily, suddenly, her voice drying to a croak. "What?"

"They can't find the baby's heartbeat," Nick admitted, baldly. He licked his lips and ran his palm over his thinning hair. "They went for a quiet drink, Bethan and your lad." That would be Kieran. "Her waters broke. Me and Hannah were out for the evening, near Cambridge, Bethan rang in a flap and I told her it would take us about forty minutes to get to her, so to phone an ambulance and we'd meet her at the hospital." He glanced at his wife.

"But Kieran rang your friend, trying to find you," Hannah put in.

"Adam." Judith nodded.

"Bethan was in a state, so your friend kindly drove them to the hospital." She cleared her throat. Her face was chalky, her eyes bright with dread. "Bethan, apparently, was fretful and crying, she said she hadn't felt the baby move all day." She wound her hair around her finger. "She was distressed. Said she had a bad feeling."

"Oh, no." Judith felt as if her own heart was trying to flutter to a halt in sympathy.

Nick blew out a broken sigh. "There's no heartbeat on the monitor or the portable scanner. They've gone in for a full scan."

"Kieran's with her?" Judith clarified.

"Yes." Nick's expression suggested he'd rather Kieran wasn't.

# CHAPTER
# NINETEEN

The full scan only confirmed the worst possible fears. There was no foetal heartbeat. No foetal movement. Nick and Hannah disappeared further into the delivery suite. Judith felt she couldn't follow without a summons. She sat on in the lobby, drinking machine-made coffee as the maternity wing awoke. Cars or ambulances brought in women in the throes. Some were serene, some were frightened, some were joyful. Their partner's anxious arms hovered or a friend trotted alongside, bright and heartening, and all followed the green line as if it were The Yellow Brick Road.

Later, visitors made a track up the open-tread stairs out of the lobby to the wards, clutching bouquets in pastel colours for new mums, and cuddly toys for new babies.

But there would be no celebration teddy for Kieran's baby.

No ceramic clown for Bethan, his hat stuffed with glossy yellow freesias.

An excited new grandma chattered by, clattering her court shoes, clutching a white wire stork. "Isn't it *beautiful*? I told the florist to fill the basket with pink rosebuds and white Baby's Breath. Baby's Breath makes all the difference . . ."

Judith flinched, and her fingers found their way to Giorgio's crucifix. It was unbearable to be a spectator to the joy of others this way. But when a sympathetic auxiliary offered her the chance of joining the Sutherlands in a little waiting room she found them clasping hands and muttering, "She shouldn't have to go through this!" and wasn't certain she hadn't been better in the foyer.

For Bethan's parents, Kieran was the black villain, the utter bastard, the cavalier rogue. Judith didn't point out that he couldn't have made a baby alone, because she sympathised. Kieran should have taken responsibility.

At nearly midnight, Bethan gave birth to a statue baby, white, but perfect apart from his eternal silence.

Back in the private waiting room while Bethan was attended to, Hannah wept for her daughter's sorrow in great gulping sobs that threatened to wrench her slight frame apart.

Then suddenly Kieran was there, bursting in through scarred blue doors, red blotches and swollen eyes of endless crying marring his pallor. "Mum?"

"Oh *darling*, I'm so sorry!" Judith pulled him fiercely to her, his chest heaving as he gave in to hopeless, roaring sobs, her son, no matter what the lawful status, who needed her.

"He was already dead!"

"I know. I've been waiting here."

"I kept hoping they were somehow wrong!"

"So did I, darling. So did I."

Kieran went back to his poor Bethan, and presently a midwife came, very grave and sympathetic, to ask the grandparents if they'd like to see the baby now that he was dressed. The parents had chosen a name — Aaron. Judith watched Nick and Hannah follow the blue uniform away without a glance of invitation for her, and her heart contracted painfully.

Kieran was shut into that nightmare of a room with his young girlfriend and his dead son! She imagined the Sutherlands giving him the silent treatment, or spitting agonised accusations at his young, bewildered head.

She clenched her fists, pacing in frustration as she tried to decide what to do.

If they couldn't acknowledge her right to be there for the baby, couldn't they find it in their hearts to let her be there for Kieran?

But her parenthood was ex-.

And step-.

And she didn't know where that left her.

But then a familiar figure was shown through the door and came to an abrupt halt before her. His furious eyes seemed to have shrunk into his puce face, his hands made big fists at his side. "What are you doing here?"

She rubbed her eyes, weary of his resentment. "Kieran asked for me. Oh, Tom!"

Suffering her sympathetic hand upon his arm, his voice was hoarse with grief. "They've just told me.

**202**

About the baby. I was away, I didn't get Kieran's message until now. And it's all over?"

She nodded. "Beth's parents have gone to see the baby."

Tom charged out immediately, of course, to demand that he be allowed to see the baby, too. Minutes later, a midwife at his side, he thrust open the door to the waiting room. "Come on," he ordered. "I expect Kieran will want to see you."

And she and Tom comforted their son, who'd just lost a son of his own, together, all acrimony and emotional baggage pushed aside.

When she finally emerged from the hush of the delivery room and the beautiful, soundless baby, she was dazed by grief, by the unfairness of life that petered out for no apparent reason.

"Thank you." She stood beside Tom on the edge of the car park that stretched away from them. "For letting me see Kieran. And Aaron." She felt now the daze that comes with missed sleep and the unreal sensation after being wrung by emotion. Every inch of her ached, and she suspected the base of her spine wouldn't be the same for weeks after so many hours on moulded plastic seats. Probably none of her would.

He thrust his hands into his pockets, and stared over her shoulder at the silver clouds heralding a cold dawn. "It's always you. Always you he wants."

The Sutherlands drifted past like ghosts, without speaking. A harsh light pierced the silver clouds on the horizon over the distant houses on the main road.

She wiped her eyes and blew her nose. "You're exhausted."

"I'll live. Shall I see you to your car?"

"No need."

"Awkward mare." He hunched his meaty shoulders, and shambled off like a bear.

# CHAPTER
# TWENTY

The letter trembled in Judith's hand.

She'd been thinking about Tom, about the catastrophic thing that had happened to Kieran and whether it would push father and son together or further apart, when the letter dropped onto the mat with the others. And, somehow, worries about Tom faded away.

Produced on a computer, the letter had the kind of heading designed on a computer wizard, white paper, plain, an economy buy for printers and photocopiers.

*Dear Mrs. McAllister*, it read, in a font that looked like copperplate, and navy ink.

*My father was Giorgio Zammit.* Judith's heart gave a great kick inside her.

*After his death, it was discovered that my father's gold cross and chain had gone missing, causing great distress to the family.*

And then, ingenuously: *Should you know the whereabouts of this valuable treasure, please send it to me without delay.*

*Alexia Zammit*

And, at the foot of the page, *Giorgio Zammit RIP*

Her fingertips twitched upwards to Giorgio's crucifix. She wore it all the time, touching it occasionally through her clothes, reassured by its weight, as if in the way it warmed against her skin it still held some tiny glimmer of Giorgio.

All she had of him, all that she'd been allowed to keep.

But this letter was designed to cause her to feel like a thief, a grave robber, to make her snatch it off immediately and send it to Giorgio's daughter.

She felt awful. Did she have good cause?

She thought of Cass, standing on the hillside beside Giorgio's fresh grave in her black lace dress and pressing the crucifix into Judith's hand. "*Only his body is here. You have his heart. Take it with you.*" It had given her such comfort by acknowledging and validating her status as someone important in Giorgio's life. But, for the first time, she wondered by what right Cass acted. She couldn't imagine Johanna or Maria authorising the giving of such a keepsake. Probably it was just Cass's soft heart that had urged her to do something for Judith.

It had a value beyond that indicated by the hallmark imprinted on the back in the dusky gleam of Maltese gold as yellow as the sun.

The muted chime of the clock in the sitting room jerked her out of her thoughts, reminding her that there was something else that needed her full concentration right now.

Shakily stuffing the letter inside her bag, she swept on a mac that belted at the waist, the only black coat she owned and nowhere near as warm as the unsuitably vivid emerald cocoon, and let herself out into the chilly day on her way to pick Molly up.

Molly had dressed as suitably as Judith. "We look like a couple of waitresses," Judith observed as they drew up at the crematorium.

"The car park's nearly empty." Molly tucked her long hair inside her coat to keep it from the wind that swirled leaves across the tarmac.

"I don't think there will be many of us."

Inside the modern building, the tile marked *Aaron McAllister Sutherland* hung on the glass of a door. It was the smallest, most intimate room, but still their footsteps echoed as they entered.

The others were already there. Bethan's parents flanked her as if concerned someone might contaminate her with their presence in the same wooden pew. Kieran stood across the aisle in the dark grey suit he'd bought for his new job. Tom stood beside him, eyes front, as if on parade.

Judith and Molly slid in beside them.

Seven mourners for baby Aaron. Just seven. It couldn't have been sadder.

There were no hymns. In fact, no one but the vicar made a sound at all. He took the service in a hushed voice from a spot just in front of the two occupied pews, and it seemed to be over in minutes.

When he'd finished, and shaken everybody's hands with expressions of concern and offers of comforting chats, Hannah made a frigid announcement. "We're taking Bethan home, she's not fit to stand about." And

**207**

in seconds they were gone, leaving Judith, Molly and Tom with Kieran, who looked speakingly at Bethan, then turned his gaze to the blue velvet curtains that had shut between them and the small scale coffin.

One long, quiet sigh, then he allowed himself to be herded out, his face set with misery.

"What was it all about?" He hunched his shoulders against the chill as they held the door for his slow, gangling figure to pass.

Judith misunderstood. "She's very pale, she's just given birth. They just wanted to get her home, I expect."

He grimaced. "I know that. She needs looking after and I knew they'd clear off the instant the ceremony was over. No, I mean the whole thing. The pregnancy. All the pain and hate it created! For months it felt like we were part of some major disaster, a train crash or a bomb. Like things couldn't get any worse.

"But then, when . . . when he died, we realised how bad things actually can get."

Kieran stared around the crematorium grounds, the formal gardens impressive even in winter with cushions of pansies and polyanthus between the shrubs and conifers, the memorial garden for stillborn babies a quarter circle in a sunny corner. "It feels as if we're being punished, taught a lesson. *You weren't fit to look after a baby! You didn't deserve a son!* But I would've loved him. Even when we considered adoption it was because we thought it might've been, like, best for him. We'd just about decided we couldn't let him go to someone else, and he died. As if we didn't make up our minds in time."

"Of course you would've loved him." Judith squeezed the words out past the lump in her throat, although Kieran was completely dry-eyed. She blew her nose.

Tom's voice came suddenly, deep and gruff, making Judith jump. "Will they try and keep the girl away from you, now?"

Kieran's response was bitter. "Of course. Protect her from me because I've ruined her life, given her a dead baby, mucked up her A Level year. Their idea is to move away, taking Beth with them." He shivered suddenly, thrusting his hands into his trouser pockets. And he looked older, hopeless but angry, as he turned up his collar against the onset of chilly drizzle. Judith wondered how — if — he'd ever be Kieran again.

She linked his arm. "Come with us, we'll eat together."

"I'm not hungry, thanks Mum. And I don't want company." He managed a smile, and squeezed her hand with his arm, quick to pre-empt the argument she meant to put forward. "Yes, I really do think that's best. But thanks for coming. Thanks, Dad. Thanks, Aunt Molly. I'm glad you were all here."

Judith waited, heart aching, hair blowing in a spiteful wind, as he folded himself into his car, and drove away.

About to say her goodbyes to Tom, also, she looked up into his face, and her conscience smote her at the bleak loss in the gaze he sent after his son. On impulse, she tucked her hand through his arm. "I bet you were just going to offer us a cuppa at your place, weren't you Tom?"

"If you like." But he turned with such alacrity for the car park that Judith knew, despite the daggers Molly's eyes launched in her direction, that she'd done the right thing.

"What did you say that for?" Molly demanded, as they strapped themselves into Judith's car and followed Tom's navy Volvo out through the gates.

Judith indicated, and pulled into the traffic. "Because he's sad." Her tone was mild. "And when you were sad, you appreciated a bit of company. He's no different."

Molly sniffed, and looked out of the window.

In Tom's kitchen that once had been Judith's, Judith sat herself down on a beech stool at the kitchen table, and watched Tom shambling about, managing to assemble boiling water, tea bags, sugar and milk into the correct combinations.

He sat himself down, and said nothing as he drank his tea at a temperature that would've scalded most people, his eyebrows twitching like corpulent caterpillars above his eyes.

"Never had a chance."

Judith put down her own tea, untouched. "I'm afraid not," she said, quietly. "It's difficult to understand."

"Only a babby."

"I know."

Tom's face worked, his complexion deepening to the brick red it seemed to be so much of the time. "When Kieran was a babby I used to watch him in his cot. Make sure his little chest was moving. And Pam. She'd

210

get up in the middle of the night sometimes, just to check."

Molly stirred. "I used to, too, with Edward. I think all parents do it."

Tom let out a huge, wavering sigh. "I've been thinking a lot, lately. How different things would have been if Pam hadn't died."

Judith's thoughts whipped immediately to Giorgio. "I know what you mean. But you still have Kieran."

Tom stared into his empty cup. "Do you think so?"

An hour later, she was back at Lavender Row, having been firm with a protesting Molly that she would be perfectly OK alone. It had all been over so quickly, she scarcely felt as if there had been a funeral at all.

But there she was on the sofa, a hot drink in her cold hands and her shoes kicked off. Recently, she'd painted the sitting room walls a dignified pigeon grey. She'd been going for understated but ended up with disappointed. It was such a dull result. Until Adam, who, like many photographers, had an arts background, took a pale dawn pink and a deep cream to the ornate white plaster ceiling roses and patterned coving. Just the lightest touch, the smallest highlights to a flower here, a teardrop there, and the whole room took on life. Stylish. Unusual.

The fire was roaring as it fed on the wind in the chimney, when Adam rang the doorbell. "I was passing, and saw your car."

She let him in, and prepared to set the kettle boiling again. He wore a midnight shirt that accentuated his

**211**

spare frame, and gave a whistle as he followed her up the passage. "Jude, you have legs! I suppose it's not funeral etiquette to tell you that they're good?"

"Probably not." But it was quite nice.

Over the second mug of tea, she dug the letter from Alexia Zammit from her bag, and showed it to him.

His eyebrows shot up into his hair as he read it. "This is extraordinary." His eyes moved over and over the page. "What do you intend to do?"

She leant closer to reread the letter herself. "It makes me feel like a thief."

"It's meant to, obviously. But you were given the crucifix, you didn't steal it, or even ask for it! Even if you suppose, just for a minute, that you're not entitled to it — how can you be sure that Alexia is? It could've been left to anybody: Giorgio's sister, or his parents. Or the local cat's home. No one's offered you sight of the Will."

Letting the page flutter from her fingers, she shrugged. "So what do I do? Just grimly cling on to it and see what happens?"

"Get a solicitor." He hesitated, looking faintly embarrassed. "If the fees are a problem, I think there's assistance available. Or I could . . . you know. If you were stuck."

She retrieved the letter, folding it neatly between her fingers, troubled and uncertain. "Thanks, but it's not the money. I just hate the thought of setting a solicitor on Giorgio's family."

"And being proved to be in the wrong isn't your strong suit."

212

She acknowledged his grin. "True. I probably am the one in the wrong, because I doubt that I'm in any Will that exists. The executors would've written."

"They might not have this address."

"So where did Alexia get it?"

The diagonal frown lines appeared on Adam's forehead as he thought. "The aunt? The only explanation for the whole thing is that she admitted she'd given you the crucifix, and coughed up your English address."

She shoved her now empty mug onto the table. "But then she would've rung to warn me that trouble was on the way."

He yawned, and stretched. "Your faith's refreshing."

She stared. "Cass wouldn't drop me in it!"

Briefly he took her hand. His unharmed hand, of course, the fingers strong and healthy as they curled around hers. "Think about her husband being furious, and probably all the rest of the family, too. It would've been difficult for her to resist the pressure."

She sighed and let her eyes close. "So I presume too much upon Cass's loyalty?"

His voice came very close for a moment, his breath brushing against her cheek. "I think, realistically, she might've had to choose — loyalty to you, or loyalty to her husband."

She sighed. And she'd choose loyalty to Saviour and the rest of the Zammits, obviously. Covering her eyes with her arm, she groaned. "I bet the damned thing's valuable."

Adam confirmed the arrangements for the next photo shoot, and left the fireside reluctantly.

"Friday, 8am," Judith noted. "And, of course, for Matthias and Davina's wedding on Saturday!"

Adam stuffed his phone in his trouser pocket. "I wish they hadn't asked me to do it. I'm no bloody wedding photographer." He frowned.

She threw him his jacket. "A photographer's a photographer to them, I expect. Would you enjoy the wedding more if you were simply a guest?"

He pulled a face. "Probably not. You are staying for the reception, aren't you? Shelley's going to be there with her new bloke, I don't want to be all on my own, ain't-it-obvious-Adam-has-no-date."

She laughed. "Get a date, then!"

"You forget how long I was married. I've forgotten how."

She gave a disbelieving sniff. "I bet your mates' wives are always inviting you to dinner parties! I bet they line up divorcées and you could get eight dates, if you wanted."

He lifted his eyebrow. "I do get invited to dinner parties, do you think that's why? Shelley was always dragging me out to sit at someone's ugly dining suite and talk to people I didn't know, and I took it as a perk of the separation that I could give those nightmare evenings a miss. Anyway, a date would expect phone calls, after."

"Dire," she agreed gravely, watching him push his feet into shiny black shoes. The laces were elasticised, and didn't need tying. "How do you know that *I* won't?"

His eyes gleamed with laughter as he straightened. "But that's what I like about you, Jude, you never expect me to phone unless I've got something to say. Neither do you dredge things up from a week last Thursday and leave me to guess what's wrong. You don't create tenuous cases to make things my fault, you don't tell me what to wear, you don't put on stupid heels and then bitch because your feet hurt, or scream over a broken fingernail or sulk because your hair's only 99% perfect." He grinned. "In fact, you're not like a woman at all!"

It took her several moments to find her voice. "Is that meant to be a compliment?"

His grin faded. "Um . . . it was *meant* to suggest that you're pleasant, easy company. But it came out a bit . . ."

"As if I'm some ancient bloke in drag?"

This time his smile blazed right from his eyes. "Never a bloke. My compliments might be skewed, but my sight is excellent." He smoothed his shirt collar neatly beneath his jacket, thoughtfully. "I've annoyed you, haven't I?"

Then he swung back, an expression of alarm flashing across his face. "Just don't say you won't come to the wedding!"

As Judith showered, she reminded herself that frowns and pouts would only add unwelcome lines to those she owned already, but, nevertheless, kept finding she was

**215**

frowning and pouting, Adam's words circling annoyingly in her mind.

Dressed in new black trousers and a cream jumper, she awarded herself a soothing read to take her mind off things before picking Molly up.

It was the thump of her book sliding off the sofa forty minutes later that woke her, crick-necked and left foot burning with pins-and-needles. Easing her head upright and the foot painfully into motion, she glared at the baroque silver clock on the mantelpiece, a rare extravagance from a jeweller in Valletta. "*Blast!*"

She definitely hadn't intended to sleep. Naps seemed so middle-aged. Pins-and-needles so un*womanly*.

Maybe because she wasn't a woman at all . . .

Oh, for goodness' sake! Madness to take any notice of Adam's teasing. Didn't she know how he loved to wind her up?

What was more important was that she and Molly had arranged to take their mother out. Wilma thought the sky would fall in if she weren't home by nine o'clock, and would therefore be in a stew if they hadn't collected her from The Cottage by seven.

Damn.

Because Judith hadn't yet made the phone call.

But she should be leaving now.

Double damn.

Decisively, she reached for the phone. The call would only take two minutes and she wanted it over. She dialled.

Click. Click. Silence. Then the single ringing tone, sounding far away. But the voice that answered unnerved her with its clarity. "Hallo?"

She caught her breath at the sudden realisation that she was breaching the citadel of Giorgio's till-now-unseen family, and had to concentrate to make her voice work. "May I speak to Alexia?"

The voice became guarded. "I am Alexia."

"This is Judith McAllister."

A pause. "Yes?"

"I'd like to speak to you about your father's crucifix."

Alexia's calm English was excellent, no doubt she practised it every day in her job in the pharmacy. "You have it," she said, with calm satisfaction. "Please send it to me. My address is on my letter." And the line went dead.

Swearing, Judith redialled, speaking the instant Alexia answered. "I don't know whether I can do that. I need information."

The voice that came across the miles was controlled and dispassionate. "Please send back my father's cross. Thank you."

Gritting her teeth and thinking of Giorgio, Judith dialled a third time. She made her tone gentle and reasonable. "It was given to me by a member of the family, I accepted it in good faith. I —"

For the third time, the dialling tone cut her off disdainfully.

"Bugger you," she snapped, then fetched her cocoon of a coat — this English winter was killing her — and slammed out to the car.

Molly always expected to be picked up, she complained to herself, shoving the grape-coloured car into first gear, checking over her shoulder for traffic and peeling out. Molly was such a girl.

She never drove if she could get someone else to, never attempted to move furniture or take something apart to see if she could mend it. Molly cooked casseroles. She'd made all the floral curtains for her new Frankie-less house, a modern, detached property that had been squeezed into a plot of four houses a few streets from Lavender Row. The plot was off Fairbank Street and named Fairbank Close. Bloody close, Judith thought as she whipped into Molly's meagre, shared drive.

Sliding into the car, Molly looked pointedly at her watch.

Equally pointedly, Judith made no apology for tardiness.

In five minutes they were at The Cottage, a glaringly inappropriate name for a three-storey stone town house of some magnitude, obviously once a terribly well-to-do establishment. Smaller properties behind had been demolished to make way for a large, single-storey extension where many of the residents were domiciled, and the car park where Judith zipped into a space and yanked on the handbrake.

Wilma was waiting on one of the rose pink vinyl chairs beside the counter and pigeonholes covered in chipped, off-white Formica that was the nurses' station. "You're late," she observed politely, accepting simultaneous kisses, left cheek Molly, right Judith, and moving a boiled sweet around her mouth.

"Nothing to speak of," breezed Judith. "I'll get your chair."

Wilma pulled her hairy maroon coat more tightly around her. "So we're still going?"

"It's only seven minutes past, Mum, we can easily get you back for nine."

Wilma pulled herself up onto her walking frame with a little grunt at the effort. "I don't want to be any trouble."

"You won't be. We're going to drive you to a new café by the embankment where you can see the river." Judith hooked the wheelchair with one hand and with the other made an entry in the appropriate book to allow for the taking out of a resident, signing it, *J McAwigglewiggle*. She didn't feel like waiting for Molly to sign it clearly *M R O'Malley*, with the capitals, the apostrophe, a loop on the Y, a curly flourish below, and a careful full stop at the end.

Once she'd gained her balance, Wilma hotched her way down the hall that was carpeted in a funny shade of honey, pushing the walking frame out in front of her and shuffling to catch up to it, her handbag swinging from a hook at the front. "Isn't it too dark to see the river?"

"They have lights shining on it. It's pretty."

Wilma chuckled creakily and rattled her sweet against her dentures. "Pretty wet! Is it raining?"

"No, not at the moment." Molly's voice was made for reassurance. She took up her station beside Wilma,

**219**

ready to catch her arm if she wobbled. This was the way they usually divided the responsibilities: driving and wheelchair, Judith, giving an arm and being soothing, Molly.

"Is it going to?" Wilma persisted.

Judith wheeled the folded chair. "Perhaps later."

Her mother halted, and Judith almost ran her over. Wilma sucked vigorously. "Do we want to go, if it's raining?"

"The car's right outside, I'll put your chair in the boot while you hang on here with Molly, then I'll open the car door. You won't feel more than two drops, even if it pours."

Wilma didn't budge. "Only I've just had my hair set. It was a new girl came round, and she's done it lovely, hasn't she?"

"Lovely." Judith joined Molly in chorus, and successfully smothered a sigh. Making her mother happy was getting increasingly difficult. Wilma was losing her confidence about being taken out of The Cottage, but didn't always want to be left in it. She worried if her daughters phoned instead of visiting, but she admitted that their visits tired her.

"Do they do scones, at this new place of yours?"

"Yes!" Judith paused for effect. "With *oodles* of jam."

"One oodle will be enough, dear." Spurred on by the promise of jam, Wilma set off again. Then, hovering in the doorway with Molly, she observed Judith's struggles to fit the wheelchair in her boot. "Pity you didn't bring Adam, he's good at lifting the chair."

And better at charming Wilma, Judith thought, exchanging a look with Molly. Molly, having long ago conquered any antipathy towards Adam, often teased him that Wilma had a crush on him. Wilma never seemed as tiring when Adam was there to make her laugh, and never checked her watch and wondered if she'd be back in time for cocoa.

"There," she said, when she was settled. "Now, Judith, how's Kieran? He hasn't been to see me for weeks."

Molly rubbed her forehead as Judith pulled up outside the house at Fairbank Close. "Gosh, Mum is exhausting these days! Not her fault, of course, bless her. Coming in for a cuppa?"

Although she'd planned to go straight home for a couple of hours with the latest Harlan Coben thriller, Judith found herself accepting the invitation. Home meant not only the seat-edge thrills of Harlan Coben, but a lot of time to think. About Alexia, the crucifix, and who it actually belonged to. About today's bijou funeral for a bijou life. About Kieran, his face floating before her eyes, empty, shattered.

She followed Molly into the dead neat, dead plain home decorated in beige and peach. She could certainly do with a cosy sisterly chat, she thought. If only she had a cosy sister rather than one who was convinced of her duty to deliver opinions on Judith whenever possible. They made for the kitchen — beige units, peach walls — Molly fussing over her long, wool coat as she slid it on a hanger and hung it in the cloaks cupboard.

Judith tossed the emerald cocoon over the newel post. "Do you think I'm blokish, Moll?"

"Blokish?" Pausing in the act of washing her hands, Molly's eyes grew round. "What, *butch* do you mean?"

Judith considered as she hopped up onto a stool. "Not butch, exactly. But . . . unfeminine?"

Molly shrugged. "Depends which definition of unfeminine."

Judith felt her eyebrows fly up in horror that Molly hadn't shrieked in protest at "unfeminine" and "Judith" arising in the same sentence. "Using any definition!"

Molly whipped a broderie anglaise apron around her waist and fastened it in a bow. "You're very independent, of course, and you're often — almost always — natural."

Judith's voice sharpened. "What do you mean, 'natural'?"

"Without make-up or artifice. Also, perhaps because you're quite tall, you *stride* everywhere."

"I have a naturally long step."

"You hardly ever wear heels."

"They'd make me taller!"

"You overtake a lot when you're driving."

"And *overtaking* makes me blokish?"

Molly dropped two teabags into a pretty china teapot, white-and-peach. "*I* never said blokish! But it is manly to overtake, isn't it? I always queue behind any traffic, but men rush by, even when they can't really see what's tearing up to meet them."

Judith sighed. If it was "manly" to overtake, this conversation was never going to evolve as she'd like. "I don't think I meant the way I drive or walk. Go back to *independent*."

"Overly independent," said Molly, thoughtfully, as the kettle made its first grumbles and hisses. "Fiercely independent. Non-clinging. Clear. Not requiring advice. Some people call it being bloody-minded."

"But it's good, isn't it, not to cling?" Judith ignored the bloody-minded bit.

Her sister shrugged shoulders that had grown plumper since she'd left Frankie although Frankie, conversely, looked thinner every time Judith saw him in town, undoubtedly because he had no one to cook him dinners and puddings each evening.

"Depends who you are and what you want. When I left Frankie there was no one I'd rather have had in my corner. You were encouraging and supportive, you have a built in scanner to detect lies and nonsense, and you're overawed by no one and nothing." Molly used a small pair of scissors to slit open a packet of shortbread, the expensive, thick and delicious kind, and began to set it out on the plate like the hands of a clock.

"So? I still don't see the problem!"

Molly spaced out her wedges of shortbread with military precision. "I didn't say there was a problem. I lean on you, Mum leans on you, Kieran does, even Tom still would, if you'd let him."

"But?"

Molly sighed, and washed crumbs from her fingertips at the tap. "But if I was a man who liked women to be frilly and girly, I suppose I wouldn't be yearning after a Judith. I'd be after something more malleable, someone who'd demand my attention, look to me to solve things for her."

Judith's stomach clenched. "You'd be looking for a Liza?"

"Oh gosh." Molly's hands froze in mid-air, and she looked stricken. "Sorry! That was a bit close to home, wasn't it? I didn't mean to go there."

Judith pursed her lips. "Anything else?"

Molly smiled, and passed her the biggest piece of shortbread. "You could do with tidying up. But that's just you, Judith. Your hair needs cutting, you stride about in your jeans and boots, efficient and practical. But men's eyes still follow you!"

"Except men who like feminine women?"

Molly hopped up onto a stool and took the second-biggest piece of shortbread. "Well, you can't expect to attract all of them."

# CHAPTER
# TWENTY-ONE

"There! first exit from this roundabout . . . don't *miss* it, dummy!"

Cutting up the car behind Adam managed to turn in time, muttering darkly about signposts and "dummy" and lifting an apologetic hand at an angry honk from a Toyota almost on his bumper. On the other side of the roundabout, the traffic braked once more to a halt. Adam muttered, and glanced at his watch.

From the mobile phone, Judith made an apologetic call to the day's victims, the Donlyns, a family in a mag feature about childhood sweethearts. Nigel Donlyn, the father, snorted into the phone. "I took a half-day off work for this, you know."

"I *know*." Judith was gravely sympathy. "We *do* appreciate your co-operation. But the M1 is closed and we're having to navigate the A roads along with all the rest of the motorway traffic. We won't be a *moment* longer than we need, I *promise*. I can only ask you to hang on just another half-hour for me."

"You're an ace crawler," Adam observed as she shut the phone as the traffic actually allowed the car up to thirty miles per hour. "That bloke didn't stand a chance against your *for me* and *promise* in that soft, sexy voice you put on."

"It's a talent," she owned. "When I was a surveyor I used to leave all the yelling to the men. I won more arguments with my syrupy voice than I lost."

Adam launched the car onto yet another roundabout. "I've had no problems with picture desks since you took over my queries. You just sugar them into submission."

"More like saccharin," she observed, cheerfully. "Artificial."

Finally, they arrived at a 1970s chalet bungalow, liberally clad with overlapping semi-circular tiles the colour of wet bark. "Ugly," Adam remarked, grabbing his case. Judith loaded her arms briskly with tripod, stands and umbrellas.

Nigel Donlyn flung open the door as they knocked. "You only just caught me. I was going to give you up and go to work!"

Judith summoned her best smile. "We can't thank you enough, we're so grateful. We would've flown if we could."

Nigel Donlyn looked slightly mollified, stepping back to admit them to the house. "Is it you what's been ringing me, then? You don't look how I thought."

"Sorry, were you expecting a twenty-five-year-old dolly?" Judith made a comic face.

Mr. Donlyn looked discomfited. "I didn't mean —"

In the sitting room, the other Donlyns waited, mother, Hayley, generous of figure and dark of hair, and two teenagers, Samuel, a loud show-off, and

Jemma with a practised line in rolling eyes and petulant tuts. Both teenagers gazed open mouthed at Adam's right hand. Judith gauged by the deepening of his frown lines that he was uncomfortable with their stares.

But as he needed both hands so couldn't jam the right one in a pocket, he got straight down to work, moving the Christmas tree out of sight, shoving chairs around, murmuring, "Jude, see if you can get Hayley's blouse and lipstick changed, or her skin tone's going to look horrible."

While Adam got into conversation with the kids to try and put them at ease, Judith coaxed Hayley out of an unflattering lime green top and into a soft raspberry pink that brought out the roses in her creamy cheeks, and to replace her blood red lipstick with a toning mulberry.

"It's not you," she promised reassuringly. "But certain colours argue with the camera. We want you to be lovely, don't we?"

Next she chatted Nigel out of his England football shirt that rode up to exhibit the underside of his hairy paunch and into a hyacinth blue polo shirt that didn't.

Adam wanted shots of Nigel and Hayley washing up together in the kitchen. Hayley's disappointment with this idea was obvious. "But the kitchen needs decorating!" she objected. "Why can't we be taken in the lounge, like the children? The wallpaper's lovely in there, and the suite's only a year old."

"It's the spirit of the feature." Judith turned up her palms, as if she totally agreed, but what could you do?

227

"To give the reader a glow, you know, the idea that you deal with everyday life together and stay happy."

"I wouldn't be happy drying up in this shirt," objected Nigel.

"You wouldn't be happy just 'cos you've got hold of the tea towel," pointed out Hayley, comfortably. Then she launched into the story of how she and Nigel started going out together at the third-year Christmas disco and had never looked at another person, not neither of them.

Judith slotted a slave flash onto a stand while Adam got the couple laughing guiltily about how their parents had been outraged when they got engaged on Hayley's sixteenth birthday without seeking permission. The parents had accused Hayley of being pregnant. She wasn't, but they'd had their moments, heh, heh.

It was typical for the victims to believe that the photographer would want to hear their story, although that was obviously the province of the freelance writer who'd identified the Donlyns as a case history in the first place.

Then Judith's mobile phone went off with a loud rendition of a Mexican dance, distracting Nigel and Hayley just when Adam was beginning to get them relaxed and to forget they were the subjects of a photo shoot. He looked at Judith sharply, brows raised as she scrabbled for her phone. That, from Adam, was like a ferocious scowl from anyone else, and she felt herself flushing. "Sorry, sorry," she muttered. And whizzed out into the hall.

Immediately, she whizzed back. "It's for you, Adam." Her voice was solemn but her eyes danced as she offered him the phone. "It's Matthias. He says, do you know your phone's off?"

With a curse, Adam swiped the mobile from her hand. "It's switched off because I'm on a shoot, Matthias! No, *obviously* I haven't forgotten about tomorrow, son, and *obviously* I'll be on time! Whatever else you have to worry about, it's not me!" He switched the phone off. "Flaming boy. Since when have I been a *wedding photographer*, anyway?"

Judith winked at Hayley and Nigel. "It's his son's wedding, tomorrow. Sounds like a few nerves are creeping in."

Adam was quiet on the drive home, twin lines engraved between his eyes and his expression troubled. After trying unsuccessfully to make him smile, Judith touched his arm. She knew that Matthias's wedding had preoccupied him recently, but his flare up today had been uncharacteristic. "You're not wound up about shooting Matthias's wedding, are you?"

He flexed his fingers on the steering wheel and sighed. She had to wait until he'd negotiated the next swarming round-about for his morose reply.

"No. I'm wound up about seeing Shelley."

# CHAPTER
# TWENTY-TWO

Shelley Leblond was a striking woman. Her hair was pale peach and she got away with clothes that were too young because she was tiny and glamorous. Surely most women of her age wouldn't choose an outfit in grass green and daffodil yellow? And, if they did, they wouldn't look so damned good in it?

She had a big laugh and a great smile, and posed between her tall, attractive sons with proprietorial pride, talking easily to Adam while his whirring camera captured the moment. Matthias, of course, took stunningly to the stark formality of morning suit, and must have filled both parents with pride.

A cheerful Caleb, ponytail down his back, hands in his pockets, looked as if he were wearing the outfit for a bet.

Shelley's boyfriend, apparently, had elected not to attend the wedding after all. She joked, "I'd just never be able to spare him any attention! I have to keep an eye on the wedding photographer." Then, "Adam, you've got to be *in* some of these photos! Get the shot set up and then come and look gorgeous! I'm sure your assistant can push the button." Adam suffered two such shots, one with Matthias and Caleb and one with

Matthias and Davina, Shelley's hand tucked lightly through his arm throughout.

But, as Adam moved to disengage, her hand tightened. "Adam and I, please," she called to Judith. "Take two or three." And Judith let a few shots run while Shelley tossed her hair and smiled up at a rock-like Adam.

But he was soon back behind the camera. "Got an empty memory card, Jude?"

"I'll change it." She took the camera off the tripod, then flipped open the camera and slid the empty card in place, stowing the full one safely in a wallet in a pocket of the case.

He lifted his voice. "Matthias and Davina, please." Then, to her again, "We'll finish out here with the bride and groom by that towering weeping willow. I'll need some reflectors, or everyone'll be green and gloomy." Absently, he fired off three candid shots of Caleb and Matthias laughing together, Matthias's hand at his new wife's waist. "Can you manage the smaller case? Then we'll go indoors for the cake and speeches."

Judith filled her arms with equipment and set off awkwardly across the grass. But when she reached the willow, she discovered that she was alone. Shelley, she saw, had intercepted Adam and was laughing up into his eyes. He was stooping slightly to listen to her, hand in pocket.

She looked petite and very feminine, making Adam appear as if he were looming over her protectively.

Judith made a return journey for the large case and the tripod, cursing herself for dressing foolishly for this wedding. Her newly purchased dress, spangled with meadow flowers, was pretty, but suitably elegant heels were hell on the ankles over the winter-softened lawns. And she wasn't warm enough. She missed her jeans and boots, and especially her coat.

"It would've been better if I'd worn a suit and flat shoes," she grumbled, when Adam finally joined her. "Whenever I bend over, I have to hoist up my neckline."

The corner of his mouth twitched as he assessed the sky and then the willow. "Don't hoist on my account."

There's nothing so turgid as a wedding reception, for the lone guest.

For what seemed like hours, Judith watched Matthias and Divine Davina on the dance floor rotating slowly in one another's arms, Davina a vision in heavy satin and cobwebs of lace. The palest pink of the satin made her look like an angel at daybreak, and Matthias, tall and handsome, his silver cravat still neatly tied, gazed at her adoringly. Neither danced with others. The dance floor heaved around them and children circled in endless games of chase.

To occupy herself, she tried to establish who was who among the family. Adam's mother was easy enough, Judith heard both Matthias and Caleb call her Grandma, and Adam call her Mother. She was stooped, and leant on a stick as if afraid she'd tip over without it. Two tall, rangy men just had to be Adam's brothers, Terence and Guy, even if she hadn't heard them also call the stooped woman Mother. They each had family with them. A woman with improbably platinum curls seemed to be Mother's sister, someone with too much time to consider other people's business and express her opinion on how they ought to conduct it.

Yawning, Judith lost interest.

God, she was bored.

This endless evening was giving her far too much time to brood about Alexia's letter, now tucked into the drawer of her dressing table. As Adam pointed out, she was none too keen on being in the wrong, and it was beginning to seem to her more and more that that was where she in fact was. Sending the crucifix back to Alexia was a simple enough remedy. But how did she know that Alexia was the one who was entitled to it?

She made an effort to unknot her mind from this problem, and gazed about the room festive with shiny silver and blue balloons and great displays of sea holly and tortured hazel.

Adam seemed to have been commandeered by Shelley for hostly duties, which could be viewed as reasonable, Matthias being just as much his son as hers. And Judith was trying not to blame Shelley for acting as if Adam still belonged to her, particularly as Judith had no claim to him. But it did rankle when Adam had particularly asked Judith to stay for the reception so that he wouldn't be Adam-no-date. She smothered another yawn.

Leaving aside the bride and groom, Caleb was the only other guest she really knew and he was part of a scuffling crowd in the corner, jacket off, shirt ballooning from his trousers as he participated in gusts of laughter and tipped pints of Diesel down his throat. Briefly, she considered joining the mob around him, but, as she'd be roughly twice the age of anyone else in the group, discarded the idea.

Would it have been worse, or better, if she'd accepted Adam's invitation to join him at the top table? She'd waved the idea away and insisted that she'd be fine for the duration of the dinner. Then they'd have the final atmospheric shots to take during the speeches, and after that the formality would go out of the seating arrangements, anyway.

But that hadn't quite worked out. Because Shelley had sprung to her feet almost as the final flash popped, beckoning to Adam and the parents of Davina, leaving Judith to pack away the camera equipment. By the time she had, in several trips, lugged everything to the car of an obliging cousin that Adam had put in charge of delivering it to his flat, events had slipped so far behind schedule that the evening reception was in full flood and Adam was involved in greeting the new guests.

Judith should have hopped into a taxi then. In any event, she decided, with a final yawn, she was going to do so now.

Skirting the dance floor and threading through the press of bodies, she escaped The Magnolia Room, the glittering pride of Brinham's only country club. In the privacy of the Ladies' Cloakroom she was able to switch on her phone and dial a cab. A minute later the lining of her jacket was settling over her shoulders and she was ready for a discreet escape.

But, outside the cloakroom, she found Adam lurking, obviously waiting for her. He frowned. "You're leaving?"

She wondered whether she should feel guilty that she'd intended to melt away without telling him. "I've just rung for a car."

He cast a hunted look towards The Magnolia Room. "I've talked to almost every guest at this bloody do except you, the one I actually want to speak to. And you're *my* guest. I'm never normally guilty of such atrocious behaviour. Are you totally fed-up with me?"

She smiled, but said, firmly, "Totally. Next time you need a date for the sake of appearances, ask Mum."

"One dance?" he wheedled.

"Don't think so."

Disconsolately, he fell into step with her, sleeve brushing hers as she crossed the softly carpeted foyer to the big double doors where she'd arranged to await the taxi. "I'm so sorry! Every time I turned to look for you, Shelley found someone else she decided I just had to talk to. I don't suppose you'd change your mind, and stay?"

She managed not to shudder. "I don't think so, Adam. You go back and do your father-of-the-groom bit, Matthias will wonder where you've gone." She was pretty certain that the moment Shelley saw her with Adam, she'd find Adam a positive shoal of people who needed his attention.

Adam hunched into his jacket as the doorman opened the door and let them out into a frigid evening. "Shouldn't think so. He's about to slip off to the bridal

**235**

suite with a bottle of champagne in one hand and Davina in the other. Do I really have to stay here on my own?"

A car turned in between the stone gateposts and up the drive, its tyres crackling over the gravel. "Here's the taxi," Judith pointed out unnecessarily, stepping forward to meet it.

The taxi deposited them outside Judith's house in Lavender Row, and drew quietly away into a clinging grey mist. "I'm sure you should've stayed." Judith, teeth chattering, tried to open her door, which seemed to swell a little more with every wet winter day that passed. For several moments she thought longingly of a hot, dusty country where freezing, dank evenings like this were unknown.

"For whose benefit?" Hands in his pockets, he turned up his collar against the damp as he fidgeted on the step below her. "Matthias and his divine wife will by now be tucked away in the honeymoon suite. Caleb is in his favourite spot, the middle of a crowd, getting thoroughly and mortifyingly drunk. They don't need their old man at the moment."

"And Shelley?"

He paused. "I hope she's enjoying the party." He reached over Judith's shoulder and struck the door a swift blow from the heel of his hand. The door flew open.

Judith shuffled into the inky black hall, wishing that she was like Molly and always remembered to leave on a light when she expected to return after dark. "I think your presence was required for that."

He sighed, stepping in close behind her as she wiggled the door key to free it from the lock. His voice was neutral. "You noticed, did you?"

The key came free. "Difficult not to."

"She tells me it's time for us to talk about our future. See what can be salvaged, now we've both had time to think."

Oh. Judith concentrated hard on not letting her heart sink. She wanted Adam to be happy, didn't she? It was selfish of her to let her mind fly to the conclusion that Adam would have no time to be her friend if he returned to being Shelley's husband.

Shelley had hurt him.

But now she was going to make it better.

So that was good. Good. He deserved to be happy. She turned in the narrow confines of the hall to give him a beaming smile, and a brief kiss on the cheek to go with her enthusiastic, "What a surprise! Congratulations! I hope it works out for the best."

He touched his cheek, lounging against the wall as she searched for the light switch. "Oh come on, Jude, we both know there's not going to be any salvage," he chided, softly. "She scuttled the ship, and it sank too deep. I think the boyfriend she's been toying with has moved on to pastures new, making her temporarily insecure. I'm just an old habit she's tempted to take up again, for comfort. You know how hard it can be to break habits like that." Stopping abruptly in the act of closing the door, he hesitated, swearing under his breath, then swung it open again with an exaggerated air of resignation so that Judith could see the large man slamming his way out of the pick-up truck slewed to a halt half on the opposite pavement. "Right on cue! Here's *your* ex!"

Alarmed, Judith peered past him. Chest out and fists clenched, her ex-husband was barrelling across the road. "*Judith*, there you are! I'm going to part your bloody head from your shoulders, girl!"

"I suppose I ought to offer to give you privacy," Adam murmured, removing his hands from his pockets. "But I can't leave you alone with a man with murder written so clearly on his face."

Judith felt her lips turn numb. It wasn't that she was scared of Tom. But he could be very . . . scary. "He's angry."

"Seems so."

Tom arrived with a clumsy jump up the two steps to the front door. "*Bitch!*" he swore, slamming his two powerful fists against the doorframe. "I can't believe what you've done! I thought even you would behave better than this!"

"Tom, you'd better come in and —"

Tom shook with fury. His voice dropped to a malevolent hiss as he talked rudely over Judith's attempt at diplomacy. "This evening I've been harangued and insulted by that Sutherland bloke, trying to find Kieran! After blood, he is! Because my son Kieran who *got the man's young daughter pregnant, a girl who subsequently suffered a stillbirth,* has now run off with her!" He struggled for control.

"And you *knew!* You knew, just like you knew about my grandchild, and you didn't tell me!"

Pinpricks of sweat sprung out on Judith's face. "I didn't!" Then she amended hastily, "Well, yes, I did know about the baby, but I know nothing about them going away together."

Punctuating his words with his fists against the doorframe, Tom blazed, "He's *my* son! *Not yours!*"

This inarguable truth made her very still. "I know," she whispered, miserably. She forced herself to meet Tom's infuriated glare. His face was puce and his eyes bulging, he looked as if he might be flung to the floor by the giant hand of a heart attack at any moment.

His eyes narrowed meanly. "And Aaron was my grandchild, not yours! You meddling, interfering mare." His breath bunched up and began to come in gasps between insults. "It was you who spoilt him rotten," gasp, "made him so wishy-washy he was too scared of me to bring me his troubles!" Gasp. "Well, I hope you're happy now? Because they're gone! Both of them. She's disappeared from her home and Kieran's room has been emptied! Her poor parents are out of their minds!"

He paused, heaving for breath, spittle dotting his livid lips, teeth bared. "Be truthful. Do you know where they are?"

She shook her head. "I haven't seen either of them since the day of the funeral."

Snorting his scepticism, Tom shook his fist under her nose. "If I ever find out you know where they are and don't tell me, by Christ I'll —"

"Enough." Adam pushed Judith coolly behind him, grey eyes steady. "You're crossing boundaries. You need to calm down."

Tom crowed for breath. "*Calm down?* I could *kill* her —"

"No, you couldn't," Adam corrected softly. "Not while I'm here."

Tom glowered into his face. He lowered his head at Judith head like an animal considering a charge. "Who's this joker? A new boyfriend?"

"No one who concerns you."

Tom stared for several seconds. "*Bloody bitch!*" Then he was spinning away, stumbling down the steps, slamming into his pick-up and stampeding off like an enraged rhino.

A silence enveloped them. Adam pushed the door shut. "That was pretty awful. You OK?"

She nodded, fearing to speak in case it let the tears out.

"You're shaking." He slid his arms around her, giving her shoulders a reassuring squeeze.

She nodded again, and let her head rest against the warmth of his shoulder. A great wave of reaction shook through her as she clung on to his mist-dampened jacket. Tom had been so venomous that she'd found herself actually frightened. Judith, who'd seen enough of his temper over the years to be desensitised. The violence of his anger had shaken her.

In the unlit hall the smell of the winter's night rose from their clothes, mingling with the typical wedding fare of sherry, champagne and wine, and Adam's

240

aftershave. "You're OK," he murmured. "You're OK. He was scary, but he'll calm down."

Her head jerked up, recalling Tom's words abruptly. "My God, where can have Kieran and Bethan have gone? What if something happens to them?"

Adam breathed a laugh, tightening his embrace and pulling her head back down to his shoulder. "Try not to worry, they're probably supremely happy in some love nest bedsit at this very moment, snug and safe from all the endless parental outrage. Eating chips from the paper because they haven't got plates. Finally able to comfort each other over Aaron and trash everyone else's feelings."

She let his warmth comfort her as she breathed him in. His good sense made her pause and think, the picture he painted reassuringly credible. Kieran was of his generation. Made a mess of things? Throw that life away, and begin another . . . Go on, mate, no one can stop you. You got rights, you know. The police won't drag your girlfriend home at her age. You're not doing anything against the law. And no one knows where you are, do they?

Gradually the constriction eased from her throat, and her trembling eased, her mind clearing. Tom was angry. Well, that was nothing new. Kieran had "done a moonlight". Not altogether unexpected, she supposed, a bit underhand, not very brave, but he wasn't good at confrontation. "I wonder whether Tom's right, whether it is the way I brought him up that made him wishy-washy?"

He stroked her hair. "If all his life he's had to face uncontrolled rages like the one we've just witnessed, I don't blame him for developing ways to avoid conflict. He's not wishy-washy. He's just gentle."

She sighed and lifted her head, slowly this time. Light from the street shone through the fanlight of leaded glass above the door, illuminating the planes of Adam's face, light then shadow on the taut cheekbones and angular jaw, creating gleaming highlights in his eyes.

His arms slackened, as if he expected that she meant to step away. But the prospect of putting the customary distance between them made her feel hollow and bereft and instead of letting her arms slacken, she tightened them. She found her body relaxing against his. Softening.

He was solid and safe, but it was no seeking of security that made her nestle against his warmth.

For several moments, Adam seemed to hold his breath.

And then his embrace shifted subtly, and, somehow, the way he was holding her was no longer that of a friend. And the contact between their bodies wasn't incidental.

"Jude." His whisper was a caress.

She looked into his face. And their lips touched. Softly. The merest brush.

Then he swooped, and pleasure prickled over her at the sensation of his tongue seeking hers while his urgent hands pressed her so close that she struggled for balance as the rhythm of his heartbeat gathered her up and made her head spin. No heart had beaten against hers since Giorgio's.

It felt . . . well, welcome home. No one since Giorgio had taken pleasure from her mouth. Adam's hand cradled her head and his hot, hard body pressed with passionate intensity that lifted her clear of the floor as if she were a lightweight. She was being kissed — she was kissing him back. And her bones were melting.

Suddenly unbearably hot and uncomfortably encumbered, she dropped her arms and shook off her coat. It made a scratchy, synthetic sound as it slithered down her arms to the tiled floor.

It seemed to bring him up short. He paused, his breathing all over the place. Like hers.

She could hear his quirk of a smile in his voice as he steadied himself. "I didn't mean to do that." Another pause. "At least, I didn't mean to do that *yet*. Because Giorgio —" Then, gently, "You're not wearing his crucifix."

"It's the first day I've left it off." And it felt odd not to be aware of it moving against her skin. She shook her head. "I don't know . . . The letter made me feel different." She didn't try to explain how.

His embrace slackened. "I leapt on you. If you want me to apologise, then I do. It's been a long time, and I miss . . ."

Her embrace tightened, her voice husky. "You miss human contact, the affection and pleasure of it. You miss being held. It's typical of you to kindly take the blame. But I leapt on you, too."

243

After a moment he kissed her again, this time with extraordinary tenderness. "I lost control. I've wanted you since you were a stroppy fifth year. I've built up quite a yen."

Her face heated in the darkness. "You hardly noticed me!"

He laughed, stroking her hair back, the back of his hand brushing her cheek. "I noticed all right! I noticed whether you wore a ponytail or a plait, black shoes or brown. I also noticed that after our riveting conversation about Polos, you looked away whenever I tried to catch your eye. And you were more than two years younger. They were pretty sinful thoughts I had — about a fifteen-year-old."

He flicked his tongue to the corner of her mouth and she heard a tiny groan that must've come from her. "I *couldn't* look at you. I wanted you to talk to me again so *much*."

His lips moved to her eyelids, her temples, exploring her in the dark. "Tell me how you're feeling."

"I feel alone," she whispered, giving in to the honesty of the moment. "And so *weary*. Of Tom's fury and Kieran's despair, Molly's unhappiness. Mum's defencelessness. I'm tired of being strong for them all. I want . . . to be comforted."

Adam was more frank. "I want to go to bed with you."

Adam made love to her with total concentration and all of his body. Apart from his right hand, which was pretty much excluded from the party.

In her bedroom that used to be his, he undressed her slowly. First her uncomfortable shoes, then the bodice of her dress, and the forest-green ribbon lacing at the front. "There's a zip," she pointed out, trying to guide his hand. "You don't have to struggle with the ribbon."

He smiled, easing her away. "But I've been fantasising about this all day." He plucked at the ribbon, pulling it slowly through each loop with a whisper of sound, fumbling sometimes with its slipperiness, pausing to kiss the swell of her breasts as each fresh millimetre was exposed. "Have you any idea how erotic it is, unravelling you?"

She shuddered, letting her head tip back. "Pretty much."

He laughed, pushing his hand through her hair so he could kiss her hard then kiss her gently, continuing to unfasten every possible fastening that would reveal her — including a left-handed struggle with her cream, satin bra — before sliding out of his own clothes. Until there was nothing left to prevent the delicious heat of flesh on flesh as he rolled her down to the lemon-yellow pillows.

Bliss. Judith gave herself up to the pleasure of being made love to by Adam.

He was tender but not shy. At all. He absorbed himself, engaging all of her senses, his lips coasting around her body as if to compensate for the loss of sensation from the missing fingertips on the right hand that he held away from her.

She watched him. His body was all bones and hollows, she could see how he was put together and the

245

working of his muscles. Examine his little frown of concentration. Feel the warmth of him beneath her palms, the tickle of his body hair against her skin.

And when he poised himself above her, he looked down into her face as if checking that she wanted him to go on. Then he dipped his head to kiss her. And let his body sink over hers.

It wasn't really daylight until seven-thirty at that time of year. And she'd been awake and staring at the ceiling for an hour, the duvet pulled to her chin, when thin, pearly light stole around the curtain edges.

Then fingertips trickled across her ribcage, raising a swathe of goose-pimples in their wake. She turned her head on the cool cotton of the pillow. He was smiling, his hair falling in his eyes and more silver-streaked in the daylight, the bedclothes falling away to display whorls of grizzled chest hair. "You're transparent," he observed.

She raised her eyebrows.

"I can read every thought rolling around your head: where do we go from here? What have we done? What have we changed or sacrificed? Did I want to wake up with him? What will he think this means — that he has some rights over me? Will he expect to make love again this morning?" His smile twitched. "He's nice and warm to put my feet on?"

She hadn't noticed that the soles of her feet had found a cosy home against his warm flesh. She flexed slightly, feeling the brush of his leg hair.

**246**

He slid closer. The smile faded. "Where *do* we go from here?"

She looked away. And tried not to hear the tiny change in his breathing that wasn't quite a sigh. "It was too soon for you," his tone was suddenly flat. "The cold light of day has made you wretched. You're thinking of Giorgio. The guilt's killing you."

She wriggled around to face him, trying to be honest with his grey-eyed gaze. "I'm not wretched, and I certainly don't regret the lovemaking. In fact, I feel . . . at peace. As if, for months, I've been wound up in elastic bands, and now you've picked them all off. As to guilt . . ." She drew a breath. "I think my only guilt is in not feeling guilty. I do understand that Giorgio's gone. And you?"

His eyes smiled. "No guilt," he decided firmly, his hand moving on to the roundness of her stomach. "I'm the man — I feel smug." His fingertips began to make tiny circles. "But I do feel strange. Special. As if I'm beginning a clean slate. As if that were my first time." His hand slid lower.

She put her hand on his wrist, feeling the coarse hairs on top and the softness of the underside. "You didn't perform like a first-timer." She sighed. "But what do you want? Because we might not want the same things. I'm afraid you might be more ready than I am for a normal relationship."

His hand continued on its journey. "Take your time. There's no rush to decide where we go next."

She groaned. She should have explained before this. She only hadn't told him because she wanted to get her

247

motives straightened out in her mind. She reached up to stroke his face, gently. "Adam, I know where I'm going . . . back to Malta."

His hand stilled.

# CHAPTER
# TWENTY-THREE

While Adam showered, Judith went down to begin breakfast, more to occupy her than because she was hungry. From the stairs, she noticed a folded piece of paper on the floor of the hall. It was scuffed and dirty, they must have walked over it in the darkness, last night.

She opened it out as she turned towards the kitchen. Then halted at the sight of Kieran's hurried handwriting.

Mum, I came round to see you, but forgot it's Adam's son's wedding today. I wanted to tell you that me and Beth are going away. We need to be together and don't want any more hassles from Beth's parents. I'm dead sorry I didn't get to see you, and will be in touch. Don't worry about me. Love you. Kieran.

She sliced bread and broke eggs mechanically, lips set, her heart banging angrily.

It seemed to her that between Tom McAllister and the Sutherlands they'd shoved her son away, and he'd gone without trusting her enough to tell her where. Did he and Bethan even have a place to go? Her eyes prickled threateningly, and she wiped the corners with the back of her hand. Guilt struck her that it was at her insistence they'd done the right thing and told Bethan's parents about the baby.

And look what a mess her parents had made with the knowledge! Forced Bethan to choose between them and Kieran.

It was all very fine Adam supposing that those two tender young kids were safe in some little love nest, but what if they weren't? She pictured them trying to live in Kieran's small car, surrounded with their bags, chilled to the bone. Or battling to stake a claim to a corner of some horrendous squat.

Kieran wasn't the type to stick up for himself in such a hurly burly environment, and Bethan would be scared to back him up. She was as much a softie as he was. Judith had a sudden vision of herself bursting into some squalid terrace with boarded windows and extracting Kieran from under the noses of the lawless and the hopeless.

She set about the eggs with unnecessary gusto, splashing her hands and wrists as she beat. Of course, technically, crucially, Kieran wasn't actually her son. That's what Tom said. Despite all those years of cuddles and bedtime stories, bruised knees kissed better and homework explained, Kieran had only been on loan to her. And, according to Tom, when she'd written her marriage off she'd written off Kieran with it.

Kieran could visit her as much as he liked, but Judith had no rights, no legal kinship.

**250**

Kin or not, she was pretty sure she wouldn't have driven Kieran away, if she'd been able to exert control over the situation.

She showed Adam the note when he came down. "Perhaps I should have let them move in here. Then at least we'd all know where they were, and that they were OK."

He squeezed her waist and kissed her hair. "You can't put everything right for everyone, Jude. If they'd lived here they would've been under constant attack from Tom, and Bethan's parents. And so would you. You might've stood it, but could they?"

They sat facing each other at the table. Adam cut the corner from his toast and scooped up fluffy egg. He had no gizmo to fit around his hand and the knife was obviously a struggle. "Are you going back to Malta for good?" His voice was casual.

She sighed, dragging her mind from whether Kieran and Bethan could actually have done what was best for them. "It's an option."

He waited, clear grey eyes fixed steadily upon her.

She sipped her coffee. She was aware that it was always the person who filled a silence with explanations who was considered the weaker negotiator. And she was aware that, however obliquely, they were negotiating the terms of their relationship. "I want to speak to Giorgio's daughter about the crucifix. It's becoming a burden instead of a comfort. I owe him and her some honesty."

"Debatable." He continued to watch her, pushing his food around.

"Then I owe it to myself."

"You couldn't make your enquiries from England?"

"Probably. And it would prove to be frustrating and unsatisfactory. Also, Richard rang last week, he's organising his retirement. If I'm not going back to the business, he wants to buy me out, so he can pass Richard Morgan Estate to his children."

"But you have the option to keep your stake? Reclaim your old desk?"

She chewed mechanically, picturing herself back at Richard Morgan Estate with the constant flow of traffic beyond the window, and the sea beyond that, bobbing with small boats at anchor. God, sometimes she felt driven to go back, feel the warmth again, smell the sea. And now to add to the mix was her unquiet conscience. "I could pretty much reclaim my entire old life."

He paused, thoughtfully. "Except Giorgio."

She swallowed. "Except Giorgio. But it's not just him. I miss Malta. I miss the sea, the people and their approach to life. I miss hot days and warm evenings, the food, the beer, the fireworks at festa time, the amazing amount of traffic in the tiny streets. I even miss the storms."

"But you'd feel closer to him, there?" He laid down his knife and fork.

She flinched. His calm couldn't disguise the hurt in his eyes. She should have organised this conversation earlier, not when they'd been to bed together. It was . . . uncaring. And still he remained the same decent

Adam, he didn't bawl or glower or throw things or crash his fist on the table to make her jump.

She tried to be candid, but gentle. "I don't know. It might be comforting. Or it might be torture. I'll find out."

He abandoned his meal altogether. His brows cut thoughtful lines above his eyes as he helped her stack the dishes into the washer.

Then he leant against the table and folded his arms. "Can I go with you?"

She knew her expression must be ludicrous with surprise. "To Malta?"

"For a couple of weeks. I realise you might stay longer. Months. For ever. But I think you could do with someone for a while, a friend. I'm your friend. You know that?"

She nodded, swallowing a lump.

She picked up his hand, the one with only finger and thumb. Turned it over to examine the white scars and the pink knuckles. Casually, he changed hands so that he could curl a full complement of fingers around hers.

"You're one of the kindest men I ever met," she said, looking up into his eyes. "No one treats me with the same consideration that you do, no one else is quite so much in my corner. It's probably harder to find a friend like you, than a lover."

He stiffened. "Suggesting that I ought to be *pleased* to be your friend rather than your lover?"

She fidgeted, subdued by his unfamiliar anger. "I'm not trying to organise your feelings. But let's think of you for a minute. What do you want? Where are you on

253

the road to recovery? What comes next? Forget making me happy, tell me how you'd arrange your world, if you could."

He squeezed her hand, his expression softening, lines shifting so that they edged his fine eyes. "I'm ready to go forward. I wish we could do that together. But, so far as I can see, I'm still travelling on my own. I'll settle for dawdling for a while. See how steep you find Recovery Road."

"I might never catch you up."

"You might even turn back. I'd have to give up on you."

"It seems a bad bargain for you, because I can't offer much."

"I don't expect much. Are you going to Malta immediately?"

She dropped her eyes. "Not straight away."

With one finger, he lifted her chin. "Because you'll be like a dog with a tick in its rear until you find out something about Kieran and Bethan?"

She grinned, viewing him through a sparkle of tears. "You reveal me."

The pad of his thumb wiped gently beneath her eye. "By the way . . . I would."

"Would?"

"Would like to make love again this morning."

She blinked away her tears and slid her hand deliberately onto his thigh. "Bring it on."

The winter ground along, wet, cold, windy, and for ever.

254

Judith didn't get any fonder of it, and Adam declared that she'd need surgical intervention to prise her from her cocoon coat when the warmer weather eventually arrived.

He was quieter, these days.

His boys' lives were diverging steadily from his. Matthias and Davina had moved into an apartment in a building that used to be a Victorian factory, in Kettering, a market town deeper into the county. Adam helped them to decorate what he deemed upside-down rooms — spice-coloured ceilings and white walls.

And Caleb, to everyone's surprise, landed an advertising job and bought a grey suit and five white shirts. Then put cobalt blue streaks in his hair to celebrate becoming a London commuter.

Judith knew how troubled Adam was that Shelley put her heart on the plate with the fresh cream cakes she bought when she knew he would be dropping in, and asked him to go back to her. Something, he told her, that he couldn't do.

Judith felt sorry for Shelley. But couldn't help being glad, for herself.

However, to Judith's dismay, Adam took a unilateral decision to return his relationship with Judith to platonic. It wasn't a decision he voiced before he put it into practice, but, nonetheless, he stepped back into the old ways, without touching, without sex. "Less confusing, for the time being," he explained, when Judith frowned over his resolution.

He wavered only once, when Judith found an old cannabis stash of Caleb's tucked into the frame of the spare room cupboard, and tried to dispose of it by tipping it on the fire. Adam flung himself full length to snatch it from her hand. "Are you mad? What are you trying to do, Jude? Get the entire street stoned?"

And he laughed so much that he went weak, and somehow she ended up in his arms on the floor, her shirt open to her waist and two of the buttons on the floor as a testament to his impatience with his own lack of dexterity. They threw the cannabis in the wheelie bin, later.

But that had been their swan song.

Their old friendship was intact, but that didn't keep Judith warm these frosty nights. She knew that she wasn't being fair to want a loving relationship to comfort her while she decided what to do with a life that may or may not include him. But that didn't stop her wanting it.

Snow set into Northamptonshire, which Judith hated more than the rain. Trying to walk when it lay in a cottonwool-like six-inch layer had yesterday broken the heel of the only elegant pair of boots she owned, and today was putting white streaks in her new chocolate suede trainers as she slithered through the salted pedestrian area in town, the late winter afternoon as dark as midnight. It didn't cheer her any to look up and see Tom ploughing past in clumpy steel toe-cap work boots, looking dry-shod and certain of his step.

"Tom!"

Ignoring her, he flung through the aluminium-framed doors of the Norbury Centre.

She pulled a face after him. Awkward boor. Then went to reattach a hanging orange flier more securely to a post, one of many the Sutherlands had scattered through the town. *Have You Seen Bethan?* it asked. There was a picture of Bethan, laughing into the camera, in happier times, obviously. The posters were already shredding and blowing away.

They'd been a forlorn hope, at best. But parents soon got desperate as to the fate of their children.

Judith had received two visits from Nick and Hannah Sutherland. One hostile, when they refused to step over her threshold but bristled on the doorstep, insisting, "You *must* know, you *must* know, you *must*!" The next conciliatory, accepting Earl Grey in the sitting room and being earnest. "If you know anything, anything at all, if you can just reassure us that she's all right . . ."

Judith had shaken her head sadly. "I've heard as much from Kieran as you've heard from Bethan. Nothing."

She missed Kieran. A constant heartache, daily misery. Even when she'd lived in Malta they'd shared weekly phone calls, and e-mailed in between. God, she missed him!

She missed his trick of rushing his words together when he had a good story to tell, the way he laughed so much he could scarcely get the funny bit out. And she couldn't help cocking an eye for him as she slid through the town centre, as if he might suddenly emerge from a shop, or a pub, laughing with friends as the cold pinkened his face.

*No news is good news*, it was said, she reflected, as she, not unexpectedly, failed to spot him. Well, whoever mooted such an optimistic view had never lain awake at night picturing her son sleeping rough, being beaten up for his cardboard box and left shivering in a shop doorway.

Trying to banish such images from her mind, she swung left at the edge of the precinct, stepping off the riven block pavers and onto the simpler flagstones of Henley Street as she made for Rathbone Leather, the leather goods shop that had been on the same spot ever since she could remember. Wilma had asked her to buy her a new purse.

"The zip's gone on this one," she'd said. "Can you get me a black one to match my bag, with a zip not a clasp — you know my hands — and a separate bit for the notes? But don't pay much, duck, it's not worth it. Go to the pound shop." Wilma always insisted on buying the cheapest available, in case she didn't last long enough to get the wear out of anything of greater quality.

It was a habit that irritated Judith, and she had no intention of shopping for Wilma's new purse at the pound shop.

She got into Rathbone Leather just before they closed. The lady member of staff, smart in her maroon smock, slid a drawer full of black purses from beneath the glass counter. Judith fingered rapidly through them, selecting the one she thought Wilma would like most. Roomy, with chunky zips that should be easy to grip, supple and soft and smelling satisfactorily of leather.

258

Outside, she picked off the price tag, and discarded the thick, pale blue paper bag in favour of a thin, pink-striped carrier, knowing that was what Wilma would expect from the pound shop.

She felt like a teenager preparing elaborate lies to pull the wool over her mother's eyes, but Wilma was so staunch in her refusal to let Judith or Molly "treat" her to nice things that a little subterfuge was called for, occasionally.

As she slithered through the slush to the car park, she sighed over the lacy fingers of the bare trees edging the pavements, and longed for spring to provide frothy dresses of pink blossom. After dropping her car keys and having to locate them by feel because the big orange lights of the car park weren't working for some reason, she drove to Molly's house with numb fingertips.

After two big mugs of Molly's "real" coffee to warm her through, and biscuits to keep her from fading away, Judith was ready to take Molly on to visit Wilma. She and Molly would eat together later.

Molly tucked her mittened hands beneath her voluminous red cape. "I'm glad you don't mind driving, because I just can't be doing with this white stuff," she grumbled, shuffling down the path in crepe-soled boots and angling herself cautiously into the passenger seat of the car.

"Me neither," said Judith, seriously, hopping into the driver's seat. "I hope we don't crash, or have to get out and push." She threw her head back and laughed to see her sister's horror. "For goodness sake, Molly! Don't clutch the door handle, I was joking."

But Molly hung on as if the car were a roller coaster about to dive down a precipitous slope, and actually shrieked as the car got into a skid in Northampton Road. Rotating the steering wheel rapidly to correct matters, Judith shook her head at her sister's feebleness. Driving in it was the only thing she liked about snow, still childish enough to be exhilarated by the odd skating moment.

Wilma waited in the residents' lounge that was set aside for receiving visitors. Her hair looked freshly "done", and she was wearing passion-pink lipstick that didn't suit her, probably meaning that it came free on the front of a magazine. "You made it without huskies and sled!" she beamed. "Did you remember my purse, Judith?"

Judith settled into one of the high-backed chairs. They were the only visitors in the visitors' lounge, but there were several unaccompanied residents. Watching other people's visitors was a bit of a spectator sport when there was nothing good on the telly, and so there were several grey-haired ladies craning to watch Judith hand over the carrier containing the purse.

Wilma beamed as she fumbled the black leather out of its wrapping. "Ooh, isn't it a lovely one?"

"Lovely!" chorused around the room.

"But you didn't get this from the pound shop?"

"Yes, I did," Judith lied. "I've kept the receipt at home, in case you want me to take it back."

260

"I won't want you to take this beauty back, m'duck!" Wilma creaked her laugh. She began unzipping compartments with stiff fingers, dropping her voice. "Did you put a coin in it?" Wilma believed that it was bad luck to give a purse without.

"Of course."

"Ju*dith!*" Wilma had found the coin. "It's a *pound*! That's all the purse cost! Here, let me give you some change."

Laughing, Judith protested. "You can't give change for a good luck coin, Mum, it's bound to stop the luck working! Adam put it in there, anyway. You can't hurt his feelings by refusing."

Beside their mother, Molly's dark brows rose in big sister reproof that Judith was slithering into bigger and bigger lies, just as she had when they were children.

"Was that purse really only a pound?" demanded a silver-haired lady in a bobbly cardigan in shades of oatmeal. "My dear, I need a new purse. I don't suppose you'll be going to that shop again, will you? Could you get me one?"

"And me!"

"And me, m'duck, if you're sure it's not too much trouble."

With sinking heart, and grinning sister, Judith found herself collecting five one pound pieces that she was supposed to exchange for five genuine leather purses from the pound shop.

When the others had drifted off to the television room or were nodding over newspapers, Wilma grasped Judith's hand anxiously, her own flesh chilly despite the central heating. "Were all them purses alike?" Her whisper was almost a wheeze.

Judith understood instantly. "I think the rest were smaller."

"Oh." Wilma sat back, looking satisfied. "They won't mind theirs being smaller."

She left much of the conversation to Molly, after that. Her sister was good at talking trivia, storing up little nuggets of information about her neighbours — people Wilma had never met — what Edward had told her about his skiing holiday, in his last phone call, and what seeds she intended to grow on her conservatory windowsill.

Wilma followed it all with fierce interest, until the residents' cocoa was ready. Visitors were welcome to join in the nightly cocoa ritual at a cost of 30p per cup. Judith waited until the frothing drinks had been served, then, knowing that when it was drunk visiting hours would be over, decided to break her news.

Until the moment arrived, she hadn't given much thought to the actual words she'd use, or having to watch Wilma's face as she delivered them. Faced with the reality, she found that the more she attempted to make her tone casual, the more falsely contrived it emerged, and the fewer words she seemed to have at her disposal. "I have something to tell you," she began. "I'm probably going back to Malta, Mum."

A silence. Molly frowned, her face sharp with disapproval, glancing at Wilma and laying a comforting hand on her forearm. "For good?"

Judith realised that she'd been too blunt, and wished she'd talked to her sister, first. Moll was good with Wilma, she would have done something to prepare the ground, used some of the endless comfortingly inconsequential chat she had at her disposal to talk around the subject, how much Judith loved Malta, how she wouldn't be surprised if Judith went back some day. So the seed of possibility was sewn somewhere on Wilma's narrow horizon. "Not definitely," she muttered. "I've got to see Richard, anyway, and discuss what's going to happen with Richard Morgan Estate."

Wilma gripped her hands together. "But it might be for good? Just when I'd got used to you, again." Her words were forlorn, and there was a hint of a tremble about her round chin. Then, "I've got my new glasses, did you notice? The frames are called 'Amethyst'. That means mauve." The tremor gaining strength, she removed the glasses to display them, then surreptitiously blotted her eye with the back of her hand.

Dismayed, Judith gazed at the teardrop glistening on the soft white skin. Gently, she rubbed it away with her fingers, taking the hand, swollen with age, in both of hers. "They're lovely glasses. Even if I stay in Malta, I'll come back, often, to see you, Mum."

"Of course you will, dear!" Wilma blotted the other eye. "But I just thought . . . I thought you might settle here, now, so that I could carry on seeing you all the time. Adam's such a nice man."

"He is." Judith didn't pretend not to understand. "He's coming to Malta with me for a couple of weeks, possibly."

Wilma fumbled to push the new glasses back on her face. "Lucky for you he's patient."

They got their usual table at The Three Bells in the little dining room. Molly didn't like to eat in pubs unless it was in a separate dining room.

A log fire roared in a stone fireplace ornamented with a companion set, andirons, bellows, horse brasses and a warming pan. The beams were hung with corn dolls and more horse brasses. A young lad with red hair and a serious expression wiped their table and presented them with cutlery wrapped in white paper napkins, and a little round pot of sauce sachets.

Molly was working now as a volunteer in a charity shop. Usually, she seemed to enjoy sitting across the table from Judith and talking about her customers, those who came in every week to stretch their budget by trawling the clothes, and the occasional middle-class matron who couldn't resist a Royal Doulton tea service at about one-tenth of its value. Normally, she'd sniff about the man from Brinham market's thriving Antique Corner, who liked to buy cheap in charity shops and sell dear on his stall.

But today she could scarcely wait for the first sip from her coke before starting in on her sister with a huge sigh. "Just when I thought you'd settled here! But, no, you're off again." She folded her arms with a little huff of annoyance. "You can't keep shuttling backwards and forwards for the rest of your life, you know, Judith." She didn't sound cross so much as anxious.

Judith couldn't resist taking her literally. "Actually, I can. I wish you wouldn't talk as if I need your permission or approval. The days when Mum used to put you in charge of me have gone."

"Pity."

"Come off it, Molly —!"

"I'm just thinking about Mum."

Judith sighed, and drank half her lager in one swill, instead of making it last as she normally did when she was driving. "I'm aware that I handled it badly. I didn't think she'd take it quite so hard," she admitted gloomily.

Molly picked up the menu as the red-haired teenager returned with his pad and pen, and ordered chicken and chips. "I'm afraid she's well aware that she's old," she said, when he'd returned to the kitchens. For once she didn't sound judgmental or bossy. Just sad. "Every time she sees you, she'll upset herself over whether it's the last time." She held up her hand. "And I know that the same could apply wherever you lived — but when you're in Lavender Row you're only ten minutes from her. Malta, in Mum's mind, is an unconceivable distance away. She can no longer grasp the reality of it, a little country in the middle of a big sea. The longer you're away, the further it seems, to her. And don't waste your breath trying to convince me otherwise. I've had three years of being cheerfully comforting when all she wants is to see you!"

Judith sank into guilty silence.

Molly unrolled her cutlery from the paper napkin to inspect it for watermarks. "How much was that purse?"

**265**

Judith groaned. "Eighteen pounds."

Molly burst out laughing, schadenfreude diverting her momentarily from worrying about her mother. "*Eighteen?* And you've got orders for five more? You'll have to pretend they've sold out, won't you? Eighteen pounds!"

Finishing the rest of her drink, Judith shrugged. "I wouldn't buy them the same as Mum, you know what she's like, it'll take the shine off for her if everyone gets the same. I'll get them the smaller size. They're only eleven."

"That's still fifty-five pounds!"

"Well, I'm not disappointing them!" Suddenly, Judith wanted to cry. At the thought of those old ladies watching other people's visitors and waiting for their wonderful one pound purses?

Or was the indigestible lump of emotion lodged in her throat at the memory of Wilma trying to hide her tears?

# CHAPTER
# TWENTY-FOUR

But it was a week until the tears finally fell.

They'd been to take pix of twin brothers who'd married twin sisters, and now the sisters were each expecting babies — single births, disappointingly — during the summer.

A magazine was doing a feature on this convoluted family branch, and intended follow-ups in one year and two years, keen to see how alike or unlike the children would prove to be.

The shoot had been an easy one, and they were home by mid-afternoon with the images downloaded for Adam to look at the next day.

Judith shut the machine down. "I've got the ingredients at home for a Thai green curry, fancy joining me?"

"You get me where I'm most vulnerable. You know I love Thai curry."

"Play you at paper-rock-scissors for who's going to cook it?"

Adam studied his right hand thoughtfully. "I'll be OK so long as you don't notice I can only make a rock."

Judith grinned. "Don't try that stuff on me — we'll both play left-handed."

Adam still lost, leaving him to cook a curry in an iron wok in Judith's kitchen, while, free of domestic responsibility, Judith switched on her computer to download her e-mails. She clicked on *send and receive*, and watched four messages download. A message from Richard. One from Microsoft. And from her book club. Then an unfamiliar electronic address.

*Kierycakeeater@yahoo.co.uk.*

It was a moment before it made sense, a moment of her mind hunting for the right memory to tune into, like a hound circling for the scent. Kiery Cake Eater. And the words kicked her heart into a gallop.

That silly nickname, used only between her and Kieran in the days when Kieran was a child and life was simple and Judith was always aware of her son's whereabouts and that he was safe, her greatest problem likely to be how to prevent him from sneaking a third slice of cake from the fridge. She had a sudden vision of playing a silly, raucous game of chase around Tom's sprawling house, she roaring, troll-like, "Where is Kiery Cake Eater?"

Kieran, breathless from giggles and the delicious panic of the pursued, "Eating all the cake!"

The scalding tears welled as she fumbled over the two simple clicks it took to open the message. She had to swipe them away before she could read.

Hey Mum. Me and Beth are fine. We live in a house we rent from a bloke. I got a job and Beth's doing her A2s at a college next year, so she can go to uni. She's temping till then. *Impatiently, she used her sleeve against her eyes again.* Sorry I haven't been in touch, I could've e-mailed u earlier, but we needed 2 get our heads round things. You know how it is. <u>U</u> know how it is! Clearing off and coping on your own is sometimes the only way. I know all the things u r going 2 ask, so I'll save you the bother. 1) Yes, Bethan sent a letter to her parents, so they know she's ok. But she posted it when we went away on a coach for a day so they won't know where she is. 2) Leaving was her plan, but I wanted the same. 3) No, I haven't contacted Dad. If you want to tell him I'm ok, that's up 2 u. He'll be completely peed at me, anyway. C u again, luv luv luv, Kieran.

Judith wiped her cheeks with the backs of her hands, and then dried her hands on her jeans. *C u again!* It didn't matter so much when. Just so long as it happened. So long as she knew he was safe, and one day she'd see his brown hair sticking up at the front and his lip creasing when he smiled.

Shaking, she began to type a reply, careful to let him know how much she loved him, how much it meant to hear from him and know him to be out of harm's way. Not giving even a hint that her cheeks were wet and her fingers rubbery with emotion, as she ended:

I shall certainly let Dad know that you're OK, darling. He was distraught when you left. I'm glad

Bethan wrote to her parents, they must've been so relieved . . . any chance of you doing the same for Dad? Please? Tons of love forever, Mum xxxxxxxxxxx

And then Adam was beside her, sliding his arms around her and pulling her head onto his shoulder, not asking any questions, just stating, gruff with dismay, "I don't like it when you cry."

But she only sobbed harder. "He's OK! Adam, he's OK! He's living in a rented house and he's got a job . . ."

He rocked her while relief shook through her, stroking her hair and letting her tears soak his shirt while the curry stuck and burnt, and the rice he'd been watching like a mother with a baby, boiled dry.

They ordered a takeaway while the pans containing the ruins of Adam's green curry steeped in hot soapy water.

Adam watched as she ladled rice from *The Oriental Garden* — never as fluffy as his — and creamy yellow korma out of the foil cartons and onto hot plates. "Are you going to ring him?"

"Him" meant Tom. She blew on a steaming, fragrant spoonful of curry that she was suddenly ravenous for, but which scorched her lip when she approached it. "He'll hang up on me."

Adam nodded, annoyingly managing a spoonful of succulent chicken and plump sultanas as if it wasn't hot at all. "And if you knock on his door?"

270

Judith sucked air into her mouth in inelegant whoops as she put the curry sauce in anyway, and it stung her tongue. "Big risk of having door slammed in my face. I'll have to write the stupid man a letter."

"Perhaps he'll thaw. He'll realise that you didn't have to put yourself out to give him information about Kieran."

Blowing gustily on her second spoonful, she shook her head. "Not Tom. He bears a grudge. But at least if he doesn't want anything to do with me I won't have to worry about him any more. It'll be a relief in a way."

"You haven't *had* to worry about him since you separated."

"True. Maybe I should've accepted that sooner." Then she added, honestly. "I hope Kieran does write to him, though, and that they make up at some time in the future. Tom's later years ought to be happier than they are."

He cracked open a cold can of Strongbow, and shared it between their two glasses, his eyes exasperated. "I hope you still worry about me when I'm as old and grouchy as Tom."

"Of course." She took the glass up and toasted him. "To the coming of your grouchy old age."

He clinked his glass with hers. "But not too soon."

Old age that was occasionally grouchy had already come to Judith's mother.

Judith was glad Adam was with her, because Wilma wasn't in one of her sunnier moods. She was waiting for them in her pink-and-white room, rather than in the

271

lounge, her walking frame before her chair like a barrier.

Her first words were, "Did you get them purses?"

Judith was ready for the question. Experience told her that Wilma wouldn't want the shine being taken off her lovely — cheap — new purse by her companions getting newer ones the same. Petty jealousies and one-upmanship seemed to feature large in communal living. "Well, I have, but they're not as nice as yours." She displayed five purses without the section for cards or the stitchery design on the front that Wilma's boasted. "Do you think the ladies will mind?"

Wilma took a purse in swollen hands, turning it over and unzipping compartments with stiff fingers. "I'm sure they won't have to! Goodness me, if they send you out for their shopping they'll have to put up with what you bring them, won't they, duck?" And then, "Smaller than mine, aren't they? Same price?"

Judith agreed that they were, feeling that one more lie in the Great Purse Deceit was scarcely important.

Wilma looked sharply at Adam. "You haven't put a pound coin in all of these, have you?"

Looking slightly surprised but forbearing to enquire why the devil he should, Adam confirmed that he hadn't.

"Ten pee in each, that's all." Judith dropped the purses back in the carrier. "Shall I hand these out, or will you?"

Wilma looked suddenly much mollified. "I will, duck, to save you the bother."

Hiding her grin, Judith handed the carrier over, knowing Wilma wouldn't be able to resist reminding all her friends that they must remember to thank Judith.

"So," Wilma turned to Adam. "You're letting her go off back to Malta, then?"

Adam raised a rueful eyebrow. "I'm afraid I have no power to *let her* or prevent her."

Rattling her dentures around her mouth, Wilma looked thoughtful. "I thought you might have. Will you try?"

He raised both eyebrows this time, and seemed to consider carefully. "I don't think there would be much point."

Wilma sighed. "No, there never was." She shook her head dolefully, folding her hands. "But you're going with her, aren't you?"

"For a couple of weeks."

"You're a good man. I hope she'll let you look after her."

"Shouldn't think so."

As there was only one chair apart from Wilma's, Judith perched on the corner of Wilma's bed, listening with rising irritation to this discussion of her behaviour. "I have lived in Malta before, it's a safer environment than Brinham," she pointed out.

Wilma lifted her stick and used it to push her Zimmer aside. "Do you miss Kieran?" she demanded.

Taken by surprise at Wilma's swerve to another subject, Judith hesitated. She hadn't told her mother that Kieran and Beth had run off, wishing to be in possession of a happy ending in the form of hard information of Kieran's whereabouts first. Kieran's visits had always been sporadic, so Wilma hadn't complained about not seeing him lately. "Yes," she agreed, cautiously.

"I know about him and his young lady doing a moonlight." Wilma ruminated over her dentures again. "He came to say goodbye."

Distantly, the rattling of the cocoa trolley beginning its evening circuit could be heard, and the loud and clear voices of the carers talking to other residents. But in Wilma's room the hush swelled until Judith's ears buzzed with the pressure. "I see." Her voice somehow sounded as if she were under water.

She minded, she realised, with a rush of hot anger. She minded that Wilma had seen Kieran to say goodbye, when Judith hadn't. Dimly, she was aware of Adam leaving the room, of the murmur of his voice, of him returning with cocoa for three. Automatically, she let him pass her a cup and saucer. The crockery used by The Cottage had a matte feel to it that she disliked, and now it positively set her teeth on edge as she sipped to ease her rigid throat.

Wilma took saucer in one hand and cup in the other. "He told me about the baby. Poor little dot, wasn't he? Poor, poor little dot."

Judith's voice seemed to be coming from someone else. "And what did you say to him?"

The light reflected off Wilma's glasses. "I told him how much you'd miss him, duck. Have you heard from him?"

274

"Yes." Judith swallowed more of the milky cocoa. "Did he tell you where he was going?"

"Back to Sheffield." Wilma said it as if there should be an "of course" at the end of the sentence.

The cocoa was gone and Judith felt sick. It had been too milky, too sweet. Kieran hadn't trusted her enough to tell her where he was going to live. Of course, Sheffield, where he'd been at university and knew the area, had friends, was an obvious choice. Easy for him to organise accommodation and a job. Why had she never thought of it? And what possible use was the information now that she had it?

In the darkness of the car Adam delayed starting the engine, and took her hand instead. "He may have been trying to protect you. He knew his father's temper, he probably felt that you'd be more comfortable facing Tom if you genuinely didn't know where he'd gone."

"You're probably right," she agreed, dully.

"I don't think Wilma realised she might hurt your feelings."

"Probably not." It was raining now, the droplets on the windscreen shattering the car park lights into fragments in the navy blue evening.

His thumb stroked her knuckles. "I think she was just hinting that she'll miss you in the same way that you miss Kieran."

"I expect so," she muttered, by way of variation. She knew the leaden emptiness of missing someone. The way you got used to it, learnt to live around an absence.

"She's bound to miss you. So will Molly. And so will I."

"I'm only going for a recce, that's all. If I decide to live there again it'll take time to organise."

His breath came out in a heavy sigh, steaming up the windscreen. "I suppose . . ." He considered his words, then began again. "I suppose none of us can see quite what would keep you here. We feel the 'recce' is just a formality. You're humouring us."

# CHAPTER
# TWENTY-FIVE

Adam pulled up outside Judith's house, where the windows were dark, as usual.

She screwed up her eyes and stared across the street. "Hell's blood, is that Tom waiting in his truck?"

He followed her gaze. "Looks like it. Shame. I quite liked it when he wasn't speaking to you." His tone of voice told her that he wasn't entirely joking.

They listened to the hiss of the rain, the warmth generated by the heaters quickly seeping away. The rain increased, until the hiss became a grumble. Grudgingly, Adam offered, "I can stay out of earshot while you talk to him." The inference being that he intended to remain within eyesight.

Judith unfastened the seat belt and let it slither over her shoulder. "Let's make a run for the door. If he spots us, I suppose we'll have to let him in."

"Run quickly, then."

But he did spot them.

By the time Judith had jiggled the key in the lock and Adam had hit the door to make it open, Tom was on the garden path behind them, huddled against the sting of the rain.

Switching on the hall light and hanging her wet coat over the newel post, Judith faced Tom in the hall while Adam went down the passage to the kitchen, discreet but not out of sight. "Not cutting me dead, tonight?" Judith challenged.

Rain dripped from the peak of Tom's navy baseball cap with the name of a builders' merchant embroidered on the front. He ignored her question. "Do you know where he is?"

"He didn't tell me."

In the kitchen, Adam coughed.

Tom scowled. "I suppose it's too much to ask that we do this privately?"

Judith folded her arms. "Yes, actually."

He stepped closer to loom over her. "Did he phone, or write? Where's the letter?"

She felt her temper rising. "Get out of my face! You really are lacking in all manners and grace!" she challenged. "Leave my house, or allow me to breathe."

Another glower, but Tom stepped back.

She let enough silence elapse to annoy him. Then, "I can't tell you more than I have. He contacted me. He gave me permission to let you know he's all right. That's it."

In the kitchen, the kettle bubbled to the boil, and clicked off. Adam turned the pages of a newspaper as loudly as it was possible to turn them, lounging against the kitchen worktop. Tom removed his sullen stare from Judith and narrowed his eyes in Adam's direction. "Do I have to worry about him?"

"In what way?" Judith hadn't quite meant to inject the astonishment that coloured her voice.

He turned his angry eyes back to her. "Are you *together*? A *couple*? An *item*?"

She laughed. "Mind your own bloody business! The days when who I slept with was your concern are long gone! Very long gone, you ridiculous arse!" She turned to glance at Adam, to find that he had lifted his head, and was staring at her.

"I don't like the way he hangs around," Tom persisted, obstinately.

Adam snapped the paper shut. "I was just thinking the same about you."

With an exasperated tut, Judith shoved past Tom and yanked open the door. "Well, I like him hanging around," she snapped. "Good night, Tom."

On Thursday, she accompanied Adam to shoot pix of Podraig Mahoney, a man who kept losing his short-term memory and had to be constantly reminded of his surname. He was highly reliant on his dark-eyed wife, Loraine, because if he left the house for too long alone, he forgot his route home.

He treated his highly unusual and frustrating condition with humour, and had to be constantly reminded not to smile into camera, as the magazine wanted a pensive mood to the piece.

By the time the shoot was over, Podraig had to confess that he'd forgotten why it had happened at all.

Helplessly, he smiled at his wife. "You'll have to remind me. I forgot to write it down."

Seated at Adam's computer, downloading the pix into a fresh folder ready for Adam to select his submissions to the commissioning magazine, Judith wondered how often Podraig asked his wife to be his memory, and how often his wife patiently complied. How strong love had to be to withstand the constant drip of a frustration like that.

Adam concentrated silently on his own work. He'd been almost morose since Tom's visit.

From her pocket, Judith's mobile began to ring, vibrating disconcertingly against her hipbone. An unknown number flashed up on the screen.

But the voice that went with it was achingly familiar. "Hey, Mum."

She swallowed. A rush of love surged through her, making her hot and dizzy, and any resentment that he'd confided more in Wilma than in her, evaporated.

"Mum? It's me."

"Hello darling," she managed. Her voice cracked. She was aware of Adam looking up suddenly, a smile clearing his faint frown lines. She closed her eyes the better just to listen to the sound of Kieran's voice as he told her a little about the house they rented, "Red bricks, black roof, white windows. Nowhere to park." And his job, "I left the one in Brinham without working my notice, so they wouldn't give me a reference. So I'm working in a shop, now, but it's cool. I'll be able to work my way up. They've already put me in charge of ordering stuff for the CD section."

"That's wonderful." She smiled. Her heart expanded in relief. He had a roof over his head and a way of keeping it there.

"So, I've rung to ask a favour." Kieran cleared his throat awkwardly. "You know . . . at the cemetery? We ordered this little —" He cleared his throat again.

She said it for him. "The stone tablet? For Aaron?"

She heard him take a couple of deep breaths. They whooshed down the line. "Yeah. It's supposed to be in place by now. We were wondering . . . could you ask Adam to take a digital photo of it and e-mail it to us? Bethan's a bit stressy about whether it's been done right, so when we've seen it we'll be cool." His voice became gruffer. "Well, we might be upset, but we want to see it. We need to."

Without waiting for the conversation to be over, she passed the request on to Adam.

"Tomorrow, as soon as the cemetery opens," he promised. "The light will be pretty decent, this rain's due to pass over tonight."

The cemetery was silent apart from the breeze through the naked trees and cautious, end-of-winter birdsong. Adam's camera bag containing the black Nikon swung from his shoulder as he walked at Judith's side.

The stone was easy to locate; palest grey veined marble with gold lettering, set into the grass. Adam took overhead shots so that Kieran and Bethan would be able to read the inscription, *Aaron McAllister Sutherland*, and of Judith laying white roses beside it, her hair blowing back from her face.

Crouching, touching the engraved inscription, the bleak, single date that reflected the baby's failure to draw breath, Judith felt claws of pain around her heart. She glanced up at the weedy, watery English winter sun, and wondered how it could possibly be the same that beat on Malta.

Adam helped her to her feet. "Let's go back and send the pictures straight away." He kept her hand all the way back to the car. Adam knew exactly when she needed these little expressions of support. She might get a bit of silent disapproval from him where Tom was concerned, but he forgot that the instant she needed him.

Next day, it was Adam who found a message from Kieran in his inbox. *Really cool. Thanx mate. Tell Mum we're really, really ok, don't think she believes me. Thx again. Means a lot. K&B*

Reading the mail for the fourth time when she should be typing invoices, Judith mused, "It sounds as if he's truly growing up. As if they both are."

Adam nodded as he sucked out one of his equipment cases with the brush on the nozzle of the vacuum cleaner. He didn't like dust on his equipment. "Tough breaks tend to chase away immaturity."

She clicked to print out the invoice she was working on, and began a fresh one. "I think they'll be OK. It's still hard to accept that Kieran's chosen not to confide where he's living, and I expect Tom's still livid. But if a twenty-two-year-old decides to resign from his job, pack his clothes and leave, there isn't very much you can do about it. There isn't much you can do about a seventeen-year-old girl doing the same thing, the Sutherlands have discovered." She looked outside to where rain had begun to fall in a cold, heavy curtain. Again. "It's time for me to go back to Malta."

Adam fitted the crevice nozzle to clean out the smallest compartments where the brush wouldn't reach. When all was satisfactorily dust-free, he switched off the vacuum, wound up the flex, and stowed it in the cupboard under the stairs.

He came back into the room, and picked up the diary with the navy-blue cover.

"I can clear the last week of April and the first week of May," he observed, after quickly flipping through. It wasn't a question or a hint, just a statement of a fact she could, or not, take advantage of. He shut the book with a snap.

She smiled to herself as her rapid fingers opened another invoice template. "I'll ask Richard if we can stay with him."

# CHAPTER
# TWENTY-SIX

Judith stood, motionless in the soft darkness, and listened. The crickets, the *werzieq*, were making their endless background buzz. Sliema Creek lapped at the edge of the pavement, a gentle noise that was soothing and comforting, and the occasional car whooshed past between the silent shops and the broad pavement where she stood, headlight reflections wheeling over those of streetlights that lay across the black water like golden scribbles.

The smooth railings that edged the harbour were cool beneath her hands. She breathed in salt water and boat oil, pine trees and dust, listening to the pull and suck of the water, feeling the utter peace.

Quiet footsteps made her turn.

Hands stuffed in the pockets of his black canvas jacket, Adam had the creased appearance of someone who'd been woken from a nap. "Are you safe out here at two in the morning?"

She smiled at his disgruntled air. "Probably. There's not much crime here — not that I have any valuables on me — and any self-respecting Romeo would be looking for someone younger."

"Good thinking," he yawned. "And maybe even Romeos are put off by madwomen who hang around alone in the dark."

"I like the dark." A long, slow, even breath, as she inhaled the essence of Malta.

He stifled another wrenching yawn.

"Go to bed," she suggested. "Erminia's given you a lovely room, and she's wonderfully hospitable. Your sheets will be scented with lavender, your pillows plump and inviting."

Groaning longingly, he leant his forearms on the rail and studied a rowing boat that rocked beside a faded red buoy. "Richard made me come out to look after you."

"Don't say he's waiting up for me, too!"

He yawned again, saying sourly, "Not now I'm out here."

Her laugh was loud in the still air. As he didn't seem inclined to leave her to a private wallow in the Maltese atmosphere, she decided to illuminate his surroundings for him, nodding first to a bulk of land across the narrow ribbon of sea. "This is Manoel Island, here in front of us. It is an island, but only just — it's joined to this road, The Strand, by a bridge. This part of The Strand's called Triq Marina or Marina Street on some maps, but everyone still calls it The Strand."

She turned to their left. "Those are the ferryboats; see the little one with *Lowenbrau* on the side? That shuttles all day to-and-from Valletta, there, look. We can go across in the morning. Or stay in Sliema. Whichever you prefer."

He turned, resting his backside on the rail, regarding her curiously. "Can we? I thought you had plans? Giorgio's family?"

Slowly, she nodded. She did have plans involving Giorgio's family, of course, wasn't that one of the reasons she'd come? But now she was here, a little rest and relaxation wouldn't hurt. She wanted to show Adam her Malta. "I'm going to take a couple of days first. I need thinking time."

He didn't comment that she had had most of the winter to think in, but glanced around with weary interest, as if resigned to the fact that sleep wasn't immediately in the offing. "So where's Richard's office?"

She pointed down The Strand the other way, towards Ta' Xbiex. "Just about in sight — see the restaurant with the bright yellow sign? Immediately past that."

"And your apartment?"

She swung back. "Behind the ferryboats and the bus stops. Second floor." The outside of her old home was so familiar, although someone else's home at the moment. She remembered the warmth on the soles of her bare feet when she stepped onto the balcony, the evening she waited for Giorgio but Charlie Galea showed up instead. She shut out the recollection. "You were supposed to be seeing all this in the morning."

"Yes, I remember the idea being to go straight to bed after our late flight. I missed the bit where it got changed to wandering about half the night."

She let her exasperation show. "Go back to Richard's without me!"

286

He adjusted his position on the railings and showed her a peeved scowl. "You are a bloody woman, Jude. At one time if a man put himself out to protect a female she used to damned well let herself be protected! Now he has to be apologetic, in case he offends her. Go on, you carry on with your tour guide bit. I'm sure I can cope indefinitely without sleep."

*Tour guide.*

*Giorgio, standing at the front of the bus and making all the passengers smile with his easy charm.*

She made herself relax. "If you're going to pout about it, we'll wait till morning." She took his arm and they crossed the road, turning up the tiny street further up The Strand that led to Richard's house with a courtyard behind. A typically Maltese house of limestone with tiled floors and staircase, a scroll of wrought iron swelling over each window like a belly. On older buildings it would have signified that the building had needed to be defended, the bulge at the bottom to allow a lookout to be kept down the street for enemies. On Richard's house it was an ornamentation Erminia liked to fill with potted red geraniums.

"Look, lizards!" Adam pointed up at the geometric shadows on the pale limestone, legs making right angles against still bodies that ended in long pointed tails.

"Geckos," she corrected. "Wall Geckos. You'll see plenty at night, they hang out near a light to eat the insects it attracts. Geckos have shorter, broader bodies than lizards and are dull, like speckled sand. Lizards like to bask in the sunshine and have shiny scales, sometimes a beautiful dark green."

287

She let her explanations fade away. Adam was watching her mouth as she spoke.

Geckos aren't that interesting a subject when your onetime lover is looking at your lips with a particularly intent expression that starts the memory of desire uncoiling inside. She reached out. Her fingertips collided with his scarred palm and she let her hand close around his. "Adam . . . why don't we sleep together any more?"

He betrayed by only a blink that her bluntness had caught him off guard. "Self preservation," he offered, with a quirk of his lips. And he inserted his left hand into the cradle of her fingers to extricate the right as they walked into the lofty, cool interior of Richard's house.

The next three days were a holiday.

With pride in her adopted country, she showed Adam up and down the steep streets of Sliema with the shops packed tightly from corner-to-corner. The following day they drove Richard's car to the beautiful beaches of Paradise Bay and Ghajn Tuffieha, where the sea had never looked so blue, and then the impressive silent city of Mdina in all its medieval splendour. Despite the fact that it was far from silent as extensive cable laying works were going on, Adam shot so many photos of the carved buildings and narrow streets that he had to use a computer in Richard's office to download the pix and e-mail them home to himself in order to free up his memory cards.

**288**

On the third day she took him on the ferry to the lovely, unspoilt, ancient capital city, the citadel of Valletta, pointing out the landmarks as they approached: the steeple of St. Paul's Anglican Cathedral — known as the British Church — the dome of Our Lady of Mount Carmel, and the turret of the Grand Master's Palace. The way up into the walled city that hung above them was cruelly steep, but Judith was merciless as she steered him onwards and upwards to one of her favourite spots, the heights of the Upper Barracca Gardens.

There they stared out over the glinting blue splendour of Grand Harbour, watching as far below ant-like passengers disembarked from a towering white cruise boat with its own swimming pool. Adam gazed silently over the depths of incredible blue to the church domes and bell towers of the three crowded little cities of Vittoriosa, Cospicua and Senglea on the opposite shore, their fingers of land creating the creeks to shelter the clutter and clatter of the docks.

She took him into the city and showed him the central thoroughfare, Republic Street, a particularly pleasant place to shop as no traffic was allowed. The streets were beautifully decorated for the Feast of St Augustine, the *bandalori* or bunting showing the city at its best. They lunched on pasta and calamari at Caffe Cordina in Republic Square, and she told him how in the sixteenth century the Ottoman Turks had laid siege to the Knights of St. John in Valletta, floating dead Knights across the harbour waters in a savage attempt to destabilise the besieged order. And of La Valette, the grandmaster of the time, who gave the grisly order to fire back the heads of Turkish prisoners in brutal response.

They strolled between the golden Baroque buildings along dusty streets so narrow it seemed impossible that they'd survive the cars whipping past them, and others where they felt pretty safe from vehicles because the road was actually a giant flight of steps.

She showed him the city gate in the huge ramparts that had protected the city for so long. They bought cake and ice-cream from stalls standing around the circular bus terminus, and he took photos of her sitting on the coping of The Triton fountain in the middle, laughing, her face dusted with icing sugar and crushed almonds, her ice-cream melting over her fingers.

Judith enjoyed playing tourist with Adam, watching his face as he studied the buildings and the views of the sea to be glimpsed down almost every street. Meanwhile, a family dinner was being prepared at Richard and Erminia's house so that upon their return, Judith's family — her cousins, their spouses and all the children they'd brought into the world — were waiting, surrounding the long table beneath the chandelier in the dining room.

The evening was full of laughter and finger-licking food, *lampuki*, peppers, sausages. Children clambering down from the table between courses to let off steam, Lino and Raymond competing to entertain Adam with unflattering stories about Judith.

It was late when the party broke up and it seemed very quiet once the various arms of the family had

290

returned to their own homes and Richard and Erminia were in bed. Judith and Adam went out to sit in the courtyard among big dusty pot plants, the night air chilly enough that Judith needed her jacket. Adam entertained himself by spotting geckos on the house walls.

And then Judith said, "Will you be able to look after yourself tomorrow? I have stuff to do."

Adam placed his hands slowly behind his head and watched the moths battering themselves against the orange light. "You're beginning your mission?"

"If you want to call it that."

"And you want to do it alone."

She frowned as she tried, unsuccessfully, to interpret the odd note in his voice. "For the moment."

He rocked his chair, thoughtfully. "Well, thanks for the last few days. I've enjoyed having you with me." His tone was polite, and Judith couldn't quite tell whether he was being sarcastic.

They lapsed into silence, and for a while she thought he'd fallen asleep. But then his voice came suddenly. "How does it feel to be back in Malta?"

"Nice," she said, carefully.

"Nice," he repeated, as if he'd never heard the word before.

# CHAPTER
# TWENTY-SEVEN

The sun was getting some real heat into it, making her roll her shoulders in satisfaction beneath the butterscotch yellow cotton of her light shirt as she approached her cousin Raymond's three-year-old blue Peugeot that looked at least three times as old. After a brief tidy up inside the borrowed vehicle, which involved throwing all the papers from the front into the back, she drove cautiously out of Sliema. She'd decided to begin her "mission", as Adam termed it, by searching out some way to feel close to Giorgio.

It certainly hadn't happened just by coming back to the island, a little to her surprise. Even in Sliema, where both she and Giorgio had lived, her present life intervened. Perhaps because she wasn't in her own apartment. Perhaps because of Adam, she was tuned in to him in the usual, easy way and that might have interfered with the slide back into the past that she'd assumed she'd achieve by coming back. Instead, she felt like a visitor.

On her last visit, the island had seemed full of Giorgio, ringing with his voice, bright with his smile, unbearable without him. Of course, that had been when his loss was so new.

But now . . . the office was self-evidently running perfectly well without her, and she had the uncomfortable conviction that it would suit Richard and his family if she simply sold out to them. The small hotel venture had proved profitable, the funds were available. Rosaire had taken over her client list.

She knew that if she declared her intention to take up her old position she'd be greeted with nothing less than a warm welcome. But Richard was spending fewer and fewer hours in the office, his children had formed a team of pleasing symmetry without her.

It seemed to her that the issue of the crucifix, though, was not so clear-cut. She was intent on gaining some sense of what she should do. What Giorgio would have wanted. She desperately wanted to do the right thing — whatever that was.

The roads were no quieter than she remembered, and she felt nervous of the lanes of weaving traffic on the regional road as she became reaccustomed to the Malta driving experience. It all seemed uncomfortably rapid and busy after Brinham, which was usually choked up with cars, and therefore slow. Dust blew in through the open car window on a breeze that held a firm edge of heat, auguring the rigours of the summer just beginning. The sun was harsh as it bounced from the pale new limestone blocks of a building under construction, the site hemmed about by other buildings and the road, a precarious-looking crane lorry swinging the large blocks into what would be the building's basement.

Construction in this style was a particularly Maltese skill. A building was cut from between its neighbours, and the site excavated into a yawning hole. She was sure that the occupants of the houses on either side must breathe a sigh of relief when the new building grew to fill it.

Joining the queue of traffic threading past the crane, she began to relax as she left the busier roads behind and reached less crowded residential areas with prickly pear trees lolling over dry stone walls like spiky green Mickey Mouse ears, and actually began to enjoy her drive.

The cemetery, when she parked the car, was enjoying an early morning peace, the flower sellers still setting out their wares on the sloping car park. Stepping through the tall, decorative gates, she had no trouble remembering to take the left avenue, uphill under the pine trees to the Zammit family plot. Her previous visit was pretty well scorched into her memory.

But having searched it out, she came to an uncertain halt before the monument.

Nobody was there to observe her, but still, somehow, she felt like an uninvited guest. Perhaps because she could imagine the fury of Maria and Agnello Zammit if her visit happened to coincide with one of theirs!

The plot was tidy. Fresh white and yellow flowers stood in a central vase. A new plaque had been created before the older ones, pale compared to their deeper tones, and an oval photograph of Giorgio making her flinch. It looked like the photograph that appeared at the back of his tour company's brochure.

*Giorgio Zammit*
*1962-2003*
*RIP*

Her stomach hollowed. Already it was almost a year since the accident in the twinkling waters of Ghar Lapsi. At the other end of the summer it would be a year since his death. She would be *another* year older than Giorgio as he lay here alone, the flowers nodding in the breeze, the still carving of the angel standing guard.

After a further brief glance about her, Judith lowered herself to the floor. She sat cross-legged, propping her forehead on her fist and closing her eyes, preparing to remember Giorgio, to feel close to him, talk to him in her head, as she used to. Tap into the grief from the familiar point of lament. *If only I'd been there . . .*

If she had been there to keep him safe, she thought, struggling to keep her eyelids shut in the inappropriately cheerful sunshine, she'd have a completely different life now — presumably — her old life, living in Malta with Giorgio.

She interrupted herself. Those should be two separate statements.

She would still be living in Malta.

She would still be "with" Giorgio. Behind closed doors.

Letting her eyes open, she gazed at the flowers, having difficulty losing herself in mental images of *if only*. Perhaps it always was difficult to envisage one life

**295**

when living another? And having accepted Giorgio as being dead for some time now, it made it difficult to imagine him alive.

But she was back in Malta, specific things had brought her back, and she'd come here to focus on one of them. Fishing in her bag, she brought out Giorgio's crucifix. It gleamed in the palm of her hand, some of its lustre lost now that it was no longer worn every day against warm skin. She closed her eyes again, reaching out determinedly to Giorgio with her mind.

*What am I supposed to do with this?*

She tried again with less impatience. *Cass gave me this so I'd have something of you. And now I don't know what to do, because Alexia says it's hers.* The memory of her conversation with Giorgio's daughter intruded. There had been positive dislike in the young woman's tone, and no chord in common with Giorgio.

She sighed. She so badly wanted to do the right thing about the crucifix, the right thing by Giorgio's daughter. She just wished she knew what that right thing was. Maybe she should have let Adam come with her, as he'd so obviously wanted to, because Adam was such a rock in a crisis.

All she'd had since she met him was one crisis after another. He must be used to coping with them by now.

For goodness' sake, she wasn't meant to be thinking about Adam!

Pushing herself to her feet, she brushed glumly at the dust and dead pine needles that now coated her jeans, dropping the crucifix into her bag, feeling foolish over sitting cross-legged like some old hippy and attempting to gauge the opinions of a dead man. An insect had bitten her ankle into a white lump with a pink halo, and it itched already.

She tucked in with the other flowers the single orange gerbera she'd bought at the gate. It blazed out from the tasteful, muted whites and yellows. She hesitated. When his family brought fresh flowers, they'd surely notice this floral stranger.

Oh, let them.

It was unlikely to be Johanna, she hadn't even liked her husband.

If it were his children or his parents . . . well, they'd just have to accept that she'd loved him, too, no matter how they'd frowned.

*I wish I knew what to do.*

She swung away down the hill, legs like pendulums, to climb back into the hot interior of Raymond's car, disappointment and dissatisfaction creeping up on her like a scudding black cloud. Only Giorgio's name remained at Santa Maria Addolorata Cemetery, inscribed upon a plaque. And the posed photograph that would keep him smiling and forever forty-one.

She thrust the car into gear and drove away.

Ghar Lapsi was an area of outstanding beauty by the standard of any nation.

Sauntering along the cliff top from the car park, Judith made for the same slab of rock where she'd waited out the day of Giorgio's funeral. She squinted past the glitter of the sun, almost too much for the eyes, at a red fishing boat and the dark shape of the rock of

Filfla. The oil rigs still cluttered up the horizon to her left, standing gawkily in the distance like a prehistoric monster.

She shaded her eyes to search the green, frothing sea. Then she wandered back to the steps and made the descent to the foreshore.

She passed no one on the way, but there were a couple of families at the restaurant at the bottom. A pretty waitress with melting brown eyes and a ready smile brought her cappuccino, and she watched the waves from a green chair on the terrace, as she drank. Substantial waves, today, thrashing the shore. Divers would be foolhardy to go down, the rip would carry them away or fling them against rock without warning. Smash, dash, flip, tumble, hold you down, drag you out into angry, jade-green depths. The sea had a soft belly but a hard head, as the Maltese said, and only the incautious went down when it was so restless.

Gently, slowly, she closed her eyes and listened to the crash of the waves and the crack of water falling back into itself.

She remembered the feeling of being down there, finning along above the weed, brilliant fish darting away, octopus reversing into rocky crevices, red starfish prone on the bottom. The sun filtering into the water in diagonal bars.

But she couldn't make the shady shape of the diving buddy into Giorgio.

Her cup empty, she went right down to where the water boiled inside the arm of rock and the sea was forced through a tiny fissure in a smoke-like puff of

298

spray as the wind rattled in her ears. It was like standing on the edge of a cauldron. On a projecting rock stood a lone fisherman, his bait in a white plastic box at his feet. He glanced around and she saw it was Paul Vella, his skin glowing golden from spray-laden breeze. Pawlu, the men called him. Giorgio had fished with him from a boat sometimes for the local big fish, *lampuki*. They'd thought it a great joke to cast near the baited floats laid out painstakingly by other fishermen, effectively intercepting their catch.

Pawlu's silver hair was damp. He raised a hand to her, then secured his rod and stepped back over the rocks.

"Catch much, Paul?"

His smile transformed his face. "Sure, *vopi*. Little silver fish, big red eyes. *Vopi Imperial*."

"What are you using. Shrimp?"

"No, just damp bread, smelly cheese, and patience." They studied the bubbling sea together for several moments. "You OK?" he ventured.

She nodded. She'd shared many a beer with Paul and the rest of the boat's crew returning after an excited day's pursuit of yellow fin tuna or Mediterranean Marlin. One of the funniest, sweetest men she'd ever met, he'd made her cry with laughter with his knack for telling stories, there was nothing he liked better than to have a crowd in stitches. It seemed a long time ago, now, another lifetime. Another life. "I'm OK." She hesitated, then added, "I came to remember Giorgio. But I can't seem to feel close to him."

His eyes showed that he understood. "You find him somewhere, maybe not where you're looking. I think of him today, too, at Ghar Lapsi. He was a good man, Giorgio Zammit, and we always raise a drink to him on the boat."

She could imagine them, those old friends of Giorgio's, joking in the sunshine over their rods and nets and noisome bait. Imagine them raising their cans of beer to Giorgio as they fished from the little boat that lurched on the waves.

"It's good to see you in Malta again. I remember you at mass."

"You're kind." She managed a smile. "Give my love to Massie. I hope she doesn't mind cooking all those fish."

"You want some?" He gestured towards his keep net, his mischievous eyes twinkling now. "Put them in your handbag. They stop wriggling by the time you get home."

The memory of his gentle humour helped her ignore an aching knee as she climbed back to the car. Joints that had never ached before did now that she no longer swam.

Once she'd driven back to Sliema, she left Raymond's car in his parking space behind the office. Through the large windows she could see Raymond talking to Richard and Adam. Adam was sitting sideways on a desk. But she turned and strode away without letting him know she was back, without even telling Ray that she'd returned his vehicle.

Twenty minutes later she paused. She was at The Chalet Ghar id Dud, its pier-like skeleton still reaching into the sea and meeting the waves as it had stood for so many years letting the sea gradually wear it away. Her hair writhed in the wind that blew on shore, stinging her eyes as it obstructed her vision, and she zipped herself into her jacket.

No teenagers leapt with joy from The Chalet today.

There was an even bigger sea on this side of the island, running with green rollers and smashing angrily against the pilings. The waves submerged the surrounding rocks, spewing spray that rose high enough to be blown onto the promenade thirty feet above. As one wave subsided with a roar of streaming water, the next roared over its head.

Judith selected one of the green-painted benches furthest back, out of range of the spray.

It had begun here.

Giorgio had materialised at her elbow one day to enjoy her fascination with the kids and their perilous descent into the sea. Here he'd lingered almost daily to intercept her. Here she'd watched him meet his buses, charm the tourists and swap jokes with his drivers. Here he'd enchanted his way into her heart with his brown velvet eyes.

But he wasn't here now.

Back at Richard and Erminia's house, Erminia had made *kawlata*, one of Judith's favourite meals, a thick stew of pork and sausages with vegetables. Richard packed a generous portion into his rotund body, talking cheerfully about the day, the weather, the way the wind was up. Erminia chimed in with her observations on their grandchildren.

Adam ate quietly.

Judith could scarcely eat at all. Her insides fluttered and her head ached. She'd got precisely nowhere today, and was no nearer knowing what to do about the crucifix.

When the crockery had been cleared away Adam thanked Erminia charmingly for the wonderful meal, then his eyes went back to Judith. "Fancy a walk to the marina? I thought I'd get a look at those floating palaces."

She managed a quick smile. "I have to see someone, and I think they'll be coming home from work between seven and eight."

His face closed, and he turned away.

"Adam?"

He paused, politely, without smiling.

She pressed the cool back of her hand against her aching forehead. "I could use some company."

He smiled. "That would be me."

# CHAPTER
# TWENTY-EIGHT

The house was set back slightly from the pavement and tight against its neighbours, with one upstairs balcony and square windows with green shutters. It wasn't quite at street level so a few stone steps led up to the front door of varnished wood, and a longer flight down to the basement.

Judith had already been aware in which street Johanna and Giorgio's daughters lived, and Erminia had discovered for her which house was theirs.

She breathed in deeply. Throughout her time with Giorgio the figures of his estranged family had lurked in the shadows, figures in Giorgio's past that, she'd been shown quite plainly, didn't concern her. But now she was about to make them real, give them faces and voices. Feelings.

The wind was gusting, bringing the temperature down to one that was low for the final day of a Maltese April. In fact, it was quite like being back in Northamptonshire. Adam's warm fingers slid around her chill hand and she looked up into the concern in his eyes.

"Don't put yourself through this, it's not obligatory. You don't have to challenge these people who feel antipathy for you, the time for that was when Giorgio was alive and there might have been some purpose to it. You can keep the crucifix — it was given to you — or send it to them by messenger. Or stuff it through the letterbox and run away! Whatever you feel is the right decision."

"But I don't know, that's the point. Once I was quite certain about everything. Giorgio was trapped in a state of separation, it was unfortunate and unfair. He'd parted from Johanna a long time before I came on the scene, and it had been her decision. We were blamelessly in love. When Cass gave me the crucifix I took it as my due. It was a part of Giorgio when I needed a part of him most, he'd worn it every day and it was as if it represented his heart." She shivered. "But now . . . I'm not quite sure why I was so convinced I was due anything."

He pulled her lightly to him, sharing his body heat. "Take a little more thinking time."

She let herself sag, closing her eyes and thinking how good it was to have contact with him. Then she straightened. It wasn't common, in Malta, to get physical in the street. She raised her chin. "No, I have to do something about this. It's a weight on my shoulders. Will you wait here for me?"

Her knee protested again and almost gave as she climbed up to the front door. She must make swimming part of her life once more, even if she never dived. A small, thin woman answered the door, her eyes black pebbles the instant they lit on Judith. "Yes?"

Judith pushed her hands into her pockets in case they began to shake. Facing her lover's widow was less easy than she'd once supposed. "Johanna Zammit?"

The slightest of nods.

"I'm Judith McAllister. May I see Alexia, please?"

After a long stare, Johanna turned away, shouting into the depths of the house in Maltese. Judith caught the words for "now" and "woman". A young woman appeared from upstairs and stood, staring with hostility at Judith.

She and her mother were very alike, slight and small, cheeks hollow, lips narrow and held in straight lines, hair glossy with chestnut lights.

"I'm . . ."

"I know who you are."

Judith swallowed. "You wrote to me —"

"And you've brought to me my father's crucifix? Thank you." The girl was overly polite.

Slowly, Judith pulled it from her pocket, the familiar weight, the chain pooling in her palm.

Alexia reached out — but Judith closed her hand.

The young woman's eyes flashed, and anger swept into her voice. "My mother says I am to have it! You have no right!" She made a move almost as if she were going to grasp Judith's hand and prise it open.

Judith thrust both her hands back into her pockets. Her voice shook. "I can see why your mother would like you to have it. But, of course, I must see the Will, just to check *in law* who it belongs to."

"Is me." Johanna spoke suddenly. "As he left this house to me. Us." Then her eyes moved to a point behind Judith. "You have a . . . friend with you?" Her voice was soft with scorn.

Judith glanced around. Adam had moved closer, his hair blowing over his eyes, his brows straight lines of concern. Johanna's tone contrived to make it sound as if Judith had, inappropriately, brought a lover to this delicate meeting with her dead lover's wife and child. It didn't make her any more comfortable that, basically, it was what she'd done.

"He's . . ." She searched for an explanation that wasn't exactly a lie. "He advises me."

She turned back. "I'll give the crucifix to the person it belongs to, but you must agree that I need proof. What if Maria or Agnello or Saviour tell me it belongs to them?"

Sharply, Johanna said, "Is not your business —"

She broke off as a car pulled up outside and a teenaged girl bundled herself out, calling thanks in Maltese and leaping for the front steps. Pulling up suddenly, she giggled as she realised she'd almost run full-tilt into a stranger. "*Skuzi*, Madam!"

"*Ma gara xejn.*" It's of no consequence. Judith managed a smile, pulling aside to let the girl through.

With a word of thanks the girl darted indoors, past Johanna and Alexia. Then she turned to smile again.

"Oh . . ." The smile was replaced by surprise, realisation, curiosity. But not the hostility of her mother and sister. "Oh . . ." she breathed, again.

"You must be Lydia?" Judith's heart clenched as she studied Giorgio's youngest child, the laughing eyes and a smile that made people smile back, the round chin

**306**

and wide cheekbones. The thick, black hair. Even the angle at which she held her head.

For the first time since coming back, she felt Giorgio's presence.

Johanna rounded on her daughter with a flurry of Maltese, Judith caught *tard*, late, and *xoghol*, work. With one last candid appraisal, Lydia disappeared into the house.

Judith looked after her. Then she returned her attention to Johanna and Alexia. "No doubt you have a copy of the Will? I expect it's in Maltese, but what I can't understand myself I can certainly get translated."

Johanna shrugged. "I don't have it."

"That's a pity."

Walking away, Judith finally allowed herself to shake. Adam took her into a bar and bought her brandy, curving her hand around the balloon and lifting it to her lips, his leg against hers, his arm along the back of her chair. She dropped her cheek against his shoulder.

He said again, "You don't have to put yourself through this. Cass gave you the cross as something to remember him by."

She'd been thinking hard about that. It was a romantic premise, but . . . Her voice emerged, muffled by his jacket. "I have other things, things he bought me. A necklace, a picture. I'm afraid I may have had my share of Giorgio."

"Difficult, hmm?"

She looked into his face to see if she could decipher the feelings that went with that neutral response, but Adam had carefully cleared his expression. She straightened up, sighing. "Let's have a couple of drinks before going back to Richard's."

The following day, Judith went to see Cass. She went without Adam, knowing any information would flow better if she were alone.

Cass, when she saw Judith at her highly polished door, looked as if she'd swallowed a scorpion.

"Sorry," Judith offered, not particularly apologetically. "But I'm back." She made no effort to embrace the older woman.

They studied one another. It was the first time Judith had seen Cass without make-up, although her dress was as smart as ever and her shoes polished.

Running a smoothing hand over her neat chignon, Cass frowned. "I should never have given it to you."

"I expect you've regretted it."

Suddenly, chariness was replaced by the warm smile that Judith remembered from happy evenings in restaurants with Cass and Giorgio. "Many times! I was emotional, but it was a stupid thing to do. I should have known that Maria would notice it was missing, she would count the tea leaves in a pack to make sure they're all there."

Proper Maltese weather had returned, and Judith found the sunshine on her shoulders comforting. "Did you get into lots of trouble?"

Cass rolled her eyes. "Enough!" Her hand was hooked onto the door handle, but she made no effort to invite Judith in. "Saviour wasn't pleased with me. Said that I'd embarrassed him."

"How did he know it was you?"

She flushed. "Once she realised it was missing, Maria talked of nothing else for weeks. Saviour began to notice how guilty I looked every time she began. He says he can read me like a book." She almost smiled at this last, as if quietly pleased.

"Is Saviour here?"

The wary expression flashed back onto Cass's face. "He's working on his old car. His darling, his favourite toy."

"I was hoping to see him."

A long hesitation, Cass's dark eyes fixed on Judith's face as if trying to read her mind. Then she stood back. "Please come in."

The house was beautiful. A pale grey marble staircase swept up from of the square hall past round windows. In the *salott*, the formal sitting room, the furniture was either heavy and polished or of painted wood. Two stuffed birds stared down from atop a cabinet, and turquoise glass shone like the sea from the windowsills. Cass led her through the *salott* and then a central courtyard dotted with spiky palms, back into the house and through a formal dining room, then out again to a tall gate. Judith reeled a little from the gleaming grandeur of Cass and Saviour's dwelling. It felt like a little palace, and they must be pretty comfortably off to afford it.

Outside the gates they approached a garage that seemed to have been built under the side of another house with a drive that was almost unfeasible, it was so steep. The black-painted doors were folded inside against the white walls.

Saviour was up to his elbows in the engine of an elderly white Mercedes, oil making black gloves on his hands and forearms, spattering his cheek and smearing his forehead. His clothes, old and baggy, were equally soiled, especially where his shirt strained to contain a belly suggestive of a love of food. He didn't seem a natural match for neat and polished Cass, but he had the look of someone happy and absorbed in his task.

Until he saw Judith.

He stared for several moments, his hand unfaltering as it worked in the depths of the car engine. He awarded her a cautious nod, and turned and looked hard at his wife.

Hoping she wasn't dragging Cass into deeper trouble, Judith plunged straight in. "I'm Judith McAllister."

He nodded again, straightening, picking up a rag every bit as dirty as his hands he wiped with it, all without speaking, as he studied her.

She held his gaze. "I'm looking for information. I've come to you because I believe you're a man to give me an honest answer."

His expression narrowed with suspicion, and he tilted his chin. "Maybe." His tone suggested: or maybe not.

Behind Judith, Cass whispered, "*Giorgio kien ihobbha.*" Giorgio loved her.

After another pause, Saviour inclined his head. "My wife take you to the house, Mrs. McAllister, and I wash my hands."

It was ten minutes before he joined them, by which time Judith was seated with Cass at a beautiful mosaic table of rich reds and greens in the shade of the courtyard, the *bitha interna*, a drink of cold peach juice beside her.

He took a dark grey iron chair that wouldn't be stained by contact with his oily gear, and regarded her. His eyes were unsettlingly direct, as if he knew more than she was aware.

A deep breath, and she began her explanation. The crucifix, how comforted she'd been to receive it when grief was crushing her. How it had reassured her for many months, shifting against the skin at the base of her throat as she went through her days. "But then I had a letter from Alexia Zammit." She paused to give him time to speak, to ease the way by making her explanation a conversation.

But he just waited, silently.

Judith eased her throat with the deliciously cold juice. "Alexia asked for Giorgio's cross back, and for the first time I questioned my right to it. Perhaps I should have done that sooner, but I was caught up in my own sorrow. But now that Alexia's claimed it, it's worrying me. And I need to know what to do."

Finally, Saviour spoke. "The crucifix is valuable."

"I suppose so. It's gold."

"But more, is old. When my wife wish to give you a thing of Giorgio, she no realise this belong to his

**311**

*nannu*. My father. Agnello give to Giorgio when he become a man. And before that?" He shrugged eloquently. "Perhaps the father of my father."

Judith felt instantly that this was the truth. There was something direct about Saviour Zammit that made instinctive trust easy. She chose her words carefully. "I've visited Johanna and Alexia. They tell me the crucifix has been left to Johanna, who wishes to pass it to her daughter." She allowed the merest suggestion of cynicism to creep into her tone.

She waited. He waited longer.

She looked into his olive-skinned face, the creases and folds of age. "I asked to see the Will. They said they couldn't show it to me. I need to be convinced of who owns the crucifix before I hand it over. So I came to you. Who does the cross belong to?"

The sun was bright across his face, engraving the lines more deeply. Bright flecks glowed in his dark eyes as he stared at her with surprise.

"You come to Malta to ask this?"

She nodded.

"*Is-Sagramewt!*" The Holy death! An old man's exclamation of astonishment.

Honesty got the better of her. "Well, partly. And to decide whether to stay in England, or to come back here."

"You let Maria think you go live England."

She grinned, faintly. "I went. I didn't go because she told me to, and I didn't say I'd stay."

He gave one of his slow nods, and sank into his thoughts, sipping juice from a thick tumbler, the oil of many hours of playing with engines riming his fingernails and defining every grain of the skin of his fingers. At length, he stirred. "You give money to Giorgio, for a bus?" He sounded suddenly tired.

She felt her cheeks warm as she flushed. "I was a private investor in the company, yes."

"And me." His voice had become deep and sombre.

She stared at him. It hadn't occurred to her that Giorgio might have involved his family with his business. In fact, she hadn't given a thought to any other investors.

"You lose a lot a money?"

She debated telling him to mind his own business. But, if he'd invested himself, there didn't seem much point in hiding anything. She shrugged. "Very nearly everything except for my house in England."

He grunted, glaring ferociously, shaking his head. "He is a silly man when he do this. A . . ." He looked at his wife and spoke in Maltese.

"An optimist," she supplied.

"And sappitutto!"

"Know-all," Cass translated.

Saviour tossed up his hands. "But still, he does not mean this bad thing to happen to us!"

Judith smiled, painfully. "I know."

"But he know, before he die, that he make a mistake with the insurance."

She heard herself make a noise, a protest. No, he couldn't have known! Surely, he would have confided in her?

Saviour held up an admonishing finger. "A mistake, only! Not a cheat! When he discover, he has horror. Horror, yes?" he checked with his wife. Silently, Cass nodded. Saviour turned back to Judith, a sheen of sweat beneath his flashing eyes. "And scare. He has scare. He come to me . . ." Saviour's voice broke, and he pushed his finger and thumb fiercely against his eyes.

Quietly, Cass excused herself.

Judith looked away to let the proud old man compose himself. "I'm glad it was a mistake."

"He no mean to cheat you!" he repeated in a voice that rasped. Saviour recovered to stare absently at the houses that rose around, the balconies and outside staircases made of stone, the sky above, china blue. He let out a long, long sigh, spreading his gnarled and grimy hands. "He come to me, but too many money is needed. Those last days he has . . ." He hesitated, searching in the air with his fingers for the word. "He has the mood. Not so many smiles." He demonstrated with a smile of his own, and Judith felt that it was something not seen too often.

Shakily, she drained the last of her peach juice. "You must be right. He was awkward — moody — with me, because I couldn't dive with him on Saturday. Unnecessarily moody. He refused to wait until Sunday."

"If he wait for Sunday, he lives now."

She didn't need reminding.

Cass reappeared with a tray of small cups and coffee in a chrome pot. Saviour tossed his back in one steaming draught, then said, abruptly, "Possessions, they go to his parents."

It took several moments for Judith to appreciate what he was saying.

"I know how Giorgio left his matters, and his possessions belong to Agnello and Maria."

"Thank you," she managed, slowly absorbing the knowledge that she'd have to speak to Giorgio's parents. A heartsinking thought.

Examining his grey hands, Saviour spoke in rapid Maltese to Cass. Too rapidly for Judith to pick up any of it. Then he rose. "Goodbye, Mrs. McAllister. I wish you well." He nodded and crossed the courtyard with a rolling, bandy-legged gait, back in the direction of the Mercedes.

Cass waited until he was out of earshot. "He said, you have honour." She sounded awed.

Even though Judith and Adam were moving swiftly through their holiday, Richard and Erminia had to go out for the evening at a party at Birzebbuga, down in the south east corner of the island. The party was to celebrate the engagement of one of Erminia's legion of great-nephews to a girl who they both agreed was beautiful and accomplished, but neither could remember the name of. At any other time Judith would have joined the party joyfully.

But, instead, she and Adam ate at a pizzerija along The Strand, on the first floor, beside an enormous plate glass window overlooking the creek. They shared pizza and dough balls, and a few beers.

Adam was quiet. He'd been quiet all evening. In fact, it seemed as if quietness had become a permanent state with him.

Judith tried to bring him out, and he smiled when she made jokes, and listened when she spoke. But she had to accept, in the end, that he wished to dwell within thoughts of his own, rather than listening to another airing of hers as they strolled back beside the slack, black, rippling water.

She let them into Richard and Erminia's silent house, shutting out the *zirzar* of the crickets as she closed the tall door, and led him into the large and homely kitchen where an enormous window that dominated one wall was covered by a fly screen. She reached for his hands. "I've been neglecting you. And you're getting fed up with it."

His answer was light. "That's what you get for inviting yourself along on someone's quest." But he didn't manage a smile.

As usual, she felt him slide his right hand from her left. She settled her hands on his shoulders, instead. "It's true that I've had a lot on my mind."

He shrugged, staring past her and out into the black night. "It's more than that. You're a different person, here. At least, you have been since you focussed on the crucifix problem. You wanted to sort your life out, I understand that. It was my fault, I offered to come, to be available when you needed me. You never promised that the reverse would apply."

**316**

Guilt flushed through her. "I am sorry! It's just this decision's been on my mind. I didn't think it'd take so long "

Abruptly, he stooped, and shut her words off with his lips.

Surprised by the swift, brief kiss, she made to explain that it was only for now that her focus was elsewhere, but that soon it would be over. She wasn't a different person, not really, it was more that she had a different situation to deal with. Different and difficult, and unhappy. She'd thought the way forward would be obvious, if she were only back on the island. But . . .

Once again he stopped her words with lips that were hard. His forehead was scored by a frown, and he looked almost angry.

She got the idea.

He'd had enough of hearing about her problems, and was too polite to snap at her to shut *up*, for crying out loud. Perhaps she ought to be thoroughly affronted, but, actually, she could see his point. She'd been self-absorbed, she couldn't blame him if he was sick of hearing her whine. Every problem she took to him, her pain over Giorgio's death, worry for her mother, emptiness and fear over her son, even her exasperation with a well-meaning big sister.

Deliberately, slowly, she reached up and fitted her lips to his. Soft lips, parted, offering a different kiss altogether. She felt the muscles in his shoulders gather, as if he might pull away. But he stayed, parting his lips as her tongue tip explored, then gradually beginning to participate, sliding his hand into the small of her back and pulling her close.

Her heartbeat kicked up a few gears and she let herself wallow in his embrace.

She tightened her hold on him, murmuring against his mouth, "Take me to bed, Adam."

He groaned, thrusting against her and making her gasp. "It's not the right time. You're caught up with Giorgio and his family. Your head's with them."

"All of me's here!" she hissed, thrusting back. "From the neck up as well as from the neck down."

"You shouldn't make me want you like this, Jude."

"I've never really understood why not."

There was to be no long, delicious disrobing, this time. Adam just grabbed her suddenly by the hand and raced upstairs with her, hustling her into her bedroom, hauling her shirt over her head, snapping off the button at the waist of her trousers with his impatience. "I want you!" As if she might not have gathered that. His breathing was hot and uneven, gusting out of him and fluttering back in. He flung back the covers and lowered her to the sheet, then shucked off his jeans and T-shirt in two seconds.

She gasped as he let himself down on top of her, kissing, nibbling, rubbing against her, pulling impatiently at her underwear, whispering her name, kissing her eyelids, cheekbone, collarbone, breast, stroking his jaw against the softness of her stomach and touching her with his tongue to leave a cool trail.

★  ★  ★

318

Moonlight shone into the room. Adam lay on his side.

She wriggled closer, seeking safe harbour in the curl of his body. "I was beginning to think that would never happen again."

"I've had the same thought." He did his half smile.

Cautiously, she smiled back, unsure of his odd tone. "You seemed fairly . . . enthusiastic. Do you still wish I didn't make you want me?"

He kissed her forehead, then her hair. "Perhaps — now I think how I dragged you up here like a caveman. Had I better go back to my own room? Will you be embarrassed if Richard and Erminia realise we're in bed together?" He seemed suddenly remote.

She shook her head. "They're so late that I should think one of Erminia's relatives has offered overnight hospitality." She slipped her hand around his waist. "I'm sorry that I've been preoccupied."

"I understand." But he made a sound suspiciously like a sigh. "It's what you came here for."

"Tomorrow, I must try to speak to Maria."

He began kissing her again, insistently, giving her mouth something else to do other than tell him her plans.

Much later, when Judith was sliding off heavily into sleep, her back spooned against his front, his bony, warm arms looped around her, she heard him in the darkness. "It's a small country."

"Malta? Of course." When she was less sleepy she could quote him facts about the Maltese Archipelago, size at widest and longest points, population, visitor numbers and even rainfall.

"A small world," he added. "Far away from Britain." She couldn't understand why he sounded so sad, and she wanted to ask what he meant, find a way to reassure him.

But her dreams whooshed up to carry her away.

# CHAPTER
# TWENTY-NINE

She was in bed alone. Even before opening her eyes she knew that the warmth of another being was absent.

She unglued her eyelids and stretched, gingerly waking muscles that had been exercised by a night with Adam. She smiled. Evidently, no one had told him that his stamina ought to have waned this far into middle age.

"About time." His voice came from the doorway. "I was going to wake you, if only to check that I hadn't killed you." Dressed already in black jeans and a black shirt with the sleeves rolled up, he'd brought her a late morning brunch of ham, cheese and crusty bread, with tea in two of Erminia's pretty butterfly-strewn mugs.

She laughed, hoisting herself up against the headboard, letting the dawn-pink cotton covers fall to her waist. "I thought I stood up to the action pretty well. It wasn't me who had to leap out of bed and cavort about the room because of cramp!"

"No, I suppose somebody was needed to stay in bed and giggle." He leant forward and kissed her naked breast, his lips hot.

She caught the back of his head, stroking his hair into his neck. "Come back to bed. I promise never to giggle again."

Slowly, he freed himself, kissed the corners of her mouth and smiled, crookedly. "Jude, if I get into bed with you again, I might never get out. And I don't want you to think that all I'm good for is no-strings sex."

He pushed himself back to his feet, leaving her to eat, shower and dress.

When she caught up with him he was out in the midday sunshine, rocking on two legs of a chair and studying a book of drawings by M. C. Escher. He was fascinated by the work of Escher, that master of mathematical mosaic, optical illusion and reflection. It was one of his favourite Sunday treats to listen to The Hollies or The Eagles while he gazed at the masterly work.

"Lizards or geckos?" he asked, indicating a drawing where unlikely looking reptiles appeared to walk in and out of a mosaic. His hair blew over his forehead, and he pushed it back.

She laid her hand upon the strength of his forearm. "Adam, I don't want you to think that I only want you for —"

He covered her hand quickly with his, and squeezed it. "Don't let's do this now."

"But I just want to —"

"*Please, don't!*" He snatched his hand away and turned a page so roughly that it should have been ripped from the book's spine.

He'd never raised his voice to her like that before, and she recoiled. "Why are you so angry with me?"

His voice softened, but his gaze remained fixed upon his book. "I'm angry at myself, not you, which is why

322

it's not the time to talk. I shouldn't have let sex cloud the issue. I turned basic, and I wish I hadn't."

She waited for further illumination. "Because . . .?"

"Because it was amazing."

"Yes, it was. Absolutely amazing, and I don't regret it at all!" She was aware that she was using what her mother would call her "difficult voice".

He turned to a page where a single drop of water captured a world of reflections. "Judith's satisfied with the way things turned out, so that's OK, then."

She'd never encountered him in this mood before, angry, rueful and troubled. Until now he'd seemed prepared to go at her pace, to wait for her while she traversed a road more rocky than his. Misery clouded her vision. She'd viewed their return to lovemaking as a breakthrough, but he was treating it like . . . like an awful error of judgement. "That's not what I meant —"

"How many times do I have to repeat myself, before you believe that *I don't want to talk?*"

There was no point persisting while he was churning with anger. Better if she went to see Giorgio's parents and got that over with — she longed for the saga of the crucifix to be done — and then when she returned, hopefully he'd be his normal self. They could talk honestly without ghosts and missions hanging in the air between them. To discuss how she'd expected to feel at home again on the island, but couldn't. Stiffly, she rose. "I have to go out for a while."

He turned a page slowly, to a house with an enormously bulbous balcony in its centre. "Thought you might."

"I honestly don't think I'll be very long."

A silence drew out. As she turned away, he said, "I'm going to see if I can change my flight. Leave a bit earlier."

She hesitated. "I'm sorry you feel like that." And then, when he didn't respond, "Change both tickets, won't you? I'll go when you do."

Siesta was a good time to find the older generation at home, and the afternoon was hot by the time Judith climbed the hill of Tower Road to find the turn off for the house of Agnello and Maria Zammit. She was amazed at how the temperature was making her head throb, considering it was only just May. She was reacting like an English tourist, wiping sweat from her forehead with exaggerated care in case she increased the pulsing ache that was building there, making squinty eyes at the sun and cursing herself for not putting her sunglasses in her bag.

The Zammit residence was in a tall and narrow street built of creamy limestone near the twin bell towers and cupola of the charming Stella Maris Parish Church, built so that sailors in the harbour could always have it within their sight. Although several houses in the street boasted traditional gallerija balconies painted dark green or plum red, it occurred to her that there was no comparison between these residences and Saviour's set on the St. Julian's side of

Sliema. Agnello hadn't made the money that his little brother had. His house would fit into Saviour's four times.

She sighed as she approached, remembering Maria Zammit's barely contained fury at their last meeting, and wondered, wryly, whether she ought to check that Stella Maris Church — the star of the sea — offered sanctuary to non-Catholics.

The door was panelled, the highly polished brass knocker looked like the result of an intimate moment between a sea monster and a dolphin. Before she had a chance to change her mind, Judith seized it by its bulbous head and rapped sharply. And in a few moments she was face to face with Giorgio's mother.

Maria looked first shocked, and then irritated. Her dark eyes narrowed into the lined skin around them, and she gave a little ladylike sniff of disapproval. Her dress bore a small, eye-aching geometric design, her hair was almost entirely silver now, and she wore little wire-framed glasses that matched it.

For an instant, Judith felt like just giving the whole damned thing up, she was tired of being a target for antagonism. She could return to Richard's house and spend a day or two being a tourist with Adam before getting on the flaming plane for England, whenever he'd arranged. Why should she continue to knock on doors and force people to speak to her who patently didn't wish to? She could even, as Adam had suggested, have pushed the crucifix through the letterbox and turned away.

But that was ridiculous! For goodness' sake, she was a perfectly respectable middle-aged woman, and not prepared to act as if she were ashamed of her existence. She pulled herself up to her full height — considerably more than Maria's — and lifted her chin. "Good afternoon."

Maria Zammit's muttered, "Good afternoon," was no resounding welcome.

It had been in Judith's mind to suggest that they take coffee and cake together in a café, like mature and civilised women with a matter to discuss. But, seeing Maria's face, she made a sudden decision to save her breath.

Instead, she reached brusquely inside her pocket. "I've brought you this." The gold, getting duller by the day, hung between her fingers.

Slowly, as if she couldn't quite believe it wouldn't be whisked away again, Maria Zammit reached out, and took the golden crucifix.

Kissing the suffering Jesus, she crossed herself, closing her eyes on a moment of pain, as Judith had done so many times. The eyes reopened, and she frowned, looking baffled.

Judith frowned back, shading her eyes against a dagger of sunlight slicing into the street. "For a while I believed it was OK for me to keep it. But now I realise it belongs to you. Saviour told me what was in Giorgio's Will." She turned to go.

But then she swung back, ignoring the way her headache seemed to move separately, painfully, anger fuelling a sudden desire to make her point. "I know that you blame me for his death. But I made your son's life happy for his final couple of years. Perhaps, in time, you'll come to think of that."

Slowly, Maria shook her head. "You take him under the sea."

Letting her breath out on a long sigh, Judith hunched her shoulders in frustration. "Not that day, I didn't!" And then, more gently, "I agree that if I'd been there, it wouldn't have happened. I believe that, as you obviously do. But I asked him . . ." Her voice caught in her throat as a sudden vision of Giorgio blazed across her mind, the angry frown lines digging grooves between his black brows as he'd shrugged off her pleas to postpone his dive. He'd been so irritated that she'd shut up. She cleared her throat. "I asked him not to go without me. But he'd made up his mind. *He* made up *his* mind. But if you want to blame me, I understand that it might help to make me a focus for your grief."

She'd probably said too much, and said it too rapidly for Maria's instant comprehension. But what use was there in pounding over the same old ground again, anyway?

Hitching her bag up on her shoulder, she thrust her hands into her jacket pockets, her fingertips finding the empty corner where the crucifix had lain in a tangle for the last days.

She wasn't sure yet whether it was a loss or a relief.

But, whichever, she'd drawn a line under the whole saga, and would, in time, feel better.

As she swung away the ache in her head took on a life of its own, and the world suddenly shimmered and pooled around her.

She halted, screwing up her eyes. The air was sparkling as if Tinkerbell had just flown around the edges of the buildings, making them glisten and warp.

The sunshine on this fairy dust made her eyeballs ache unbearably, but she forced her feet to get going again, left-right, up the street, their echo launching lance-like pains above her eyes, across the bridge of her nose and her cheekbones. Her ears began to ache, making her uncomfortable with the chatter of children, car engines echoing as they passed in low gear, and the voices of three women calling to one another from their upstairs windows.

Oh no. Migraine.

She hadn't had one since her teens, but she hadn't forgotten how savagely they used to attack. Shading her eyes with her hand she felt the pavement turn to sponge beneath her feet. Her heart rose up into her throat.

Putting out a hand to a wall to steady herself, she breathed in through her mouth, trying to quell the nausea as the world dipped alarmingly. Thankfully, she was unlikely to be humiliated by being sick in the street. If previous attacks were anything to go by she had a couple of hours of this misery before the sickness that would signify the end of the migraine swept over her. Sweat burst out all over her face, in the hollow of her throat and down her spine. She swallowed hard and breathed deeply.

Engrossed in her own discomfort, she didn't notice that Maria had followed her until her voice came from behind. "Hey!"

Pain cannoned about Judith's skull as she half-turned.

Maria was holding out the crucifix. To her. Agnello waited, a step behind his wife. He'd lost a lot of weight since Judith had seen him last. Probably grieving for his only son.

Dumbfounded, she squinted at the glint of gold, then at Maria's expressionless face. "What . . .?" She winced as the pain above her eyes grew boots and kicked at the top of her head.

Impatiently, Maria shook the crucifix in Judith's direction.

Slowly, Judith put out her hand. And Maria slithered it into her palm.

"But . . .?" Bile pulsed in her throat in rhythm with the pounding in her head, and focussing through the fairy dust became harder. "Are you giving it to me?"

A tiny nod. Then a huge shrug, reminding Judith sharply of Giorgio. "It was give to you."

She tried to think through a band tightening around her forehead. "But should it have been?"

Maria began to walk away. "Perhaps yes. Perhaps no." Agnello gave Judith a curious look, nodded, and followed Maria.

Shaking, Judith managed to cross into the shade. But her pain increased until she felt as if massive talons gripped her entire head. Her vision danced and fizzed.

She sank down against the base of the wall, legs like water, desperate to be still. Just to be out of the sun. To close her aching eyes. She prayed that the church bells wouldn't begin to peal.

She was so taken up with her discomfort that she jerked as a hand grasped her shoulder. The movement made her feel as if her skull had broken into shards and rasped sickeningly against her brain.

"You are ill?"

She sliced her eyes open a slit to glimpse Maria Zammit wearing a tiny frown of concentration. The pattern of her dress made Judith feel as if she was spinning.

"A little," she said. "Migraine, I think. I'll have to wait for it to go off a bit." She let her eyes close again.

Maria clicked her tongue and made a noise, "*Tsh, tsh*. You don't stay here!"

"I'll go soon. It'll pass. I just need . . ."

With another click of her tongue, Maria turned away.

Judith covered her eyes with her hands, craving darkness.

And then there was a man beside her. Agnello. "I put you in my car?"

Judith swallowed convulsively at the thought of being shaken about on Malta's busy roads. "Thank you, but I'm afraid of being sick."

**330**

"OK." She felt a hand under her elbow. "Come, you have a quiet room and lie down. Yes? We phone your friends."

She forced her eyes to open slightly as, one either side of her, they pulled her steadily to her feet. All she could think about was the blinding headache/seasickness/vertigo that was migraine, it was certainly no time for a prideful refusal. "That would be . . . a relief. Thank you."

They helped her through the door and into a small room with a long sofa.

She was pathetically grateful just to lie down and close her eyes as her unlikely white knights closed the thick russet curtains with stealthy movements, and fetched her a blessedly soft pillow for her poor head. She gave them Richard's home phone number, but they received no answer. Adam must have gone out. She elected not to phone Richard Morgan Estate, although Raymond and Lino would no doubt be there. She could live without their cousinly ministrations. She wanted Adam.

As she couldn't get him, she closed her eyes and gave herself up to simple gratitude for the cool, dim room.

Gently, gradually, she relaxed.

Once she was motionless, the pain in her eyes, temples, cheekbones and the top of her head settled to a lancing throb, and the rolling nausea began to subsided.

She dozed uneasily, torn between appreciation and anxiety. She'd found a haven but it had, until now, been hostile territory. Fervently, she wished she could click her fingers and find herself back in the bed she'd abandoned so late this morning. Preferably with Adam's comforting arms around her.

The church bells began, sliding into her dreams as she dozed.

The graceful Stella Maris Parish Church. Giorgio's funeral mass. Dark suits and dresses. Solemn faces, lines of grief, tears.

And, back down the years, Johanna beautiful in a white lace dress, Giorgio handsome in a new suit, young and smiling and thinking they had a love to last. Proud, beaming family, Maria and Agnello, his sister, Josephine, Saviour and Cass. Nobody knowing that one day the implacable sea, the same that almost surrounded Sliema, would take him away.

Her eyes flickered. A frightening image formed of the sea welling up onto shore after him . . . Her head banged with fresh pain as she moved unwisely on the pillow. No! The sea wasn't to blame, it was the jet ski, roaring, racing into a diving zone. And Giorgio surfacing at the wrong instant . . .

Giorgio hadn't taken every precaution possible. She swirled the idea around her mind, testing it for soundness. No one could argue with the fact that he'd committed the sin, for a diver, of not respecting the boundaries of his own limitations. Armed with his brand new open water certificate, really quite a basic qualification, he'd put himself in peril and flouted advice.

*Reckless, reckless!*

He'd risked a life that was good, a life containing her love. And paid the price. They all had.

Because she'd known that she could probably have prevented the tragedy *had she been there*, she'd blamed herself, let others blame her, too. Attempted to shoulder a burden that had been impossibly unwieldy.

According to Saviour, Giorgio had known about the lapsed insurance policy. Perhaps fear at the consequences of his own mistake was what had made him reckless?

*If only you hadn't gone without me. Had waited until Sunday. The sea would still have been there, Giorgio.* Her eyes popped open. He'd chosen to go without her. She closed her eyes again hastily as pain boomed behind them.

This time without difficulty, she summoned Giorgio's image to her mind.

And she smiled. Because the image of Giorgio was smiling, of course it would, he smiled often. The smile the image wore was the apologetic one he employed when his enthusiasms had overcome his common sense and everything had gone wrong. When he'd tried to speed up the cooking and burnt the meat. When he tried to force his way into traffic and pranged the car.

When he refused to wait one day for an experienced diving buddy.

When he forgot, in all likelihood, about listening for engines immediately prior to surfacing. Sighing, she frowned, trying not to move although she was growing cramped, anxious not to reawaken the blinding pain.

Something felt strange.

She was used to abrading her wounds and making certain that she could still feel the blame.

Forgiving herself was a new sensation. A relief.

# CHAPTER
# THIRTY

It was an hour later when she awoke from restless, fitful dreams of headache, heartache and Giorgio.

The tolling of the bells had ceased, and the house was filled with the aroma of frying onions. She could hear the murmur of voices, water running in a sink and the sawing of a bread knife.

Experimentally, she opened her eyes. The glittering fairy dust had gone. She tried rolling her head on the pillow. Bearable. Cautiously, she pushed herself upright. *Error!*

She launched to her feet and staggered out of the room, surprising Maria in the kitchen into dropping a wooden spatula. Mutely, Judith slapped a hand across her mouth, and Maria immediately grasped the urgent nature of the problem.

"*Hawnhekk!* In here!" She hustled her into a downstairs shower room, and Judith dropped to her knees in front of the lavatory as the door closed.

But after a further hour on the sofa, the migraine had passed. There was residual giddiness and a sort of hangover, but her vision was steady now and the violent headache had subsided. Sleep was still asking for her, but that could come later.

She made her way out to the kitchen. Maria turned away from wiping the kitchen table. She didn't smile, but she didn't glare or frown either. Her voice was considerably soft. "Do you recover?"

Judith's own voice sounded thin. "I'm much better, thank you. You've been so kind. I'm very grateful."

Maria shrugged, and clicked her tongue dismissively. Any kindness on her part was not up for discussion, evidently.

In the corner, Agnello shook out his newspaper. "Is good. You are not ill. You want food?" He indicated a big saucepan.

Judith looked away hastily. "Really, no, thank you, I couldn't." But she accepted a tall glass of clear, cool water, which she made herself sip. Then Maria showed her out to the street.

"You know the way to go?"

"Yes, thank you." And she did. It was quite plain and simple.

"We say goodbye." Maria held out her hand.

Judith took it, gaining a curious comfort of closure from feeling the small, rough and wrinkled hand in hers of the woman who'd given Giorgio life. "Goodbye. And thank you. Really."

Maria took her hand back, with a shrug. "I think of Giorgio."

"Of course. So do I. He'll remain in our hearts and minds."

Almost, Maria smiled, as Judith settled her bag on her shoulder and turned to walk back towards Tower Road.

★   ★   ★

Johanna's door had no doorknocker and no bell, and Judith had to knock hard with her knuckles on the timber to be heard. The impact stuttered up her arm and into her fragile head.

It was evening by now, mild and balmy. The sky had faded to lavender. Judith waited on the top step. It probably wasn't as long as it felt before Johanna answered, gazing suspiciously at Judith, perhaps unsurprisingly, her features sharpening. Judith didn't bother trying to summon a smile, but ensured that her voice was pleasant and polite before letting it out to duel with Johanna. "Would it be possible for me to speak briefly with Lydia, please?"

"Why?"

"A very quick word. I don't need to be alone with her, but I do need to talk to her directly."

Johanna looked thoughtful, but didn't turn to call her daughter to the door. She stared silently at Judith, instead, as if trying to read Judith's mind. Perhaps she would never have let Judith see Lydia if the girl hadn't come running downstairs as Judith waited on the well-swept steps.

"Hello," said Judith, carefully.

"Oh!" said Lydia, exactly as she had last time. She looked intrigued, eyes agog.

Judith ignored Johanna's impatient tuts and addressed Lydia, extracting her hand from her pocket, the crucifix looped between her fingers. "Lydia, you know who I am. I've been to see your grandmother, your *nanna*, this afternoon, and she said that I could have this. But I'd like you to have it, instead."

Pleasure blazed from Lydia's face as she took two rapid skips closer. "Is for me?" She took what Judith offered unhesitatingly, and with joy, her thick, dark hair framing her huge smile as she clutched her prize.

Judith smiled. "I think it's better if it stays in your family. Your Nannu Agnello tells me it belonged to his father, and perhaps *his* father, too." And then, she offered as much of an explanation for her actions as she was going to, to a wooden-faced Johanna. "She has a smile just like her father's."

# CHAPTER
# THIRTY-ONE

By the time she turned off The Strand for Richard's house, Judith felt stronger.

Her headache had faded, her legs had rediscovered the bones that were meant to be in them, her vision had cleared of fairy dust and the giddiness and sickness had vanished with it.

She hadn't expected that her detour to see Lydia would have a magical effect, but she felt as if she'd put down a burden. Strolling home along The Strand, watching the boats bob in the creek, she'd felt as if every step was one in a new direction. The right direction.

The house was quiet as she let herself in through the warm kitchen redolent of the evening meal. In the *salott* Erminia knitted at great speed in the pool of light from a tall lamp, her eyes more often on the television than her red wool, which was nevertheless forming into the correct shape to clothe a grandchild next winter.

She exclaimed when Judith walked into the sitting room. "*Il-hanina dinja*, have you been lost? Adam has waited for you."

Judith yawned as she dropped into a comfortable chair, and explained about the migraine. "Isn't Adam here? I suppose he's sloped off for a beer with Richard? I'll just make a sandwich, then, and have an early night." How frustrating that she wouldn't be able to speak to Adam tonight, after all.

Erminia raised her eyebrows, and cast off two stitches on a sleeve. "He has left a letter in your bedroom."

Reluctantly, Judith climbed back out of the comfy chair that had nestled her into its cushioned arms. She was disappointed that Adam hadn't waited in for her, and so she'd have to wait to rest her fast-recovering head on his shoulder and tell him about her day. And, of course, that they must talk, now.

She yawned her way up the uncarpeted stairs, desperately tired. She'd forgotten how strong was the craving of sleep that went hand-in-hand with the misery of migraine. Her eyes began water with every jaw-wrenching paroxysm.

Maybe she wouldn't even bother with a sandwich. If she just cleaned her teeth, she could fling off her clothes and be in bed in a minute. Closing her eyes, stretching out, naked to better appreciate the welcome of those smooth, cool sheets.

The envelope waited on the bedside, pale blue and square, *Jude* large on the front in Adam's familiar scrawl.

She ripped it open, still yawning, unfolding the note as her fingers began on the buttons of her shirt. Her room seemed considerably neater than when she'd left it this morning, and she felt guilty if Erminia had felt the need to tidy up after her.

**340**

Jude, I waited as long as I could because you said you wouldn't be long. But you were. No doubt you've been busy with things that don't concern me. *Her latest yawn died mid-execution.*

Do you remember, last night, that I said Malta was a small world? I think I was coming to realise that you'll stay, safe and warm in it. I'd love you to come back to the world that we've lived in together, but I don't think that you will. I'd love to think that some day you'll be ready to care for me in the way I want you to, but that seems less and less likely, too. Has Malta called you back? Or is it the memories of Giorgio? I don't know. But your head has been somewhere else for the past few days and the rest of you will follow.

I suppose Malta was the life you chose and coming back to Brinham was a knee jerk reaction to a particularly horrible episode in it. In reality, you and I are heading off in opposite directions. I thought that when I asked to spend this time with you there was a decent chance that you'd put Giorgio in the past and be receptive to me, but, instead, the opposite has happened. I've watched you getting more and more involved in your past. In Brinham, I thought that having to stay at home and wait to see whether you returned was to be avoided. But, actually, I think it might have been easier.

Of course, we were very much together last night in bed and it's a night I'll carry with me, even though I had sworn to myself that I wouldn't sleep with you again, unless things changed.

Lovely as it is, I'm unhappy in Malta, and have rearranged the flights for tonight. *TONIGHT!* But now you've stayed away all day it seems as if I should've left yours as it was — but if you don't make it, I'll fund the replacement flight. I hope I'll see you when you're in Brinham. Adam x

Judith stared at the piece of paper in her hand. Her heartbeat halted. And then started again with a giant pulse that almost burst it from her chest cavity. Adam had gone home! Without her! She'd been so absorbed in the unsatisfactory business of trying to feel close to Giorgio in order to decide what he would have wanted her to do with the crucifix, that she'd managed to push Adam away.

The single kiss beneath Adam's name wasn't much comfort. Nothing but ink on paper. After last night? The way his mouth had fed on hers? In a moment of painful clarity she realised what last night had been about. Why Adam had broken his own rule to sleep with her.

He'd been saying goodbye.

He'd gone back to Brinham *without her*, and she was suddenly positive that Brinham was where her future lay. Because Adam was there.

Judith burst back into the living room. "When did he go?"

"More than half-an-hour." Erminia's brown eyes were pools of sympathy. "1845 flight. Richard took him." She hesitated. "I've packed for you, in case you want to catch him . . . shall I order a taxi?"

In ten agonising minutes, Judith was clambering into the back of a Ford Focus, leaving Erminia behind with her knitting and her television programme as the driver whizzed towards Gzira to join the regional road.

The traffic was hell, it always was when you really needed to get somewhere. She gritted her teeth and gripped the seat as they sliced past other cars, ruthlessly feeding into the flow of cars in scary games of "chicken", even when other drivers blew their horns in long, angry blasts to go with their equally angry gestures.

She refused to glance at the dashboard clock.

The journey was a greater nightmare than usual and she gathered from the fireworks in the navy sky that there was a festa going on.

The traffic flowed through the tunnel at Hamrun well enough, though, and as they picked up the signposts for the airport the going became easier.

At least Malta's international airport was small and accessible, there was no slow approach and miles of car parks as found at monsters such as Heathrow or Gatwick. As they neared in grim silence, she felt a gust of panic to see the lights of an ascending aircraft. She scolded herself for a stupid leap of her heart. He couldn't have taken off, yet.

She knew it wasn't Richard's way to hang around waiting for visitors to queue up for check-in, so Judith wasn't surprised not to see his car in the drop-off zone.

She threw ten liri at the taxi driver with her thanks, waited impatiently for him to pull her case from the boot, then struggled through a disembarking minibus load of tourists who were in typical end-of-holiday dolour, and on beneath the arch signed *Departures*, to the big glass doors.

She normally liked the airport, it was brightly shiny and clean in its relaxing speckly shades of sand and honey, reminding her of happy events such as meeting Kieran or Molly or Wilma from the plane. But she'd never seen it so *busy*, a million tourists milling before her in snaky check-in lines as long as a football pitch. What the hell was going on with the check-ins? Tour reps patrolled the lines, being loud and jolly despite the holidaymakers' peeves about going home, queuing, and the weight of their cases, as if it were someone else that had stuffed the luggage with Mdina Glass and books about the war.

"Excuse me, excuse me, please!" Judith tried to wiggle through the tail end of the lines that blocked the door.

A broad lady with a red face turned. "It's a *queue*, lovey."

Her travelling partner fanned herself with her passport. "I don't know why they don't open more check-ins."

"That's why they tell you to be here two hours in advance, if you ask me. They've no intention of opening enough, so they know there are going to be long queues."

The tourists turned their stolid backs on Judith as they grumbled, leaving her marooned in a space by the doors.

"I don't need to check in! I just need to get through to find someone!" Judith fibbed. Still a wall of turned backs. She aimed for a weak spot in the wall and jostled her way through.

"Charming!" she heard, behind her, as she burst into the area beside the queues. And, "Don't mind my ankles!"

She rushed along the length of the queue nearest to her, gripping the handle of her case as it bounced along on its inadequate wheels, craning her neck, searching for the familiar tall shape, the hair sliding forward towards his eyes. Tiptoeing, stretching, she tried to look over into the next bunched line, and the four beyond that.

Oh, it was hopeless! He'd probably checked in by now, anyway, and was no doubt through security. With such a queue to check in she doubted that she'd even make the flight.

She swung around, aiming for the Air Malta desk. They could page him. Wherever he was in the airport, they'd get him to a phone, even if he'd gone through the departure gate and up to the first floor, she would at least be able to talk to him.

Even away from check-in the airport was busy, reps in red or blue blazers, tourists, airport staff, what looked like a delegation of businessmen making their farewells to their hosts.

And then she saw him.

He was at the head of the queue filtering between the barriers into departure security, the enclosure where hand luggage was scanned and passengers stepped through the metal detector before taking the escalator up to the departure lounge. His camera bag was over his shoulder, a newspaper in his hand. Any moment and he would step out of sight.

"Adam!"

Her voice was lost in the swirl of conversation and purr of public address announcements as he shuffled between the barriers.

Abandoning her suitcase — strictly against the advice of the posters — she took a deep breath and began battling her way towards him. "*Adam! Adam!*"

He turned suddenly, his head moving, searching for her.

"Adam!" She windmilled her arms, trying to side step and dodge her way around the mass of aimlessly milling people. "Wait!"

He glanced at the looming archway that signalled entry into the security check area. The brink of no return. He began to try to make his way back, no doubt annoying a lot of passengers as he went, some of whom moved reluctantly to the side.

The sea of people parted suddenly before her, and Judith raced across the polished floor, putting a spurt on as she realised that her dash was gaining the unwelcome attention of the uniformed security staff. Adam had become locked in a dispute with an overweight red-faced tourist who seemed too corpulent to allow passage past him, and Adam was looking

346

assessingly at the waist-high steel barrier. She jinked around a family arguing in German and broke into a sprint, counting her final steps. Her heart sank to see a man in uniform moving rapidly to intercept her, holding up a forbidding hand and shouting simultaneously at Adam in an effort to halt his unorthodox exit from the pen.

Even if she felt perfectly entitled to race after somebody who had nearly passed through security, she didn't intend wasting time in making certain.

Five, four, three, two, one . . . "Adam!"

But as she tried to skid to a halt, the highly polished tiles and the heels of her shoes conspired to prevent her. Even as her feet tried to slew beneath the barrier — a slot too small to allow the rest of her to follow — her knee folded, and she teetered, grasping fruitless handfuls of air.

And then a hand caught hers and she was yanked upright, her left wrist almost pulled from its socket as she was hauled against a long body, feeling the scaliness of his scars against her flesh. A man in uniform addressed them in severe tones as he snatched his walkie-talkie off his belt. But she didn't care. Even with the barrier still between them and digging into her stomach she was safe within the warmth and comfort that surrounded Adam.

His eyes fastened silently on her face, and it took three good breaths before she could dredge up some words.

"You're wrong!" she managed, gripping the hand that had caught hers tightly, as if he was likely to turn and run. "I came home to tell you, and you'd gone. I couldn't believe it, I got a taxi but the traffic was a bastard." She paused to suck in a breath, ignoring tutting tourists wanting to pass them to get security over and passport control so that they could spend the last of their liri in the shops.

The security guard was still speaking, but Judith simply zoned him out.

Adam's grey eyes were intense, his voice quiet. "What was I wrong about?" His hand tightened around her wrist so that she had a job not to wince.

"I had to go back, to tie up loose ends. I couldn't be happy until I had."

"And?"

"And I've done it. I gave the crucifix to Lydia, because she reminds me of Giorgio, and, although it's not very nice of me, I don't care for Alexia. I told his mother I didn't accept the blame for what happened." She thought about that, frowning. "I think she may even have accepted it. But I got this incredible migraine and I'm not completely sure how much was actually said, and what just happened in my head." She smiled at him, brilliantly. "But Giorgio's parents took me into their house and let me lie on their sofa in a dark room until I felt better. Which was nice of them, considering."

"And?" he asked, again.

"So I choose the world in Brinham," she said, as if it were obvious thing. "With you."

"And Giorgio?" His voice was tight with strain.

She looked down, suddenly becoming aware of the hand gripping hers, the tightness of the pincer grip. He was letting her hold his right hand! Trusting her with the damaged part of himself, for once not withdrawing and hiding it away.

She smiled, covering his right hand with hers. "I loved him once. But I've said my goodbyes."

He looked down, in turn, at their hands clasped between them. His smile twisted. But he didn't try the usual left-hand-for-right exchange.

Gently, he tilted her face to his and kissed her. And then again, more deeply.

"I think we've finally ended up on the same bit of road." He kissed her temples and her cheekbones, her eyelids and the crook of her neck. "We can go home together."

She let her head fall back, and closed her eyes, feeling his lips on her flesh and the beat of his heart through her hands upon his chest. "I haven't got a bloody ticket!"

He laughed. "It's waiting for you at the Air Malta desk." He peered around her to where the uniformed man with the walkie-talkie was still watching them, but calmly now, almost smiling. Two of his colleagues surveyed them from a vantage point at the top of the escalator before passport control, obviously prepared to be tolerant of these mad English. "I wonder if this nice man will help hurry you through?"

Judith felt happiness filling her up. "Bound to. The Maltese are terribly kind."

He turned her gently towards the security man. "OK. Let's see if we can move on."

Also available in ISIS Large Print:

# All Inclusive

## Judy Astley

For the last few years Beth and Ned have gone to the same luxury spa hotel in the Caribbean. There they meet up with the same crowd, pick up where they left off and leave the cares of real life safely behind.

Except this year. This year, home problems have somehow tagged along for the ride. Ned has been playing away — a bit of a drunken fling, that's all, nothing to worry about, Beth thinks. But although they have put it all behind them, what Beth doesn't know is that Ned's fling was with the female half of one of the couples they are holidaying with.

To make matters worse, Beth has insisted on bringing along their 16-year-old daughter, Delilah, who's been ill and needs rest and sunshine. Not so ill, however, that she can't look around for some entertainment . . .

ISBN 0-7531-7423-5 (hb)
ISBN 0-7531-7424-3 (pb)

# The Frozen Lake

## Elizabeth Edmondson

The year of 1936 is drawing to a close. Winter grips Westmoreland and causes a rare phenomenon: the lakes freeze. For two local families, the Richardsons and the Grindleys, this will bring unexpected upheaval as the frozen lake entices long-estranged siblings and children to return home for the holiday season.

Childhood friendships are rekindled, old rivalries resurface and new relationships sparkle with possibilities. Everyone's keen to put aside their troubles — money worries, love tangles, career problems, domestic rifts — and enjoy themselves skating while they can. But one visitor carries the seed of violence and not even the redoubtable matriarch of the Richardson clan can prevent the carefully buried secrets of the past from reappearing and transforming everything.

**ISBN** 0-7531-7429-4 **(hb)**
**ISBN** 0-7531-7430-8 **(pb)**